wicked WATERS

BECCA STEELE

WICKED WATERS

BECCA STEELE

Wicked Waters

Copyright © 2024 by Becca Steele

Editing by One Love Editing

Proofreading by Rumi

Cover design by Opulent Designs

Becca Steele

www.authorbeccasteele.com

AUTHOR'S NOTE

The author is British, and this story contains British English spellings and phrases.

For Catherine W.
Miss you.

Happiness resides not in possessions, and not in gold, happiness dwells in the soul.

— SOCRATES

LEGEND

Legend tells of three gods. Zeus, king of all the gods and ruler of the skies, Hades, ruler of the underworld, and Poseidon, ruler of the seas.

The three gods were brothers.

According to legend, the gods grew bored with their immortal lives, and their attention was drawn by the humans who lived in the mortal realm. Each of them took women, and sometimes men, even though it was forbidden. Poseidon, in particular, was known for his promiscuity, and stories about him began to spread far and wide.

When the Titans, parents of the gods, discovered what had been done, they threatened the gods with banishment and even death. So the gods agreed never to visit the mortal realm again.

Thousands of years passed, and humans no longer believed in the gods, although the legends remained.

The blood of the gods was strong, though. Every so often, a child would be born who would be faster, stronger, more beautiful than those around them. The inherent characteristics of the gods could be seen in these children, too, shaping their personalities and lives.

Did the gods exist?

Was it all a myth?

No one knows for sure. But eighteen years ago, a boy was born. A boy with hair as black as midnight and eyes as blue as the depths of the sea.

The boy was impulsive and quick to anger and soon became known for his violent outbursts of temper. He was at his happiest around water, and he excelled at swimming, rowing, and surfing.

The boy's parents moved around the world for their jobs, but they wanted their son to grow up in England. A succession of nannies took care of the boy's needs, but none of them could provide what the boy needed the most.

Love.

As the boy grew older and his skill in the water began to surpass those around him, his reputation as a troublemaker also began to grow until it became legendary.

The boy was expelled from a number of schools, and his parents despaired. But thanks to his family name and a sizeable donation from his rich uncle, he eventually ended up at Hatherley Hall, one of the most prestigious boarding schools in the country. For a while, things were calm.

Then, he grew bored, and the trouble started again. First, arson. It was only a small fire…

Next, there was a flooding incident. His uncle's smooth words and financial generosity kept him in the school.

It wasn't enough, though. The beast inside him wasn't satisfied. He needed to do something bigger to get everyone's attention.

Something that would go down in history at the school, that would make him a legend.

So, he planned.

The outbuildings at Hatherley Hall were perfectly situated for his second bout of arson.

He succeeded, sealing his notoriety in the process, but the restlessness remained.

Then, there came a girl. A girl who ruined everything…

Quinn

Staring at myself in the mirror, I rolled the waistband of my skirt higher. It wasn't regulation, but screw the rules and regulations. I ripped the hair tie from my hair, shaking it free, then stalked out of the toilets into the school corridor, all the way to the end, past the classroom where I should have been sitting in a biology lesson, and pushed open the heavy doors leading to the grounds of Hatherley Hall.

Freedom. I took a deep breath, filling my lungs with fresh air.

"I wasn't expecting to find one of the elite out here. Shouldn't you be in a lesson right now?" The voice came from my left. Fifteen-year-old Roman Cavendish. Tall and lean, with inky-black hair and the most gorgeously tanned skin, leaning casually against the honey-coloured Cotswold stone wall without a care in the world. He cocked a brow at me, and I blinked, realising he'd addressed me directly and I'd let the silence stretch for far too long. Wow. I hadn't known he could talk. I mean, obviously, he could talk, but I'd never heard him speak. Roman Cavendish was a bit of an enigma.

I knew nothing about him, other than the fact he mostly kept to himself, and he'd developed a bit of a reputation as someone who didn't take any shit from people. He'd beaten up Charles Pennington for calling him a dirty little orphan, even though he had parents somewhere overseas, and people whispered about him behind his back. Wild rumours that I doubted had any truth to them. Kids could be cruel, and in a place like this, a boarding school where we couldn't escape each other, gossip was practically our lifeblood.

"Shouldn't *you* be in a lesson?" I countered, returning his raised brow with my own.

"Yep." He shrugged, flashing me a small grin, his messy hair falling into his eyes.

"I…um…I had to get away, you know?" I mumbled, caught off guard by the way the smile had transformed his entire face. "Sometimes I feel…it feels like I can't breathe."

His smile disappeared as he studied me intently. After a minute where I held my breath, wondering what was going through his mind, he held out his hand. "Come with me."

Something deep inside me told me I could trust him, and I placed my hand in his. He startled for a moment, staring down at our hands with his brows pulled together, before he shook his head with a small laugh and entwined our fingers. His warm palm was a reassuring touch against my own as he led me around the side of the school and pulled me into the tree line that marked the beginning of the wooded boundary area running all the way down the left side of the school buildings and beyond. He cut through the undergrowth, ducking under the overhanging tree branches, and we eventually broke through the line of trees on the other side. A gasp fell from my lips as a lake appeared in front of us, still and glimmering in the weak sunlight that filtered through the clouds.

"Where is this?" My voice came out as a whisper. There was a large lake on the school grounds, used for various water sports. But this one was different. Smaller, clearer than the murky waters of the other, with a tangle of reeds and more trees at the far side, ducks swimming lazily in the distance, and close to where we were standing, a tiny pebbly beach that sloped down into the water next to a little wooden jetty, where a rowboat was tied, bobbing up and down.

"I don't know who it belongs to or what it's used for, but I've never seen anyone else here before. I don't think it's part of the school." He hesitated for a moment. "I…I come here when I need to get away. I like to be close to the water." His soft confession was accompanied by a squeeze of my hand before he let me go. Taking a seat on the soft grass next to the pebbled beach, we sat in silence for a while, the quiet only broken by the sound of the birds in the trees and ducks creating ripples in the still water. I glanced over at the boy by my side. The boy who was labelled as a troublemaker. The boy I'd never spoken to before today. The boy who had always intrigued me. He was so still, reclining back on his elbows with his face tipped to the sky and his eyes closed, long black lashes sweeping down. There was still an undercurrent of tension that seemed to radiate from his body, but this was the most peaceful I'd ever seen him. A soft breeze ruffled my hair, and I let my whole body relax. It felt like we were in a different world out here. Away from the drama of school and the pressures that sometimes felt like they were drowning me—for a moment, everything else disappeared, and it was just us.

Eventually, though, I knew we'd have to get back before I missed English lit as well as biology. My moment of rebellion had passed, and the need to get back to being the good girl, the perfect student, overwhelmed me.

Pulling my hair back into a smooth ponytail, I blew out a shaky breath.

"Thank you for bringing me here."

Roman's eyes blinked open, and he turned to face me, his deep blue eyes meeting mine. "Come back whenever." He gave me another small smile, and my stomach flipped. But I pushed that feeling aside because nothing good could come of being interested in the bad boy of Hatherley Hall.

Over the next few months, I continued to meet up with Roman, snatching moments whenever I could sneak away —normally during our lunch break, although I still cut the occasional class if everything got on top of me. My parents would have flipped if they'd known—he was very much the opposite of the kind of boy they'd want me to be friends with, despite his family name. In fact, they didn't want me to be friends with any boy, let alone one who had a reputation as the bad boy of Hatherley Hall.

The problem with that was that Roman was... different. He was easily as rich as the other kids who attended our school, yet he didn't have the same air of entitlement and arrogance that most of the others did. The others I spent most of my time with. Not only that, but he also didn't expect me to act a certain way—he accepted me just as I was, whatever my mood happened to be, and that was something I hadn't experienced with any of my friends other than Aria Harper, a girl I'd been getting to know recently. As we'd spent more time together, he'd begun to open up to me, telling me about his life being transferred between schools until he'd arrived here the previous year, how he didn't really know his parents since they'd lived overseas for most of his life while he'd been left in England, and how when he acted out, it was the only time he really felt anything. With every layer that I uncovered, it became more and more clear to me that my feelings for him were starting to grow beyond friendship.

"What's up?" Roman tilted his head as he studied me, his long legs stretched out in front of him, his shoes idly making circles in the dirt. I shifted on the log we were sitting on at the lakeside. How could I tell him? Should I tell him? Screw it. I was going to tell him. It was the last day of term, and my parents were taking me to Greece the following day. This would most likely be my final chance to speak to him face to face until the new school year.

"I…I was wondering." This was too hard to say. What if he rejected me?

No, I had to do it. Swallowing hard, I tried again. "I was wondering what…what it would be like to kiss you." As I whispered the words, I lowered my eyes, my cheeks hot and flushed. It felt so good to finally say the words, but I couldn't bear it if he didn't feel the same.

He stilled next to me, and my breath caught in my throat. Then he reached over and tucked a strand of hair behind my ear, his finger brushing down the side of my face. "Me too," he breathed, and then his lips were on mine, so soft and sure. We explored one another's mouths with slow kisses that filled my stomach with butterflies.

Eventually, he pulled away, clearing his throat, a slight flush on his high cheekbones. "You should probably know…I've been wanting to do that ever since the first time I brought you here."

"You have?" I stared at him, and he nodded, his lips curving upwards. I returned his smile. "Me too. I wish…I wish we hadn't waited until the end of term. Now I have to get through a whole summer without you. What if you forget about me or find another girl?"

Shooting me a grin, he pulled me into a hug, placing a kiss to the top of my head. "Not likely. We can text each other, anyway, then pick up where we left off next term."

I wished with all my heart that those words had been true.

1

ROMAN

PRESENT DAY

"Did you hear?" Tristan leaned against the door frame of our shared room, his eyes on his phone.

"What?" I stared at him impatiently as he tapped away on the screen.

"Oh, yeah. Sorry. Did you hear that our queen of the elite, Quinn Farrow, is back?" He glanced up at me then, his eyes dancing with amusement. *Fucker.* Running a hand through his thick, dark blond hair, he smirked. "Not that you'd be interested in that news."

"Fuck off."

Tristan just laughed, shaking his head. While he was my complete opposite on paper—he was the head boy, and I'd always been labelled as a bad boy—somehow, we clicked. At the beginning of the previous school year, we'd been assigned the same dorm room, and now I counted him as my closest friend, along with the final member of our trio, Knox, whom I'd known since we were little kids.

Together, the three of us were known as the "gods" of Hatherley Hall, the elite of the elite. That was a thought that constantly amused me because I'd always had a bad reputation in every single school I'd been expelled from. I never thought I'd be one of the popular kids—in fact, I'd aimed to stay under the radar. But I guess I could blame my current status on my two best mates, and there was the fact we were all on the lacrosse team.

I joined in with Tristan's laughter, but it rang hollow.

Quinn.

She'd been one of the elite back when I was on the fringes, but she'd been different from the other girls. The only girl I'd had more than a passing interest in. A friend— no, even more than that. She was once the person I'd been closest to, the person who dipped beneath the surface and actually liked what they saw. Except…she'd completely ghosted me after the term ended. All my messages went unanswered, and she'd never returned to Hatherley Hall. After a while, I stopped feeling rejected and instead started fucking stressing, wondering if something had happened to her. Tristan seemed to know everything about everyone, and so I'd asked him if he'd heard any news about her, and he'd actually taken the time to go and find out some information for me. It turned out she'd been transferred to a Swiss boarding school while her dad had moved to the Geneva offices for whatever his business was.

So, fuck her. She obviously hadn't cared enough to stay in touch, to even give me a heads-up to say she was leaving. Clearly, I hadn't meant enough to her.

And I couldn't help comparing her situation with mine. It would never even occur to my parents to take me overseas with them, even if I was at boarding school and they only had to see me during the school holidays. If I was lucky. Sure, my uncle, Arlo Cavendish, and my two older cousins, Caiden and Weston, were here in the same country as me. But they were down on the coast in Alstone, and I was stuck here in the Cotswolds in this boarding school. I was an afterthought for them, just as I was to everyone else I was related to.

I shook my head, derailing my train of thought, and turned back to Tristan. Ever since I'd confided in him, we'd become close friends, which had taken us both by surprise. Secretly, I thought Tristan liked living out his rebellious streak through me. He prided himself on his head boy status, but more often than not, he was the deviant. The one who came up with the pranks I did. Like the latest arson incident.

That had been fucking close. I'd almost managed to get expelled. Now, I tried to toe the line so I wouldn't have any more issues with anyone in authority since I was sure I'd been banned from ninety-nine percent of the elite schools in the country, and Hatherley Hall was my last hope now I was eighteen and in my final year of studies. But the need inside me to create chaos and get away with it was always there, and it would eventually grow too strong to ignore. That was when I'd end up risking my future to ease the craving.

When I'd started the fire in Hatherley Hall's outbuildings, it was only supposed to burn the empty building that normally housed the headmaster's Bugatti. How was I supposed to know the man had decided to store a load of fucking petrol cans in there? It wasn't like there was a fuel shortage. It had resulted in the fire getting a little out of hand, if you could call the explosion and flames spreading to three nearby buildings "a little." I'd been caught and suspended, and my uncle had had to get involved to smooth things over. Suffice to say, I was a lot more careful now.

"I'm not interested in Quinn." Flinging myself back on my bed, I stared up at the ceiling.

"Yeah, alright." Tristan reached out to grab the door handle. "Since I'm the head boy, I have to go and greet her, welcome her back to the school and all that. I'll just leave you here, yeah?"

I shot up from the bed. "Wait! Give me a second to grab my shoes. Don't even fucking think about leaving without me."

He laughed again as he straightened his already pristine school tie, adjusting his head boy pin badge. "Not interested? Keep telling yourself that, Ro."

"Fuck off."

I stopped dead, staring. My mouth even fell open. Quinn Farrow had been gorgeous at fifteen, but now, eighteen years old and a woman in her own right… *Fuck*. She was a goddess. Shining waves of rich brown hair, shot through with reds and golds, and those thickly lashed eyes that seemed to switch between blue and grey and green depending on the light. Her body was utter fucking perfection, even covered head to toe in the Hatherley Hall uniform—navy blazer with the school crest, a navy V-necked jumper with royal blue piping over a pale blue shirt with the school tie, and a navy chequered skirt and black tights. Her house pin caught the light as she turned towards the tall lead-paned window, talking with Mrs. Banting, the school secretary, and a grin tugged at my lips. *Good*. She'd been placed in Epi, with me. The school houses were all named after ancient Greek philosophers—Aristotle, Democritus, Socrates, and Epicurus—otherwise known as Aris, Demo, Soc, and Epi. Quinn being in Epi with me meant we'd be spending a lot of time in the same vicinity, with our house activities, meals, and shared common room, and maybe she'd be in some of my A-level classes, too. A grin tugged at my lips, but I suppressed it.

At my side, Tristan nudged me before moving towards where Quinn stood. I shot him a warning look, falling into step beside him. Quinn's head turned at our approach, and then she saw me.

Her eyes widened, her lips curving into an O. It only lasted for a few seconds before her fists clenched at her sides, and she tore her gaze away, a blankness coming over her features. Completely ignoring me, she greeted Tristan with a bright smile that was patently fake. Tristan's curious gaze bounced between us, and I gritted my teeth, unsure of what to do. Why was she blanking me? Eventually, after an awkward silence, I cleared my throat.

"Quinn."

She startled, but recovered instantly. "Roman." The way she said my name set my teeth on edge, so coolly polite it was bordering on icy. As soon as she'd completed the obligatory greeting, she turned away from me in a clear dismissal.

What the fuck? Tristan mouthed at me, his brows pulling together, and I shrugged, at a loss. Maybe she was doing this because the school secretary was here.

I needed to get her alone. When Tristan took her arm to give her a "refresher school tour," I leaned into his other side, speaking low in his ear. "Get me five minutes alone with her."

He gave a short nod before returning his attention to Mrs. Banting. Once he'd waved her away, he led Quinn towards the school hall. When the sound of the school secretary's heels had faded away, he bypassed the hall's entrance doors and turned Quinn in the direction of the doors that led outside, down to the sports facilities and lake. Not *our* lake, but the school lake that was used for a number of aquatic activities. She walked stiffly by his side, either uncomfortable in his presence or mine, and I would bet my entire inheritance that it was me who was affecting her. What the fuck was going on with her?

The school had had new, upgraded boat sheds put in while she'd been gone, and it was here that Tristan led her. Stopping outside the sheds, he opened the door of the nearest one, then gestured for her to enter. When she stepped inside, he shot me a pointed look, and I took the hint.

The door closed behind us, and we were finally alone. The part of the boat shed that opened onto the lake was currently open, letting in plenty of light, and when Quinn spun to face me, the sun's rays backlit her. My breath caught in my throat at how good she looked.

"Quinn," I said hoarsely. "It's so good to see you again. Where—"

Her jaw tightened, and she crossed her arms over her chest. "Roman. Look. Whatever you're thinking…just don't."

"What's that supposed to mean?" My words came out more harshly than I'd intended, and she flinched away from me.

"It means." Gazing down at the floor, she took a deep breath. Then she straightened her shoulders and met my gaze head-on, her eyes completely expressionless. "It means that—that I'm not the same person as I was. I'm over my rebellious phase. I'm here to get good grades and surround myself with good people. And that—" Her voice cracked, and she took another deep breath. "—that doesn't include you. You're bad news, Roman, and I want you to stay away from me. Far away from me. In fact, forget I even exist. I don't want to know you."

With that, she shoved past me, wrenched open the doors, and was gone before her words even had a chance to sink in.

I slumped against the wall, rubbing my hand over my face. My head spun, and I sucked in a deep breath, trying to push away the sudden hurt that had shocked my body like a fucking lightning bolt. What the fuck?

"I take it that didn't go well." Tristan pulled the door open, eyeing me with what looked suspiciously like concern. And that was not a look I wanted directed at me.

"You think?" A humourless laugh fell from my mouth.

"She ran out of here like the fucking hound of Hades was after her or something," he informed me. "Lost your touch?"

"Apparently, I'm not good enough for her. She doesn't want to know me." The hurt that I'd felt only seconds before was fading away, replaced by a hot rush of anger that burned through my blood.

"Seriously?" Tristan stared at me for a second, his mouth open, and then he punched my arm lightly, which I guess was his form of comfort. "She can fuck off. If that's the way she thinks, you're better off without her."

The anger burned brightly, a ball of fire inside my chest.

"She thinks she's better than me? Wants me to stay away from her? To forget she exists? I'm going to make sure she regrets ever saying those words."

Triston studied me warily. "What does that mean?"

"It means…that Quinn Farrow is about to find out just what happens when you make an enemy of me."

2

___

Quinn

"And finally…our captains. The blue team captain… Quinn Farrow! The red team captain…Penelope Byron-Clopard! Alright, ladies, take your places!" Mrs. Cox, the netball coach, blew her whistle, and we lined up on the court. Penelope stood opposite me, shooting me a quick smile, her high ponytail bouncing as she shook out her arms and legs. Just behind her and to her right, Freya stared at me, unsmiling. My attention was only partly on them, though. Because there was someone else looking at me. A boy with deep blue eyes and raven hair.

Roman stood in the shadow of a tree, leaning back against the trunk with his hands in the pockets of his school trousers. His tie was loosened, and his blazer was crumpled in a heap at his feet, on top of his school bag. From here, I couldn't make out his expression, and I couldn't afford to take a closer look in case anyone saw. Still, my entire body grew warm, and I couldn't keep the smile from my face.

That warm, bubbly feeling lasted throughout the netball match. Maybe Roman watching us was my lucky charm because my team won, the final score 38-31. After the customary team captain handshake, I made the most of the teams being distracted—the blues by their celebrations and the reds already making their way back to the *changing rooms. I jogged off the court in the opposite direction to everyone else.*

Roman was no longer in sight, but I headed towards the tree anyway. As I rounded the corner of the large trunk, I saw a shoulder, and then a second later, I was standing in front of him, watching as a gorgeous smile spread across his face.

"Hi. You played well today."

I bit down on my lip, feeling my cheeks heating. "Thanks. You played well, too."

His brows rose. "When?"

"Um. Yesterday. I watched your lacrosse practice."

"I didn't see you."

Scuffing at the leaves under my feet with the toe of my trainer, I nodded. "I know. I stayed out of the way. Didn't want to distract you, you know."

He shot me a look that was far too knowing. "Or you didn't want anyone to notice you looking at me." Stepping closer, he lowered his voice. "No one knows about this side of you apart from me, do they?" A grin curved over his lips. "Don't worry, your secret's safe with me. Just as mine is with you."

I knew exactly what he was referring to. My need to escape… with him, and for him—his softer side that he only ever showed to me. We were only fifteen years old, and yet it sometimes felt as if I'd found my soulmate.

"Always." We smiled at each other, and I felt that bubbly warmth again, that heady feeling I only ever got around him.

Tears filled my eyes as I stumbled blindly away from the boat sheds, barely even seeing Tristan as I passed him. It had taken everything in me to hold my composure while I'd thrown those horrible words at Roman, and seeing the look on his face…

A sob tore from my throat. I'd thought it would be easy enough to follow the rules my parents had set out for me, but I'd just been fooling myself. The second Roman's eyes had met mine, everything I felt for him came rushing back.

But he'd believed me. I'd seen the way he'd shut down and hardened, his hurt and confusion replaced by hatred.

I couldn't help feeling like I'd just made an enemy out of the boy that I'd once been close to falling in love with.

When I arrived at my dorm room, I threw the door open and flung myself onto the nearest bed, letting the tears free.

"Quinn?"

I raised my head at the soft voice that came from my left, swiping at my eyes. Pulling myself into a seated position, I met the concerned gaze of Penelope Byron-Chopard, current head girl and my friend. We'd been best friends, once. Our families were close, and we'd grown up together. It was completely my fault that we'd grown apart during my rebellious phase and my parents' fault that we hadn't spoken while I'd been away, but she was far too nice to hold a grudge. I hoped we could grow close again now I was back. I could really, really use a friend.

Taking a deep breath, I gathered myself. "Hi, Pen. It's...it's so good to see you. I'm sorry, I didn't see you there."

She smiled, although the concern was still clear in her eyes. "Quinn, it's good to see you again, too. It wasn't the same here without you." She paused, her gaze searching. "Is there anything I can help you with?"

"No, thank you. Just first-day nerves, I think." Thankful that my voice came out steady, I shrugged. "I know I'm not exactly new here, but you know...I've been away for a while."

"Of course. I get that." Crossing the room to sit next to

me, she sank onto the bed to give me a hug. "I wanted to be here when you arrived so you'd see a familiar face. I missed you, you know."

I glanced around the room, taking in the four beds in each corner, each with a desk, wardrobe, and shelves. Taking a deep breath, I gave her a shaky smile, so relieved that she seemed to be happy to have me back. "Me too. I missed you. I missed…everything. More than I thought I would." My gaze went to the neatly made bed across from the one I was sitting on. "Who are my dormmates?"

"Well, they didn't have much space. Most of the beds were taken." Her mouth twisted. "You've been put in with three of the other girls from Epi. They're not… None of them are girls you were friends with before. I'm sorry. The bed under the window is free."

My first day back, and I was having to share a room with three other girls that I didn't know? I tried not to let my disappointment show because I shouldn't have expected anything, rejoining the school after the term had already begun.

"Sorry, I didn't realise." As I glanced around me, I noticed my suitcases were placed next to the bed and the empty desk that sat underneath the large, leaded window.

"No need to be sorry." She reclined back on her elbows, flipping her blonde ponytail over her shoulder as she did so. "I would have roomed with you if I could, but you know the head girl gets a separate room with a private bathroom, and since you weren't here at the beginning of term…I had to choose a roommate. My room isn't big enough for more than two beds, unlike the head boy's, so I had no choice."

"You don't need to explain," I assured her. "Who are you sharing with?"

She hesitated before lowering her gaze. "Freya."

Oh. Freya Thorpe. Blonde, beautiful Freya. We'd never seen eye to eye, but she was a close friend of Penelope. They were third or fourth cousins, or something like that, and Freya was popular despite her spoilt, arrogant attitude. Thanks to her popularity and relationship with Penelope, she wasn't someone I wanted to get on the wrong side of. There wasn't any particular issue I had with her; it was just that she was one of those people who had to be the best in everything. We'd fallen out when we were younger, after I'd beaten her to the team captain position in netball. Her entitled attitude grated on me, not that it was anything unusual in this school with so many rich kids' egos crammed into one space twenty-four seven. But I could deal with it, and who knew, maybe Freya and I could put the past behind us and start over again now that I was back.

Before I could think of anything to say in reply, a bell rang loudly, making us both jump. Penelope sighed, sliding off the bed. "Come on. House assembly. We'd better not be late."

"Yeah. I don't want to draw any more attention to myself." Mainly because Roman would be there. And despite Pen's calming presence, I knew that it was going to take everything in me to stick to the agreement I'd made with my mother to stay away from him.

I quickly flipped on the selfie camera on my phone, making sure that my face showed no traces of my tears, and pulled my hair into a ponytail. That done, I ran my fingers through the length, smoothing it out. I took one last glance at the screen before putting my phone away, then Penelope and I made our way down to the hall where the house assemblies took place.

As soon as I stepped inside, my shoes hitting the worn flagstones, it was like no time had passed. The hall was exactly as I remembered—cavernous, vaulted ceilings and pillars, all stone and huge windows, with rows of wooden pews facing a small stage with a lectern and microphone. The whole thing gave off a cathedral-type vibe, although, to my knowledge, the building had never been used for any kind of religious ceremony. The carved stone statues that flanked the corners of the room were depictions of the Greek philosophers rather than saints, for a start. Although it did have something in common with the cathedrals I'd visited as a child—the hall was always cold, even in the summer with the sun streaming through the windows.

There were other students filing into the room, so I slipped in between them, losing Penelope in the crowd. As the head girl, she had to sit up at the front, and I wasn't about to draw any more attention to myself than I absolutely had to. Having said that, I wasn't going to hide in a corner either.

Before I could decide on a seat, a hand curled around my wrist. "Come and sit with me."

I spun around to see Aria grinning at me. Petite, with long, jet-black, wavy hair, huge golden-brown eyes, and a rosebud mouth, I'd heard her described as both "cute" and "fragile." Looks were deceiving, though. Aria was fierce. Her small stature belied her sometimes fiery nature, mostly if she was provoked, and she swore like a sailor, as my mother would say. We had different friend groups, so we'd never interacted much in public. Aria wasn't someone who cared about status or anything like that. She was just one of those people that most people genuinely liked, so she'd more or less been part of the elite without even trying or even wanting to be, yet status didn't concern her. We'd become friends of a sort around the same time I'd started getting to know Roman. We'd met on the night I'd sneaked out of my dorm room to the old bell tower that was off limits to students and found her in there smoking a joint, casually draped across the crumbling remains of a window ledge like there wasn't a sheer drop that could kill her if she moved an inch in the wrong direction.

Our friendship had never really had a chance to see the light of day, though, with us moving in different circles and my parents' tight control over me regarding the people they deemed appropriate for me to be around. But maybe now I was back, things would be different. It wasn't that they disapproved of Aria as such; it was more that they encouraged friendships with what they classed as "influential people." People who, in their opinion, could further my future career and my adult life. Unfortunately for them, I couldn't ever view people as commodities.

"Aria. Hi." My lips curved into a genuine smile, and I followed her without hesitation.

"We're roommates," she announced as we took seats about halfway down the rows of pews, sliding along the row until we reached the end closest to the window.

"We are?" My smile widened. This was great news.

"Your parents probably won't be happy."

"I don't think they have a problem with you specifically, but…" My voice trailed off, and I couldn't help my grimace.

Aria studied me intently, her head cocked. "Let me guess. They wanted you to be rooming with Penelope or Freya or someone else they explicitly approve of? The people who were your friends before. The elite."

We both pulled a face. She was right. It wasn't like I hadn't known the terms of my return to Hatherley Hall, but after I'd faced Roman earlier…the reality had been far more difficult than I'd anticipated. I couldn't tell her the details yet, though. Not until we could be alone, with no chance of being overheard.

The tower, I mouthed, and she nodded before turning to face the front of the room, where Professor Donnelly, our head of house, was shuffling papers at the lectern. Most of the teachers preferred to use laptops and projectors, but he was one of those old-school teachers who had a deep distrust of modern technology.

He cleared his throat loudly, the microphone amplifying the sound, sending it bouncing around the hall with the help of the speakers placed on the pillars that ran down the sides of the room. Just that small action had the hall falling into silence, students straightening up and fixing their gazes on him.

A sudden chill went down my spine as Prof. Donnelly began to speak, and it had nothing to do with what was happening at the front of the room.

It was the awareness of the gaze I felt boring into the back of my head. Without even having to turn around, I knew it was him.

Roman.

My heart stuttered, and I squeezed my hands together in my lap, my knuckles turning white with the pressure. After all this time, the way this boy held so much power over me, the way he could affect me like no one else ever could…

I could never allow him to see it. I had to perfect my mask of disinterest, even if it made me feel like a hollow shell of myself.

The consequences weren't worth risking. Not for me, and not for him.

Quinn

"We're sorry to do this to you, sweetheart. It's for your own good. Your education is more important than anything else. More important than fleeting friendships that won't last." My mother squeezed my hand.

Next to her, my dad nodded. "We just want what is best for you. A clean break is what you need. Time away from those bad influences in your life. My secondment to the Swiss office came at just the right time. You'll soon forget about Hatherley Hall and those people you should never have come into contact with. Especially that Roman Cavendish. Mark my words, that boy will end up expelled, and it wouldn't surprise me if he ends up in prison with the way he's going."

My dad tugged my phone from my grip, ignoring my shocked gasp.

"A clean break," he repeated, throwing my phone into his desk drawer and then slamming it shut. "That's what you need. No more contact with anyone from that school. We know the Cavendish boy was mostly to blame for your grades dropping. He was your biggest distraction, and we should have done something about it sooner. But he wasn't the only one." Exchanging glances with my mum, he placed a heavy hand on my shoulder. "I know some of the other students were *your friends, but you'll forget about them when we're gone. Your grades are the most important thing, Quinn. You'll thank us in the long run."*

The rest of the day was mostly uneventful, and I managed to avoid Roman. I didn't get to speak to Aria again, as she was nowhere to be found. Thankfully, Penelope came to find me after the assembly, and we ate lunch together, surrounded by the popular girls. Penelope's roommate, Freya, was at a netball team meeting, so my first interaction with her was delayed, and I was grateful for that. Although I'd probably been building everything up too much inside my head, the thought of more than one confrontation on my first day back was enough for me.

When the warning bell rang to inform us that curfew was thirty minutes away, I was already in my dorm room, collapsed on my bed, earphones in and an audiobook playing on my phone. My roommates were nowhere to be seen—my guess was that they were in the common room. Each house had its own common room, shared between two school years. Our common room was located on the same floor as my dorm, and Epi students from years twelve and thirteen, aka A-level students, shared it. In the daytime, it was mostly used as a study area, but in the evenings, it played host to board games, card games, film nights, gossip sessions, students flirting with each other…all the usual stuff, I guess. The staff generally turned a blind eye as long as everything remained discreet and no one got too loud. I should have been there, integrating myself with the members of my house and reforging old acquaintances, but the day had been a little draining, and I needed some peace. To be back at Hatherley Hall, surrounded by so many people…it had been everything I'd wanted since I'd left here the first time, but it was a big change after over two years of being homeschooled.

The door suddenly swung open, and I reached for my phone, pausing my audiobook and removing my earphones. Three girls piled into the room, the first one stopping dead when she saw me, and the other two crashed into her back with muffled cries.

From the back, Aria stepped around the other two girls, throwing them an eye roll, then turned to me. "Meet Quinn. Despite being one of the goddesses, she's actually nice."

"Ugh. Don't start with that whole gods-and-goddesses thing." Grimacing, I returned her eye roll with one of my own. It was like no time had passed between us.

She just laughed. "You can't deny it. You were one before, and you'll be one again."

There was a tradition at Hatherley Hall—every May, there was a Greek gods and goddesses–themed ball. Each ball had a slightly different theme, but it was always based around Greek mythology.

I loved the ball itself—who wouldn't love a chance to dress up, dance, and have fun with all your friends in a beautifully decorated space? But part of the ball was essentially a popularity contest, where people would vote for their favourite gods and goddesses in the run-up to the ball, and towards the end of the evening, the winners would be announced. When I was younger, I'd always hoped to be voted as one of the goddesses, for the crown styled like a laurel wreath to be placed on my head, cementing my place as one of the elite. The year I left Hatherley Hall, I'd become one. I'd been the youngest-ever goddess, according to the then-head girl, and apparently, I'd narrowly beaten Penelope to the spot—if the head girl at that time had been telling the truth since the votes were supposed to only be seen by the staff. Of course, Penelope was nothing but happy for me, even though it meant that she missed out on the prize—although we both agreed there was no way of knowing if it was true.

This time around, things had changed. While my mother would no doubt love nothing more than for me to be one of the goddesses, especially since she was a Hatherley Hall alumni and had been a goddess two years running during her time as a student, I didn't want that.

Because there was no doubt in my mind that Roman would be one of the gods.

He'd always affected me, had always been beautiful, but now? He took my breath away. That chiselled jaw, those deep blue eyes, like the depths of the ocean, fringed with thick, inky lashes, his raven hair, artfully dishevelled, falling into his eyes, that body I'd felt pressed against me today—all lean, toned muscle, no doubt from his hours of swimming and rowing and whatever else he did to get such definition—and that sexy, low rasp to his voice that sent shivers through me. Whether or not he was still a troublemaker, there was no denying how utterly gorgeous he was. Not to mention, it seemed like he was friends with Tristan now, who was the head boy, and that more or less guaranteed him a place as one of the gods.

"I have no interest in being one of the goddesses," I said firmly, and Aria raised a brow.

"You might not get any choice. Everyone's eligible." She seemed to read something in my face because she gave a small shake of her head and stepped closer. "Anyway, enough about that. Quinn, meet Samira and Gracelyn, our roommates."

I recognised both of them, although I'd never spoken to either of them before. Samira was striking, all dark hair and flawless brown skin, and Gracelyn was a pretty redhead with pale skin dotted with freckles.

They both eyed me curiously, and before the silence became awkward, I spoke up. "It's nice to meet you both. Thanks for letting me crash here."

"It wasn't like we had a choice." Samira's reply was accompanied by a smirk that changed into a bright, genuine smile, and I relaxed. "Only joking. Welcome back to Hatherley Hall." Glancing over at her friends, she grinned. "Grace is my girlfriend, by the way. I thought I should mention it upfront in case things get awkward if you start wondering why we're all over each other."

I glanced between them both, taking in the way they were curled around each other. "I did wonder, but honestly, I miss the signs all the time, so thanks for telling me."

Samira's grin widened. "No probs. Hey, we'll have to introduce you to our other new friend, Elena. Wait, Aria, have you already introduced her?"

We chatted for a bit, and I relaxed even further. By the time the curfew bell rang, I was curled up on Samira's bed in pyjamas and a hoodie, catching up on everything I'd missed while I'd been gone, while Gracelyn painted her toenails in rainbow colours and Aria sketched something that she refused to show to any of us. Now the bell had rung, we had around ten minutes before we had to be in bed with the lights out, so we all made our way to our own beds.

Aria leaned into me as she passed. "One hour."

I gave a small nod, climbing into my bed and discreetly waking up my phone under the covers, turning the screen brightness right down and making sure it was on silent. I passed the hour by playing games on my phone, and once I heard Aria's bed creak, I made myself wait another few minutes before slipping out of the room into the silent, dark corridor.

The corridors were occasionally patrolled by security, but in a building this large, it was easy to avoid them, especially since their numbers were minimal. They were mostly concerned with covering the grounds, anyway, stopping anyone who might want to sneak out. Inside, they relied more on the cameras sparsely dotted around the school, but once you knew where they were, it was fairly easy to avoid them. There were no cameras in the old bell tower, either, since the entire area was off limits to students. The entrance was completely blocked off, and most people had forgotten all about it. Except...Aria had found the hidden entrance, through a small door under a set of stairs. It looked like a cupboard—in fact, it *was* a cupboard—but it had another exit on the other side, which opened onto the set of stairs that led up to the tower.

I made my way to the cupboard, which Aria had left ajar for me, and once I was inside, I flipped on my phone torch so I could see the bit to push on the panelled wood that doubled as an interior opening for the bell tower door. It opened with a soft creak, and then I was out on the other side with the cool night breeze snaking down the stairs and wrapping around me.

Pulling my hoodie sleeves down over my hands and tugging my hood up, I made my way up the stairs to the room right below the ruins of the top level, where the bell had once stood. Aria was on a blanket on the floor, leaning her back against the wall with her legs outstretched and a joint already in her hand.

Crossing the room, I took a seat on the blanket next to her. "Where do you manage to get these things?" I indicated towards the joint clasped between her fingers.

"I have my ways." After inhaling deeply, she held it out to me, but I shook my head.

"No, thanks. I just want to get all this off my chest first, and I need a clear head to make sense of everything."

"Fair enough." She leaned her head back against the stone wall, exhaling a stream of smoke that the wind immediately whipped away through the sizeable gap where a window used to be. "Okay. I haven't had a proper conversation with you for over two years. So, I think it's time you caught me up."

Our eyes met, and there was no judgement in hers.

I opened my mouth and began.

I'd always had an expectation on me to be the perfect daughter. I was an only child, and my parents had provided me with everything I needed. Everything I needed, but not everything I wanted. They didn't believe in spoiling me, although I was never deprived of anything. Their primary goal for me seemed to be for them to have a child they could boast about to their friends and colleagues, a child who excelled at everything. No expense had been spared in my education and extracurricular activities. Ballet, tap, and jazz were three of the dance disciplines I was expected to perform. I played tennis, rode horses, and even learned to kayak (the only discipline I was allowed to choose myself). I was coached in French and German and played piano and violin. For any child, it would be a lot, and I was left constantly exhausted, under pressure to do better every time I achieved one of my parents' goals. When I received my letter of acceptance to Hatherley Hall, my parents threw me a huge party filled with all kinds of influential adults and very few people my age. Penelope had been there, though, and we'd escaped to my bedroom after the cake-cutting ceremony, which included an incredibly long, drawn-out performance from a string quartet. That night, I remember that the thing I felt most was a sense of relief and anticipation because Hatherley Hall meant getting away from my parents, and whatever the school pressures were, surely the other students would be dealing with similar pressures and expectations. We were all children of rich and influential people, after all.

Everything had gone well to begin with. I settled into the routine of school, carving out a place for myself. Penelope shared my dorm, and we'd stay up late talking about boys and our plans for the future, making up wild stories that a secret prince of some obscure European state would fall in love with us and take us back to his homeland to be his princess. Looking back, it was clear that we spent far too much time in our formative years watching *The Princess Diaries*.

As I grew older, though, the pressures gradually returned, with the weight of the expectations on me becoming clear again. My parents were friendly with several members of Hatherley Hall's staff, and they used their connections to stay updated on my progress. I'd receive regular messages and phone calls from my mother that would make it clear that my best wasn't good enough.

One day, I snapped. I'd been on my way to a biology lesson when everything had hit me all at once, the pressure suffocating me. I'd ducked into the toilets, and then afterwards…that was when I'd met Roman for the first time.

That first taste of rebellion, of the freedom to make my own decisions, was an addiction. I continued to meet up with Roman, I met and became clandestine friends with Aria, and I carried out small acts of rebellion—adapting my uniform, cutting classes, slacking on my homework, dabbling with contraband drugs and alcohol.

It didn't take long before word reached my parents. Their spies must've been almost everywhere because they somehow knew everything, except for my friendship with Aria, which had somehow remained a secret. It had to have because there was no way I'd have been allowed to room with her this year otherwise. It wasn't that they disliked her as such—it was more that in their eyes, she was useless because she didn't have an influential family name like my other friends did.

My punishment was taking me away from the school I loved. I also had to relinquish my phone, to cut ties with everyone and everything to do with Hatherley Hall, even Penelope.

Since my parents were moving overseas temporarily while my father took a secondment in Geneva, they took me with them. I was assigned tutors who homeschooled me, and while I threw myself back into my schoolwork to prove I wasn't a failure, I grew increasingly withdrawn. The simple truth was that I was lonely. So, so lonely. I missed my friends, my school, the daily routine, the old buildings surrounded by gorgeous English countryside. In Geneva, despite the beauty that was all around me and the people who welcomed our family, I was completely alone. My parents had a schedule, so I had no company day to day other than my tutors, with my father working long hours and my mother out doing whatever she did all day with her friends.

Eventually, things changed. My parents weren't monsters, and finally, their concern for me began to outweigh their need for me to succeed.

. . .

"What did they do?"

I blinked, my gaze flying to Aria at my side. I'd almost forgotten she was there; I'd been so lost in my memories.

"When we came back to England, they allowed me to come back here. I have conditions, though."

"Of course you do." She flicked the tiny stub that was left of her joint out of the window, then sighed. "Let me guess. You have to toe the line? Be the perfect student? Interact with the right people?"

"Quinn. We want to make this clear. We took you away from Hatherley Hall because your grades were slipping, and we'd received word that you'd taken up with unsavoury company." My dad clasped my shoulder. "Your mother and I don't want to see you suffer, and so we've re-enrolled you as a student at Hatherley Hall now my secondment has finished." His grip tightened. "We want you to do your best and succeed in the way we know you can. If we hear any whisper of you interacting with the Cavendish boy, or anyone who we know to be a bad influence, we will take action."

"I-I'm not planning on speaking to him," I whispered.

My dad smiled, satisfied. "Good. If Roman Cavendish comes near you, we will ensure he's expelled. Your mother and I have plenty of influence with the school board, and he already has a record. Stay away from him, and we won't have to worry about you."

"Yeah, all of that. I expected that, though. And although they've always put a lot of pressure on me to succeed, I have to look at it from their point of view. They're paying a lot of money for me to be here, and they don't want me to squander my education."

Aria's fingers tapped against the stone floor, her mouth thinning. There was silence while she gathered her thoughts, and then she spoke gently. "I get that, but, Quinn, it almost sounds like you're a commodity to them. They want you to do well because it makes them look good."

A lump came into my throat that I desperately tried to ignore. "I know," I whispered. "But that's okay."

It's not, she mouthed, shaking her head sadly, and I blinked again, sudden tears obscuring my vision.

"That's not even…there's something else. I'm not allowed to even *speak* to Roman. I can't be friends with him, and I *definitely* can't be anything more. If…if word gets back to my parents…it can't happen. They made it clear that they'd find a way to get him expelled. You know how he was in and out of all those different schools before he came here, and this is really his last chance." A tear crystallised on my lashes, then fell. "He's *happy* here. I could see that the second I saw him with Tristan. I can't do that to him. I can't risk it. This is his life, his future. If anything happened and I had a hand in it, I'd never forgive myself. My parents more or less blame him for my rebellious phase. I mean, it was easy enough for them to jump to conclusions, based on his reputation, but the thing was, it wasn't him. It was all me. *I* made all my own decisions, and *I* was the only one who deserved to face the consequences."

Aria studied me for a moment. "This is fucked up," she muttered. "You still like him, don't you?"

I pulled up my knees, resting my arms on them and dropping my head. "So much. It took me aback…I…I wasn't expecting to still have such strong feelings for him. The things I said to him, I—" My voice cracked. "The way he looked at me, Ari. I feel like the worst kind of monster for making it seem like he was nothing to me."

"Do you think it's worth telling him?"

"No. I know him, and I know he'd try and find some way around it. He lives for the thrill of danger, doing what he thinks he can get away with, without being caught."

"Yeah." She gave me a wry grin. "His arson stunt was talked about for months. But he's been quiet since then. I heard he was on his last warning."

"You see?" I raised my head to stare at her. "This is why I can't say anything. This is his last chance, and we're in our final year. I'm not going to do anything to jeopardise that for him."

"I—"

Whatever she was about to reply was lost with the unmistakable sound of footsteps on the stairs.

4

Quinn

ria and I froze, staring at each other, before she tilted her head towards the shadowed part of the room next to the stairs. As quietly as we could, we melted into the shadows, and I was glad that both of us had worn thick socks and no shoes. There was nothing to hide behind in this room, so our only hope of remaining undetected was if whoever was coming up the stairs only took a cursory glance around.

A tousled blond head of hair came into view, silvery in the bright moonlight that bathed the bell tower. My body relaxed incrementally, and Aria made a sound that was something between a huff and a laugh, then stepped out of the shadows. "Head boy," she drawled, somehow managing to look down her nose disdainfully despite her small stature.

"I should've known *you'd* be here." Tristan matched her disdain with an imperious look of his own, and I clapped my hand over my mouth to hold in my laughter.

When Aria stalked over to the wall opposite my hiding place and leaned against it, folding her arms across her chest and darting a pointed look at me before staring up at Tristan, I figured out her plan. *Distraction.* Allowing me enough time to get away.

Tristan moved farther into the room, so close to me. I held my breath, not daring to move.

"Come closer, head boy. Or are you scared I'll bite?"

"You fucking wish." He stepped up to her, and I caught a glimpse of his curled lip and arched brow before he turned to fully face her.

"Mmm, maybe I do." She gave him a blatant once-over, exaggeratedly licking her lips, but even in this dim lighting, I could see her eyes sparkling with mischief. After one last sweeping glance, she returned her gaze to his face and bit down on her lip, clearly trying to hide her amusement.

"Sorry, I don't associate with drug users who—"

Aria's hand flew up, and from the muffled sound Tristan made, I guessed she'd placed it over his mouth. "I'm going to stop you right there. Someone as…uptight as you could use a little relaxation. Ever smoked a joint? Or are you as perfect as your reputation suggests?"

Fuck, I really needed to get out of here before I laughed out loud.

Tristan gripped her wrist, lifting it away from his face and pressing it into the wall behind Aria. "I know plenty of ways to relax that don't involve weed. Do you? Have you ever…" He lowered his head to her ear, and I could no longer hear what he was saying, but I watched as Aria's mouth dropped open and her eyes flashed with something I couldn't name before her leg came up and kicked him in the shin.

"Fuck's sake, what was that for?" he growled out, collapsing against the wall and rubbing at his leg. Unfortunately, it was at that moment that his head turned, and he saw me. Shock registered in his expression, and then his eyes turned hard. "Quinn."

"Why didn't you leave? I was creating a distraction," Aria hissed, and then I had both of them glaring at me.

Tristan shot Aria an annoyed look before returning his attention to me. "What are you two doing here?"

"We could ask you the same question." Aria stepped forwards, drawing his attention to her again.

He sighed, pinching his brow. "Whatever. Look, it's late. Why don't we just get back to our rooms and forget we ever saw each other here, okay?"

Silence fell, and I tried to signal Aria with my eyes. We'd accomplished what we'd come here to do—to talk—and it wasn't like Tristan was going to let us stay up here now he'd found us. He'd probably go running to our head of house or something, and I couldn't risk anything getting back to my parents. I shouldn't have even come here in the first place, but I'd thought the risk was minimal until Tristan had shown up.

"Fine," Aria muttered eventually, pushing past Tristan and stalking over to the stairs. I went to follow her, but I was stopped by a hand on my arm. Tristan leaned down and spoke low in my ear.

"You'd better stay away from Roman. He told me what you said to him, and that shit isn't okay."

"I didn't—it's not like that." I shook my head furiously, yanking my arm away from his grip. "Is…is he okay?"

Tristan studied me for a long moment before he turned away. "You need to stay away from him." Then he was gone, following Aria down the stairs.

I'd really thought that I'd done the right thing by coming back here, by pushing Roman away, but I had a horrible feeling that my problems were only just beginning.

The sky was beginning to lighten when I gave up on sleep. No one else was awake, so I made my way down to the showers at the end of our corridor and spent way too long under the water, turning everything over in my head. When I was back in my dorm room, it was still early, so I dressed in running leggings and a sports bra and threw on a zip-up hoodie. All regulation, of course—the school had uniforms for just about every kind of sport imaginable. I pulled my damp hair into a ponytail, grabbed my phone and headphones, clipped my running belt around my hips, and then made my way down to the ground floor.

There were a few students milling around—other early risers, most dressed in some variation of sports clothes, taking advantage of the time before breakfast for exercise or extra training in their favourite sports discipline. Since I'd only just showered, I wasn't planning on exercising, but the clothes were comfortable and meant I didn't stand out among the other students.

Once I was outside, I hit a random playlist and turned up the volume, leaving the path and walking across the soft grass that was damp with the morning dew. Without any conscious thought, my feet carried me towards the line of trees that marked the boundary. When I realised where I was, I came to a stop, staring at the wooded area in front of me. Stopping my music, I tugged my headphones off and shoved them into my pocket as I lost myself in the wave of memories that crashed over me. Roman leading me through the trees, my hand clasped in his. The small smiles and sideways glances he gave me. The way he held back the branches for me so that I had a clear path.

I took a step forward. Then another, and another, until I was moving with purpose through the trees, until I reached the other side. The lake was there, exactly as I'd remembered. That still water, now a soft grey as it reflected the cloudy dawn, the reeds at the far side, the jetty, the ripples—

The ripples. There shouldn't be ripples. Not like that. I watched as they spread, a dark shape beneath them, and before I could make sense of what I was seeing, Roman burst from the water.

Fucking hell.

His eyes were closed, his lashes spiky and wet, and his jet-black hair was plastered to his head, rivulets of water running over the ridges of his muscles as he lifted himself effortlessly above the surface like some kind of water god. As he drew closer to the surface and more and more of his godlike body was exposed, his eyes opened.

Something dark and hot flared in his gaze as our eyes connected. His mouth curved into a slow, predatory smile, and he stepped upright as he reached the shallows.

He was completely naked.

Heat raced through my body. My mouth went dry, and my heart sped up so fast that I had to press back against the tree behind me, gulping air into my lungs.

When he stepped onto the shore, the water sluicing off his hard body, I closed my eyes. It was too much. Way, way too much. No one could be confronted with Roman Cavendish looking like that and not be affected.

The silence surrounded us, only broken by the birds in the trees. Then I felt a whisper of breath across my cheek, and fingers curled around my jaw, holding me in place.

"Did you follow me here?" Roman's soft rasp hit my ear, and I dared to open my eyes. He'd wrapped a towel around his waist, which should've made me less flustered in his presence, but it didn't. Droplets of water glittered all over his bare torso, and as he stepped right up to me, I felt the unmistakable press of his hardening length against my body.

"I didn't know you'd be here," I managed once I remembered how to form words.

He clearly didn't believe me, even though it was true, but he didn't comment. Instead, he released his tight grip on my jaw, skimming his hand down my throat, stopping at the zip of my hoodie.

"You're overdressed." He gripped the zip and lowered it all the way until my hoodie was hanging open, then slid it off my shoulders, leaving me in my running leggings and sports bra. I told myself that my shiver was from the cool morning air hitting my exposed areas, but in reality, I knew it was the feel of his hands sliding over my bare skin. Our interactions in the past had been more or less innocent, never going further than kissing, but there was nothing innocent about this.

"Better," he murmured once he'd thrown my hoodie and running belt somewhere. I couldn't bring myself to care where they'd fallen. His hands went to my waist, pulling me closer. When his lips trailed along the side of my face, up to my ear, a soft noise escaped me before I could stop it. I felt his mouth curve against the shell of my ear as he dipped his fingers beneath the waistband of my leggings. "What would you do if I pulled down these leggings? Would you let me fuck you?"

"*Roman.*" I gave in to the desire to touch him, winding my arms around his shoulders and gripping the back of his neck, attempting to angle his head so I could kiss him.

He scooped me up, pressing me back against the tree. I wrapped my legs around his waist as he held me effortlessly, palming my ass and brushing his lips over mine with the barest touch, nothing that would satisfy the craving I had for his mouth on mine. When I tried to deepen the kiss, he turned his head, stepping backwards, away from the tree.

"Why won't you kiss me?" I whispered.

In the back of my mind, I knew the answer to the question, but right now, surrounded by him, just the two of us in the place that had always been ours, it was easy to forget everything else. To forget how I'd hurt him with my words, how I wasn't supposed to allow myself near him. How I'd told him one thing, but I was now doing the opposite.

I dimly became aware of the sound of wooden boards creaking under his feet, but I barely paid attention. His mouth returned to my ear. "I'm not good enough for you, but I'm good enough to kiss? Good enough for a quick and dirty fuck out here where no one else ever has to find out?" He clamped down on my ear with his teeth. "I don't fucking think so."

Then he ripped me away from him, and I found myself falling, a scream tearing from my throat as I hit the water of the lake and went under.

5

ROMAN

I left Quinn without a backwards look, scooping up her hoodie as I went. Her shouts rang in my ears, but I didn't stop other than to grab my small pile of clothes where I'd left them. Quickly tugging on tracksuit bottoms and my own hoodie, then shoving my feet into my trainers, I jogged back to the school building and made my way to my room.

Tristan looked up from his laptop when I entered, his eyes narrowing. "You look suspiciously happy."

"I don't know what you mean. I'm off to have a shower."

Once I'd washed the lake water off, I headed back into the room to change into my normal uniform. Tristan was sitting on the side of his bed, holding up Quinn's hoodie.

"Care to explain this?"

"Not really, no." Opening the wardrobe, I pulled out my clothes, hiding my smirk.

From behind me, he cleared his throat pointedly. "Okay. Want to tell me how you now have two phones when you had one this morning? And why you're suddenly in possession of a pair of rose-gold headphones?"

"Who doesn't have two phones these days? And I liked the colour, so what?" I shifted so he could see my face, and he rolled his eyes at me.

"Nice try."

Moving to stand in front of the mirror, I began pulling on my clothes and made sure I kept my voice casual. "I saw Quinn."

"Uh-huh." He eyed my reflection in the mirror. "In that case, I don't even want to know. Plausible deniability and all that. But you can't keep her phone."

"Watch me."

"Ro. You can't."

"You know what your problem is?" Shrugging on my blazer, I turned to face him. "You have too much of a conscience."

"Maybe if you listened to yours, you wouldn't get into so much trouble." He flashed me a grin, and I knew he wasn't really annoyed at me. Head boy or not, he was my friend, and he was on my side. Except, he continued. "I'm serious. You can't keep this. I'll make sure it gets back to her without implicating either of us, okay?"

"You're such a good boy, Tris. Want some help polishing that halo?" I stepped over to his bed and ruffled his hair, which made him glare at me, shoving my hand away and smoothing his hair back down. With a sigh, I held up my hands. "Fine, get it back to her if it'll stop you whining about it." The truth was, I hadn't even noticed her phone was in the hoodie when I'd first taken it. If you thought about it, I'd actually done her a favour by saving it from being drowned in the lake when I'd thrown her in.

"My influence spreads far and wide. I got Hatherley Hall's resident bad boy to do my bidding." Climbing to his feet, he pulled on his own blazer and then grabbed his bag. "They don't call me the king of the school for nothing."

Swiping my own bag from the floor, I followed him out of the room just as the bell rang for breakfast. "Literally no one calls you the king of the school."

"Everyone does."

"They don't."

We continued arguing all the way down to the dining hall, where Tristan strolled to the front of the line with his head boy privileges, and I had to join the back of the queue with the other students. In front of me, two girls were talking in hushed voices. I wasn't paying attention until one of them mentioned Quinn's name.

"…and she only had a sports bra and leggings on. She was completely soaked, and I heard from Harriet that her lips were blue with the cold."

I had a sudden twinge of something that felt a lot like guilt, but I pushed it aside. Quinn deserved it.

"…yes, but did you actually see her? I did. Ugh, I wish I had her body. There's no way I'd look anywhere near that good if I'd fallen in the lake."

"Yeah, she's so pretty. I'd look like a drowned rat if it had been me. How did she even manage to fall in the lake, anyway?"

"I don't know."

The conversation segued into something about hair-drying techniques, so I tuned them back out. From the sound of it, Quinn hadn't told anyone about the part I'd played in her dunking. At least she was smart enough to keep it quiet.

For a moment there, when I'd broken the surface of the water and seen her standing frozen, staring at me with that look in her eyes, I'd forgotten the way she'd acted towards me. Forgotten that I needed to punish her. And when I'd had her pressed up against me, all soft and pliant, it had taken every bit of willpower I had not to just rip off those fucking leggings that showed off the curves of her long legs and sink my cock inside her. She would've taken it, too. Probably even begged me for it.

Then I'd remembered what she'd said to me. Throwing her in the lake had been an impulsive decision, but she made me irrational. Made my head spin, telling me one thing one day, then begging me to kiss her the next. No, Quinn Farrow deserved to be punished. I knew that no one loved me, that despite the way I looked, I'd never have a close connection with someone. I tried not to think about it, managed to ignore it most of the time, but then Quinn had come along and reminded me of everything I wanted to forget. And she'd made it crystal clear just what I meant to her when she'd told me I needed to forget she existed.

I wasn't going to let that happen. The lake was just the beginning.

By the time lessons were over for the day, the word had spread around the school, and every time I saw Quinn, she had a murderous look on her face directed at me. Good.

It wasn't enough, though.

I cornered Tristan in the common room after dinner. Knox was down in the creepy crypts with his girlfriend, Elena, so it was just the two of us.

"Hey, Tris, can I have a word?"

He glanced up from the TV screen, meeting my gaze. "Yeah. What's up?"

"Over here."

When we were in a corner of the room away from the

others, I shoved my hands in my pockets, leaning back against the wall. "Did you give Quinn her phone back?"

He shook his head. "Not yet."

"Okay, good." It was time to put the first steps of my plan into place. "You know how Blaine was talking about going down to the beach for the bank holiday weekend? What do you say we take him up on that and invite a few others?"

"I can already see where this is going." He shook his head with a sigh, but I caught the wry grin that he was trying to hide. "Let me guess. You want me to get Quinn to come. This is a bad idea, you know."

"Yeah, but we're doing it."

When he gave me a resigned nod, I called Blaine over. He was a guy that I knew from the diving club, plus he was a friend of Tristan and Knox. I hadn't seen him much lately because despite the fact I was a fucking strong swimmer and diver, I'd been kicked off both the swim and diving teams the previous year, and I'd been banned from reapplying this year. Banned from applying for anything else, in fact. The lacrosse team was the only extracurricular activity I was still allowed to be involved in at this school. The only reason I'd been allowed to stay in it was because I was really fucking good, and the truth was, the number of players that were on my level could be counted on one hand. That, and the competitive nature of Hatherley Hall —the desire to outrank the other schools and come out on top—was stronger than the desire to punish me for my transgressions.

"Hey, mate." I grinned at him. "Still planning on that beach trip for the bank holiday weekend?"

His face lit up. "Yeah. You coming?"

"Yep. How do you feel about me bringing a few friends? I can sweeten the deal with some contraband."

"No need. The beach house is fully stocked. But yeah, the more the merrier. We've got the space."

Throwing my arm over his shoulders, I lowered my voice conspiratorially. "There's a girl. I want her to come, too, but I don't want her to be pressured into showing up. I want her to realise it's gonna be a good weekend that she doesn't want to miss."

He gave me an evil grin. "Leave it with me. Who is she, and what do you need me to do?"

I glanced over at Tristan, who raised a brow at me. "Well…we have this phone, and we need it to sound like you found it lying outside on the ground…"

When Blaine returned to the common room around fifteen minutes later, he headed straight for me. "Done. Now we have a whole group of girls coming, and I kept your name out of it. I gave the phone to the scary short girl."

Tristan snorted. "Aria?"

"The one and only."

I noticed Tristan pretending to study the window intently. "Is she coming?" His voice radiated disinterest, but he was so transparent.

"No. Or, more accurately, 'Fuck no. Why would I want to come?'" He laughed. "Nah, she said she had shit to do this weekend."

"I see," Tristan murmured before changing the subject. "Okay. Who else is coming, and how many cars do we have?"

I left them to make plans and headed out of the common room. Coincidentally, the path to my and Tristan's room led straight past Quinn's dorm room. If you took a detour in the opposite direction, that was.

My timing was perfect. Just as I rounded the corner of

the corridor, I saw her disappearing into the shower room. Wasting no time, I followed her in.

Her shocked gaze met mine through the mirror, and she spun around, clutching her towel and toiletry bag in front of her like it would protect her from me. She was fully dressed, but she was acting as if I'd caught her naked or something.

I grinned. "I heard you went for a swim with your clothes on this morning. Trying to shower again to get the smell of the lake water off?"

Her eyes flashed with anger, and she bared her teeth at me. "Get out."

There was no one else in the shower room, but I wouldn't have cared either way. Stalking up to her, I ripped the towel and bag from her grip and let them fall to the floor, then caged her in against the sink unit with my hands planted on either side of her body. "No."

"Get. Out." The way she pushed at my chest, staring up at me from beneath her lashes with both anger and lust burning in her gaze, combined with her body up against mine, made my dick harden rapidly.

"I don't think you want me to." Angling my hips, I let her know just how she was affecting me. When my hard cock pressed against her, a gasp fell from her lips, her eyes darkening, and I took the opportunity to lower my head and kiss her gorgeous mouth. Fuck, she tasted so sweet.

There was a single moment when our lips met, hers plaint against mine. The next minute, there was a stinging pain as she clamped her teeth down on my lower lip, and I tasted blood. This time when she shoved me, I let myself go. Was it wrong that her actions made me smile?

"Biting isn't very nice, Quinn." I shook my head at her.

She stood there seething, all the lust gone. "Don't.

Touch. Me. Don't speak to me. Don't come near me again." Her words were spat at me between gritted teeth.

"I'm going." Making a show of adjusting my dick in my trousers, which made her cheeks flush a deep pink, I backed out of the shower room.

She knew I'd never touch her properly if it wasn't clear that she wanted it, too. The ball was in her court. I'd let her think she'd won, for now. I'd step back for the rest of the week, lull her into a false sense of security. But this coming weekend…

I knew that despite herself, despite her mind telling her I was the wrong option, she wanted me.

And with that knowledge…I couldn't wait.

6

Quinn

"I have an exciting proposition." Professor Fitzgerald paced up and down at the front of the classroom. "I know several of you are planning to incorporate history into your degrees and even your future careers." He beamed at us. "I have an unprecedented opportunity for you. One that no other Hatherley Hall history student has had before. How would you like a chance to write an extra-credit paper?" Pausing dramatically, he hit a button on his laptop, and the screen at the front of the classroom lit up. I sucked in a breath as I took in the words in front of me. This really was unprecedented.

Our history teacher went through the details. We could choose to write a paper on a history subject of our choice, and after he'd looked through all the entries, our best efforts would be judged by a panel of academics. If we managed to impress them, our paper would have a chance of being published in *The Historical Review*, a prestigious academic journal. If that wasn't incentive enough, the winner would be in the running for a summer internship at the National Archives. It was an incredible opportunity.

All I wanted for a career was to do something with history. Nothing else had ever caught my interest in that way. There was no other subject I was so passionate about. This opportunity…it was everything.

Glancing to my left, I saw Tristan narrowing his gaze at me. I shot him a glare. Yes, Roman's best friend happened to be in my A-level history class, but there was no reason why I should interact with him. In fact, once Professor Fitzgerald had given us the details of the paper, I had a feeling that only a few of us would actually be interested in completing it, considering all the extra work it would entail.

I was right. The class drew to a close, and those of us who were interested in the extra-credit assignment were asked to stay behind. Tristan sailed out of the door with a salute to our history professor, and the room gradually emptied.

When there were only a few of us left, Professor Fitzgerald strode to the projector screen, tapping it with the tip of his pen.

"I'm assuming you're here because you want to complete the extra-credit paper. Once you've chosen your subject, you need to research, research, research. The academics viewing your work will be looking for you to cite your sources. If you have a strong subject and the sources to back it up, then you will have done your best. No matter what happens, you can hold your head high. Remember, you've done all you can."

I exchanged glances with Penelope. It was clear she was feeling just as excited as I was at our history teacher's words. While his back was turned, I scooted across the rows between us until I was next to her.

"Hi."

She gave me a bright smile. "Hi."

"This is an amazing opportunity. Do you…do you want to study together? We can do this. We're good at research, Pen." It didn't matter that we hadn't studied together for a while—thanks to me being away—it was still the truth.

"You're right, and I'd love to study together." Straightening up in her seat, she tapped her notebook. "What are you planning to focus on for your paper?"

I smiled, happy that she'd accepted me straightaway. "I was thinking…"

The sun peeked out from behind the clouds, soft rays making the normally murky river shimmer in different shades of blues, greens, and greys. I couldn't help smiling because I'd missed this. The benefit of attending an insanely expensive school meant that we got to do a whole range of extracurricular activities, and kayaking down the river was my favourite of those activities.

My shoes sank into the mix of mud and pebbles as my group headed down to the point on the river shore where we were launching the kayaks. Up ahead of me, Harriet nudged her friend and subtly indicated to our left. I followed the line of her gaze to see Roman and a group of guys—mostly his former teammates from the swimming and diving clubs—heading in the direction of the lake where the windsurfing activities were taking place. They were wearing wetsuits, but the top part hung from their waists so that their torsos were displayed, and they were clearly loving the attention they were getting, based on the expressions on their faces.

When they drew level with our group of kayakers, Roman's disinterested gaze passed over us, then stopped and homed in on me. His eyes darkened, his brows lowering as he studied me. Just as I managed to tear my gaze away from his, his lips kicked up at the corners in what I could only describe as a malicious smile.

My stomach flipped, and not in a good way. Moving to the other side of the group, I picked up my pace. As I reached the area where the kayaks were stored, I couldn't help glancing back. A guy from my group was handing Roman a life jacket...then he picked up Roman's windsurfing board and crossed over to Roman's group. Penelope and Freya were part of the other group, watching as Roman switched to my group, and although the sun was in my eyes, making me squint, I caught the savage glare Freya directed my way. As if this had anything to do with me.

I dived for my kayak, pulling it into the water. Gripping the paddle, I straddled the kayak and then lowered myself carefully. The need to get away from Roman was strong, but I'd learnt the hard way that rushing only ended up with the kayak tipping me out. Once I was seated, I used my paddle to propel the kayak out of the shallows towards our guide, who was waiting farther out in the wider part of the river.

Getting away from Roman was wishful thinking. I'd barely even made it to the guide before he drew alongside me, his paddle cutting through the water with smooth, powerful strokes.

"You didn't think you could escape from me that easily, did you?"

"Leave me alone, Roman." Shooting him a glare, I paddled around to the other side of the guide, and we were soon surrounded by the rest of our group. Roman kept his gaze on me as the guide reminded us of where we could and couldn't paddle and the fact that we would stop for lunch in a small inlet farther down the river.

This is so hard. His presence was so magnetic, and it hurt to be so close to him and have to act like I was unaffected, like he meant nothing to me. At the same time, I was so angry with him that I couldn't even breathe every time I remembered the way he'd thrown me in the lake and left me, stealing my hoodie, phone, and headphones.

Bastard. Of course, he'd roped someone innocent into his twisted scheme—Aria had given me my phone back, saying Blaine had given it to her. The way she'd described it, he was almost panicked. It was clear who was behind it all, especially because it had gone missing at the same time as my other items.

Thankfully, because we were kayaking and the guide was there making sure we kept enough space between the boats, Roman didn't bother me again, and I almost managed to relax, enjoying the gentle swell of the water and the sun sparkling on the surface.

Everything changed when we stopped in the inlet.

We'd just finished pulling our kayaks up the muddy beach when the clouds rolled in, all deep, heavy greys, and then the first drops of rain began to fall. Everyone scrambled to shelter under the huge overhanging rocks at the back of the inlet, waiting for the rain clouds to pass.

"Scared of a bit of rain?"

The low voice in my ear made me shiver.

"Leave me alone, Roman," I hissed.

"Hmm. I don't think I can." His body was hot next to mine, a contrast against the chill of the rain.

Spinning to face him, I let my annoyance come to the surface. It didn't matter that we'd meant something to each other once. The fact was, he was an asshole now.

"Leave me alone," I said again, pushing at his chest. "I mean it."

Caught off guard, he staggered backwards across the muddy shoreline, his lips curving into a snarl. "Fuck you."

I straightened my shoulders, determined to remain composed in front of him. "I want you to stay away from me."

Glancing between me and the river, he seemed to come to a decision. His lips flattened, his jaw clenching, and then he deliberately turned his back to me.

"You got your wish," he ground out, and then he was gone.

7

Quinn

My smile widened as I breathed in the sea air coming through the open doors that led onto the deck of Blaine's family's beach house. Solar-powered fairy lights sparkled in the night, wrapping around the wooden railing that ran around the edge of the deck. At the far end of the deck, steps led down to the beach, sinking into soft sand. I sipped my wine, listening to the sound of the waves lapping at the shore as the moon lit the horizon with a milky glow. It was so good to be here for the bank holiday weekend with my friends, sadly minus Aria, and to see the coast again. I hadn't seen it in over two years. My parents liked to holiday at luxury beach resorts in the Caribbean and the Maldives, but there was something about the British coastline that I loved. The craggy cliffs, windswept beaches, the wildness of the sea in the winter, even the annoying seagulls that stole food from unsuspecting tourists… It felt like home to me. If I could, I'd live on the coast all year round. Maybe I would, one day. I'd already applied to Alstone College, an exclusive university on the coast that mostly specialised in business-related degrees but had an amazing history programme. It was fairly close to where we were staying this weekend—not that I was expecting to see it during the weekend, but if all went well, I'd be attending there once I left Hatherley Hall. The University of Brighton was my second choice if things didn't pan out, but either way, I'd hopefully be close to the sea for the duration of my time at university.

Penelope lifted her wine glass. "Cheers to the weekend, for unseasonably sunny weather and hot boys at the beach."

Elena and I laughed, clinking our glasses together with Penelope's. "Cheers."

"They're here! Finally!" Freya's voice came from behind us, and we spun around.

My stomach flipped.

A group of guys were strolling into the room, all popular, good-looking guys from our school, most of them from the lacrosse team. Heading them up were the three "gods"—Tristan, Knox, and the boy I'd been avoiding for most of the week.

Roman.

Dimly, I registered that I wasn't even surprised that he'd showed up. Something in me had known that he'd be here.

When he caught my eye, he smirked. Why did he have to look so good when he was acting like a dickhead? I shot him a glare that made his smirk melt into a blinding smile that gave me butterflies against my will. For fuck's sake, not again! Why did he affect me like this?

How had he even become one of the elite? He'd always been the bad boy of Hatherley Hall. Either the elite admired him for his give-no-fucks attitude, or they weren't immune to his charms. Probably a bit of both, if I had to guess. Well, that and the fact he was super rich, and from the rumours I'd heard, his uncle had apparently used his considerable influence to keep him at Hatherley Hall as a student despite the things he'd done. Money and power were the two biggest draws for the elite, after all.

I turned away from Roman and his friends, stepping out onto the decking and taking a seat on one of the loungers, watching as Freya came to stand next to Penelope, joining a whispered huddle with their friend Harriet. I would bet anything that the new arrivals were the subject of the conversation. Elena had disappeared inside with Knox, and for the moment, I was left alone.

My breath caught in my throat as it all hit me at once. I shouldn't have come here. Maybe I could avoid Roman tonight, but tomorrow, I doubted I'd be so lucky. In the evening, we were apparently all supposed to be going to a place called Chaceley Rock—a little island farther down the coast with a ruined lighthouse. It was basically an excuse to go out on the boats and get as loud as we wanted without any neighbours to complain. I'd been looking forward to it until now because I'd been avoiding the truth. Now, there was no denying it. If I was lucky, I could escape to my room tonight and stick with the girls tomorrow during the day. But when it came to the evening…I'd be stuck on a tiny island with no escape from the one person I was trying to avoid.

Was it too late to fake a sudden illness that would mean I didn't have to go?

Blaine directed me to the very end of the pier, to the ladder that led to the water. "Down here."

I paused. There was still time to turn back.

"Come on. This is the last boat. The others are already there." I could hear his barely concealed impatience.

The boat in question was bobbing below us, a shadowy figure at the helm and two other figures sitting inside. I shook my head, looking at the dark water swirling below us, and then began to descend the ladder. The metal rungs were cold under my grip, and I was suddenly aware of how cold I was. A shiver racked my body, and goosebumps flared down my arms.

A pair of hands were suddenly gripping my waist, and then I was being lifted into the air and placed down on a bench seat. I shrieked involuntarily.

"Sorry. Didn't mean to scare you," the figure spoke. They pulled a phone from their pocket, turning on the torch and shining it in my face. I recoiled at the sudden brightness.

The next minute, Tristan's low voice sounded close to my ear. "Quinn. Hi. I feel I should probably tell you to watch out for Roman."

I swallowed hard. I shouldn't have come.

Before I could think of a reply, the boat engine started up, and Tristan was moving away.

Then, it was too late to turn back. We were cutting through the dark ocean waves, heading for Chaceley Rock and Roman Cavendish.

The closer we drew to the tiny island with the ruined lighthouse, the more apprehensive I grew. I had to remind myself that I could hold my own. Roman needed to get the message that we had to stay away from each other, if he hadn't already, and if I had to hurt both him and me to get the message across, it was a price I was willing to pay. He wasn't going to be expelled because of anything I did. I'd make sure of it.

The smell of salt filled the air, and the boat kicked up

sprays of seawater that misted on my hands and face. I huddled into my thin hoodie, wishing that I'd thought to bring something warmer.

Finally, the boat slowed, and then the engine cut out. Blaine jumped out onto a small dock, the wood creaking beneath his trainers. Once the boat was safely tied up, we climbed out of the boat. I stood, blinking, letting my eyes adjust to the darkness. Huge, jagged rocks towered ominously to my left. To my right was the jetty, and up ahead, I saw the tall, looming structure of the old lighthouse. So, this was Chaceley Rock.

My feet slipped on the wet, stubby grass as I followed the light of Tristan's torch towards the lighthouse, and I slowed down, not wanting to risk falling on my face in the dark. As we reached the lighthouse, I looked around me. I could just about make out a tiny path leading to a small, pebbly beach and more jagged rocks, with waves crashing against them.

Yet again, I stumbled a little, and I reached out, touching the crumbling stone wall of the lighthouse in an attempt to support myself. Pushing the door open, Blaine gripped my arm to hold me steady. Dim light spilled from the opening, and he tugged me forwards before dropping my arm and stepping inside. "Come on."

The crowded, circular interior was full of people, talking, drinking, laughing, kissing, but I didn't see Roman.

As I stood, paused in the doorway, taking everything in, an arm snaked around my waist and yanked me back outside. I gasped as a hard body pressed me up against the side of the lighthouse, a hand coming over my mouth and nose so I could barely breathe, let alone scream.

"I've been waiting for you."

At the sound of Roman's voice, I kicked out, but he was too strong. He gave a dark chuckle, adjusting his grip on my face so I could at least breathe through my nose. "So angry, but you still want me."

He was right, but I couldn't and wouldn't admit it to him.

His lips skimmed over my ear. "We need to have a conversation about the way you say one thing and do another. How you think I'm not good enough, but you still want me to fuck you." At my attempt at a violent shake of my head, he laughed, tightening his grip on my face. "Don't even deny it. I'm not fucking stupid, baby. I see the way you look at me."

"Roman?"

Shit. That was Freya's voice. Roman growled under his breath, then released me, muttering a string of swear words, too low for anyone to discern.

"Don't even fucking think about going anywhere." He stepped back, glaring down at me.

"Ro—oh. Quinn." Freya suddenly appeared from around the side of the lighthouse, staring suspiciously between us. "What's going on here?"

I didn't trust her, and I *definitely* didn't want any word getting back to my parents. "Nothing's going on. You're welcome to him." Turning back to Roman, I hissed, "Don't try to speak to me again." Pushing past them both, I stalked back around to the lighthouse door and entered. Roman and Freya appeared less than a minute later, so I made my way to the far side of the ground floor room. I needed a distraction, but Penelope was occupied, flirting with a guy from the lacrosse team. Looking around at the others in the lighthouse, I suddenly felt alone. It wasn't a feeling I liked—I'd spent far too much time alone when I was in Switzerland. Here, the fact that I'd been away for so long made me feel like the new girl all over again. I knew I should make an effort, to at least try to talk to people, but instead, I decided to get some air.

Outside, I immediately felt calmer.

The calm lasted for less than a minute before a hand came around my waist and gripped my arm tightly.

Not again.

Roman's low rasp sounded in my ear. "You're coming with me."

8

Quinn

"No, I'm not." I dug my heels into the ground, throwing my weight back.

"You are. I said we needed to have a conversation, and now we're going to have it. Back to the boats. We're leaving." Roman tightened his grip on my arm and began dragging me away from the lighthouse, back towards the jetty. I stumbled a little, and he slowed down so I could regain my footing. Even as he did so, he frowned, and then as soon as I was steady on my feet, he picked up the pace again.

Was he seriously going to do this? "We can't just *leave*."

"We can and we will."

"People will talk."

"I don't give a fuck," he growled.

"But I can't—"

"Enough. Boat. Now. We're going to have a conversation without any fucking interruptions."

We reached the dock, and he wasted no time in manhandling me into one of the moored boats. I practically fell inside, collapsing down on the seat at the back and putting my head in my hands. I heard him moving around, and then the engine turned on, and we were roaring away from Chaceley Rock.

What was everyone going to think when they found out that Roman and I had both disappeared? I had to hope that they were too drunk to notice. I hoped that once we were done, he'd be taking us back to the island, otherwise, we were going to have a lot of explaining to do, not to mention the risk of my parents finding out.

I was so lost in my thoughts that I hadn't even realised that the engine had cut out until Roman's shout sounded from the front of the boat. "Fuck!"

"What is it?"

He ignored me, flicking switches, turning the key in the ignition over and over again. "Fuck, fuck, *fuck*."

"What's wrong? Why have we stopped?" I carefully made my way over to him, attempting to stay steady as the boat bobbed gently in the ocean.

He finally met my gaze, his eyes dark and angry.

"Know anything about boats? The fucking engine just cut out."

No.

"I don't, sorry."

"Fucking useless," he hissed, which I thought was a bit unfair since it had been his idea to do this in the first place.

"Doesn't look like you know any more than I do," I countered, glaring at him. "Weren't you on the swim team? You should know more than I do."

"Fuck you, Quinn. That has nothing to do with boats. If we can't get this engine going, we're stuck here. Do you want that?"

"No. Is there, like, a manual or anything?"

"Do I look like I know? It's not my fucking boat." He was getting more and more angry, and it shouldn't have affected me the way it did, but I couldn't tear my gaze away from him. He was so beautiful, even in his anger, cursing the sea like some kind of vengeful god.

When he slammed his hand down on the control panel, I finally looked away, glancing through the windshield. We seemed to be drifting farther away from the island. "Um, Roman? Does this boat have an anchor? I think the tide is carrying us along. Look." I pointed towards the now-distant lighthouse, which appeared to be off to the right instead of directly behind us now.

His eyes widened as he took in what I was seeing. "Shit. Yeah. Anchor." Both of us turned to scan the boat, and I immediately saw the anchor.

I raced for it, grabbing the handle of the winch. "Roman!" I called, and he was suddenly there with me, his hands on mine as we turned the heavy handle together, and the anchor released, the clanking of chains as it descended into the depths the most beautiful sound I'd ever heard. There'd been a moment there when I had a vision of us being carried away on an empty ocean, swallowed up by the night.

"We did it!" I forgot who I was talking to for a moment, turning to Roman with a huge smile.

He stared at me for a moment, his face illuminated by the moonlight, and then he gripped my face in his hands.

Then, his lips were on mine.

I froze in shock for all of two seconds before I kissed him back.

It felt like I'd been waiting my whole life for this kiss.

He pulled back slightly, his breath coming in pants as he stared down at me, his eyes wide. "This wasn't supposed to happen. Fuck, why do you do this to me?" he groaned before his lips descended again. I lifted myself up on my toes, winding my arms around his neck, and he slid his hands from my face, down around my body until his arms were around me, holding me to him.

This kiss. Everything about Roman was hard, so hard, but his lips were so soft. My tongue slid against his as he pressed into me, grinding his hardness against my body.

"*No.*" With an effort, he pulled away from me, stepping back towards the helm. "We need to get out of here," he muttered to himself. I collapsed back on the padded leather bench seat, attempting to slow my breathing and get my elevated heart rate under control. Everything in me wanted to carry on kissing him, to make the most of being alone with him here on this boat. No one would know. There was nobody to see us, no way for anyone to find out.

He was the biggest temptation I'd ever had, and I knew that if he kissed me again, out here with no one to see, I wouldn't stop him.

I watched him as he tried again, and failed again, to restart the engine, distracted by the way his arm muscles were flexing. Then a thought came to me. "Isn't there some kind of radio or SOS thing on here? I knew I shouldn't have listened to Blaine's stupid rule about not bringing phones to the island."

"Flares." His voice was suddenly hopeful. "In the—" He cut himself off, slamming his hand on the control panel. "Fuck. We cleared everything out to make room for the drinks."

"You cleared out the life-saving stuff to make room for alcohol?" My voice was incredulous. "Whose genius idea was that? There's nothing else we can do, then. We'll have to wait for the others to find us when it gets light. Or the coastguard, I guess."

"The engine's overheated. It might work again if we leave it for a bit." His voice sounded uncertain, and I was sure that neither of us believed that was the problem, but I nodded.

"Let's try it again in a bit." Biting down on my lip, I warred with myself before I let the words come out. "We can have that talk, if you want." Both of our defences were down right now, and maybe this was what we needed. A chance to clear the air.

He stared at me for a long, charged moment.

Then he spoke. His voice was low, his words carried away on the night breeze, but I read the intent in his eyes perfectly. "I don't want to talk."

He crossed the boat to me in three strides, threw himself down on the seat next to me, and tugged me onto his lap.

There was no hesitation from either of us. I poured everything I had into this kiss, grinding down against his hardness, digging my knees into the leather of the seat as his tongue swiped into my mouth. The boat rocked, making me slide across his thighs, and his hands came down to grip my hips, holding me steady.

"I want you," I whispered as he kissed along my jaw, then bent his head to drag his teeth down my throat.

"Yeah. Here, where there's no one to see," he muttered into my neck.

The hurt tore through me, and suddenly, I wanted to explain. Explain what I could, to make him understand it wasn't what he thought. I gripped a handful of his hair and tugged, making his head come up. His darkened eyes met mine.

"Listen to me." I took a deep breath. "I want you all the time. Those things I said to you in the boat sheds… none of them were true. I lied to you."

His brow creased. "Why say them, then?"

"I-I can't tell you. But I want you to know that if there was a way for you and me to be something, or even to just be friends, I would seize it. But we can't. Please, please don't ask me why. I can't tell you."

"Is this—"

Brushing my lips over his, I cut off his question. "*Please, Ro.*"

He huffed out a sound against my mouth that sounded like a growl, but then he kissed me again. "Okay. No more questions. Not tonight. I don't believe you, but I've got a much better idea for your mouth." Taking my hand, he slid it onto the impressive bulge in his jeans. "Have you ever given a blow job on a boat?"

I eyed him from beneath my lashes. Fuck. I was already so wet for him. He affected me like no one else ever had, and I wasn't sure if I wanted him to know the extent of the effect that he had on me.

I chose my words carefully. "Not until now." Licking my lips as I palmed his erection, I was rewarded with a groan. Then I slipped off him to kneel on the floor.

He opened his jeans, revealing his thick, hard length.

"You're so big," I whispered, and he smirked down at me. There was something more in his gaze, though. Something that I wanted to take advantage of. He could act like this was nothing, like I was just another mouth, another body to satisfy him, but we both knew the truth.

"You like what you see, huh?" He swallowed hard, trying to sound casual, steadying me with his legs on either side of me as I gripped the bottom of his erection, not wanting him to go too deep while we were on a rocking boat.

Instead of replying, I leaned forwards to place a kiss to the head of his cock, followed by a long, slow lick. One of his hands came down to grip my hair while I licked around the head again, then down his shaft.

"*Fuck.* Your mouth. Stop teasing me and suck me." His voice was hoarse, and his legs tensed on either side of me.

Lowering my head farther, I took him into my mouth, down until I reached the place where my hand was gripping him. Getting into a rhythm, I sucked him up and down in tandem with the movement of my hand, swirling my tongue, getting him wet and messy until he was panting above me and groaning out my name.

"Fuck. Fuck. Quinn. *Fuck.* Baby. I'm—"

His hips stuttered, and he pulsed in my mouth, his release hitting the back of my throat. I swallowed him down, as much as I could, his cum spilling out of the corner of my mouth as I raised my head.

For a minute, he just stared down at me, breathing hard, and then he cupped my jaw, his thumb rubbing across the side of my mouth. "Open."

I opened, and he slid his thumb inside. As I sucked lightly, he stroked through my hair with his free hand. He didn't say anything more, but a smile curved over his lips. It lit me up from the inside and brought a lump to my throat because that was his proper smile. The smile he used to give me.

While he was doing up his jeans, I took a minute to compose myself, swallowing down the emotions I couldn't allow myself to feel. When I straightened up, he lifted me onto him again and gently tugged my bottom lip between his teeth.

"I think it's time I returned the favour."

Just as he spoke, I felt the first drops of rain. My release was forgotten as we both scrambled to get under the tiny hardtop at the front of the boat while we were pelted by the rain. It was little more than a sunshade and barely provided any shelter, especially with the way the wind was picking up and driving the rain sideways.

I began to shiver. Why had I worn this stupidly thin hoodie?

Roman wrapped me in his arms, but as the rain started coming down harder, I knew that we'd both be cold and soaking before long.

Raising his head, he looked towards the back of the boat. "The island doesn't look too far away," he said slowly. "I think I can make it."

"*What?*" There was no disguising the horror in my voice. "You can't seriously be thinking about swimming it!"

"I'm a strong swimmer. I can make it." He nodded decisively before releasing me to rip off his T-shirt and tug down his jeans.

"But—but look! Look how far away we are from it. I can barely even see it. What if there are rocks? Or sharks? And it's pitch black and raining! What if you get disoriented? You could *die*, Roman." Panic was clawing at me as all the ways that it could go horribly wrong hit me at once. "Please, please don't do this."

A sob tore from my throat, and I began to shake. Roman glanced towards the island, then back at me, and gave a heavy sigh. He stepped forwards and hugged me to him, rubbing his hands up and down my arms. "I have to. We can't stay out here all night, not like this. You'll get hypothermia, and so will I. There's no proper shelter on this boat." Tugging me into a corner of the boat, he directed me to sit down on the floor where the seats were providing some protection.

"Put my T-shirt on under your hoodie, and stay as dry as you can," he instructed. "I promise you I can make it, okay?"

Before I could reply, he made a run for the back of the boat and dived into the deep, dark water.

"*Roman!*" My scream was carried away in the night as I desperately scanned the waves for any sign of him.

All I could see was darkness.

He was gone.

9

Quinn

"**O**h, Quinn." My dad took a seat next to me. I stared out of the window, the stunning mountain view barely registering as I blinked back tears. "We're so sorry you've had such a difficult time here. We only ever wanted what was best for you." He sighed. "I've spoken to the executive team, and I've arranged to finish up the remainder of the financial year in England."

Settling on the other side of me, my mum patted my knee. "You're going back to Hatherley Hall. Your father and I agreed that it was in your best interest, as long as—"

"You stay away from trouble. All trouble. Any bad influences. That includes the Cavendish boy." My dad's voice hardened. "There will be consequences if you disobey us. Consequences for him. Consequences that will affect his future. Listen carefully, and I'll explain everything so there's no confusion..."

The sky gradually lightened, so slowly that I wouldn't have been aware if I hadn't been lost at sea in a small boat, attuned to every tiny change that was happening around me. I hadn't slept, and my stomach was churning, my entire being focused on Roman.

He has to be okay.

I'd reassured myself over and over again, but nothing made a difference. I wouldn't feel any better until I saw him for myself. And…I'd also feel better when I was rescued. There was a thought at the back of my mind, wondering if he'd left me for dead, but I ignored that. I had to ignore it. Otherwise, I'd fall apart.

The rain had stopped overnight, and the sun was high in the sky.

And still, no one came.

The sun had moved, the shadows beginning to lengthen, and I guesstimated it to be some time in the afternoon. I curled into a ball, pressing against the side, swallowing hard as the gentle sloshing of the waves sounded next to my ear. My stomach ached with hunger, and the motion of the boat made nausea rise in my throat. Thankfully—if there was anything to be thankful for—the rain had stopped soon after Roman had left, but I was still damp, and despite the sun, I hadn't been able to chase away the chill that had settled in my bones.

Amidst my despair, there was a tiny thread of anger wrapping itself around my consciousness, hot and savage. If I got out of here, and if Roman Cavendish was okay, he was going to pay for leaving me here.

The monotonous lapping of the waves was broken by the purr of an engine, followed by a shout.

"Quinn!"

My body was aching everywhere, but I gradually unfolded my stiff limbs and carefully rose to my feet, grasping onto the nearest part of the boat to keep myself steady. Figures swarmed the deck, and I turned to face the person who had called my name.

"Elena."

She blew out a heavy breath, her eyes brimming, and then she pulled me into her arms. We barely knew each other, yet she didn't hesitate to comfort me, rubbing my back with soothing strokes. "Quinn, I'm so sorry. We're going to get you back to the house as quickly as we can." There was a pause, and then she added, "I want to make it clear that Knox and Tristan knew nothing about this, and believe me, they are not happy with Roman after he did… *this*." Her final word was spat between gritted teeth.

It took me a moment to wrap my head around what she'd said, but when it registered, I inhaled sharply. When I spoke, I couldn't disguise the tremor in my voice. "He left me here *on purpose*?"

"I'm so sorry," she said again. Releasing me, she handed me a water bottle and instructed me to drink. "None of us realised what had happened. Everyone was drinking and partying, I was with Knox—not that it's any excuse—and by the time we found Roman, he was so drunk he'd passed out. He was still drunk on the boat back to the mainland. Tristan made him drink some coffee when we got back to the house, and that sobered him up a bit. By that time, it was already close to midday. I asked him if he'd seen you, and he suddenly shouted, 'Fuck, isn't she here?' I said no, and it was like the colour drained from his face. He was…frantic. He kept asking where you were, and none of us could work out what was going on. The second he said that you were out here on the boat, we came as quickly as we could."

"So he actually left me here. On purpose," I managed to say after I'd gulped down the rest of my water, gripping the bottle with shaking hands.

"I know, and he doesn't deserve your forgiveness. I wasn't even the one affected and I want to castrate him. He's such a—" Her hands waved in the air.

"Fucking heartless bastard?" My voice cracked on the words as I blinked back tears.

"Yes. At least." She glanced at Knox, who was directing a random guy to pull up the anchor. Moving closer to me, she lowered her voice. "Roman deserves nothing. Even though he told us you were here, it means nothing because the fact is he *left you*. He deserves to pay."

Amidst the relief I felt, knowing he was okay and hadn't drowned at sea, my anger was morphing, turning into rage. *He fucking left me*. Who cared if he told his friends that I was here? The fact was he'd made it back to the lighthouse, and instead of telling someone I was stranded in the middle of the fucking sea, he got drunk. Who did that?

Squaring my shoulders, I cleared my throat. "You're right. Roman Cavendish is a callous, heartless bastard who deserves to pay. And he will."

"Quinn?"

Glancing up, I found Knox with his hand outstretched, concern in his dark eyes. He handed me a bar of Dairy Milk.

"Chocolate's good for shock. Eat it." As I unwrapped the bar, he continued. "If you want to go back to school, I'll drive you."

Elena nodded. "Honestly, Quinn, I think it'll do

everyone some good to have a chance to cool off. If I see Roman now, I might commit murder."

"You and me both," Knox muttered under his breath, and my brows flew up. "Yeah, he's one of my best friends, but he was completely fucking out of line." His gaze slid to Elena's, and his mouth curved into a wry smile. "I did some things to Elena in the past that I'm not proud of, but there's a line you shouldn't cross, and he went way over it."

"Thanks," I whispered. "I think I'd like to go back, if you're sure you don't mind taking me. Otherwise, I can—"

"We're taking you," Elena said firmly. "Don't worry about anything else. We'll take care of it all."

A tiny bit of the tension I was holding drained away at her decisive words. And then my fingers brushed against soft fabric.

Roman's T-shirt. I'd done as he instructed, putting it on under my hoodie.

Bile rose in my throat. I mumbled something about feeling sick and staggered towards the bow. When I was alone, I stripped the T-shirt from my body while covering myself with the hoodie, a process that took far longer than I wanted. But finally, I was free, and with another glance around me to make sure no one was paying attention, I balled up the T-shirt and dropped it over the side of the boat.

Saltwater licked up the fabric until it was soaked through, and then it sank beneath the waves.

ROMAN

"Where's Knox?"

Tristan exchanged glances with Blaine and Lincoln across the beach house deck. "Gone."

"What do you mean, gone? He was supposed to be coming with me to meet up with my cousins."

Shaking his head, Tristan stepped closer. After giving Blaine and Lincoln another pointed glance and they took the hint, disappearing back inside, he leaned his elbows on the railing as he stared out to sea. "Mate, I don't really know how to say this."

"Just say it," I growled, yanking off my sunglasses so I could glare at him properly. The pounding in my head increased dramatically as I screwed my eyes up against the brightness of the late-afternoon sun. Shoving my sunglasses back on, I pointedly cleared my throat, and he sighed.

"Okay, okay. Fucking hell, what pissed you off today? Wait, don't answer that. I know what it was. The same thing that's been pissing you off ever since a certain brunette beauty made a reappearance in your life."

I gritted my teeth. I had the hangover from hell, and I didn't need to deal with Tristan's shit on top of everything else. "*Tristan.*"

"While you were still wasted from yesterday and sleeping it off, Knox left with Elena to drive Quinn back to Hatherley Hall. He won't be coming back."

"What?" My jaw dropped at the utter fucking betrayal from one of my best mates. "What the actual fuck?"

Tristan pounded his knuckles on the railing. "No. Look, I didn't say anything when you pulled that stunt at the lake, but what you did last night…leaving her on that boat… that's seriously fucking unhinged. Anything could have happened. Fuck, man, she could've *died* or something."

I reeled back, struck by his harsh tone, at the fact that, somehow, everyone seemed to have turned against me. "I thought you were on my side."

"I am, but when you make stupid decisions, I can't support them. I stood by you with the arson and all that shit—" He cut himself off, pacing up and down the deck while I stared at him in disbelief. Finally, he came to a stop in front of me. "That's all irrelevant, in this case. You know I'm down for fucking with people, and you know I've got your back, but you took it way too far this time. And as your friend, I'm here to tell you the truth, whether you want to hear it or not."

I couldn't listen to him. Not then. I needed to be alone, to cool down before I said something I'd regret. And I didn't know what the fuck had happened last night, so how was I supposed to defend myself? Ignoring the nausea that was rising inside me, the insistent feeling that everything was so wrong, that I'd fucked things up irreparably with Quinn, I slammed my fist down on the railing. "I'm going out," I muttered, pushing past him and stalking back into the house, ignoring his calls after me. Heading into the hallway, I didn't stop, pulling the front door open and letting it slam behind me as I stalked down the driveway. Passing the cars parked up against each other, it hit me that I'd come here in Knox's SUV, so I didn't even have a fucking car to drive anywhere.

As if the universe was fucking with me, my phone started vibrating in my pocket, and when I pulled it out, I saw my uncle's name on the screen.

"Roman. Caiden tells me you're in town. I know you're supposed to be meeting him and Weston while you're here, but I'd like to meet with you first to discuss a few things."

Fucking brilliant. Not only had my best mate decided to give me a lecture, but now I got to hear one from my uncle. All so he could delude himself into thinking he was doing his familial duty since my parents were out of the country and he was their de facto representation.

"Arlo." I never referred to him as "uncle." "I'm unfortunately without transportation."

"I'm in the car. I'll pick you up. Send me your location," he said, and then disconnected the call.

Well, fuck.

When I was seated inside my uncle's spacious SUV, I tipped my head back against the headrest and closed my eyes, steeling myself for his words.

"Roman. It's good to see you. I want to apologise."

My eyes flew open. "Huh?"

He laughed. "Not what you were expecting?"

"Uh, no. I was expecting our conversation to go the way it did last time. With you telling me I needed to get my shit together."

"Ah. Yes. Well, you have, haven't you? Being suspended from the swimming and diving teams seems to have done its job. But I shouldn't have been so hard on you before. I know your parents entrusted me to keep an eye on you in their absence, and that should mean supporting you, not just bailing you out of trouble. I've…well." Gripping the steering wheel with one hand, he rubbed the other across his jaw. "Suffice to say, I've learnt where my priorities lie. What's important is family, and that includes you. You'll have to bear with me because no doubt I'll make mistakes, but I want you to know that if you need anything— anything at all—I'm here for you. Your cousins are, too."

My hungover brain took much longer than usual to parse through his words, but when they eventually registered, I had no fucking clue how to respond. It had always been me looking out for myself, with everyone I was related to being so far away. The girlfriend of my cousin Caiden's best friend had attended Hatherley Hall, but we'd been in different school years and different houses, and she'd always kept to herself, so we'd never interacted. And I rarely saw my cousins as it was. Maybe a couple of times a year at the most.

"I want to show you how serious I am," my uncle continued. "I'd planned to come up to visit you to do this, but since you're here…" The SUV slowed down to a crawl and then came to a stop. My jaw dropped as I stared out of the windscreen, taking in our surroundings.

We were in supercar heaven. Everywhere I looked, gleaming machines were parked up outside a glass-fronted showroom with even more luxury vehicles inside.

"What is this?"

My uncle grinned at me. "It's both your belated eighteenth birthday present and bribery to ease my guilty conscience for not taking better care of you. Take your time, and let me know when you've made a decision."

"A car? For me? Seriously?" Fucking hell. Suddenly, my

hangover was gone—or not gone, but banished to the back of my mind.

"Yes."

Two hours later, and I was the proud owner of a Jaguar F-Type, and my uncle had arranged for a custom matte-black paint job and delivery to Hatherley Hall the following week. He dropped me off at Alstone's pier, where I'd arranged to meet my cousins, and I couldn't stop my grin as I headed down to the seafront, stepping onto the wooden boardwalk. Seagulls cawed loudly, diving and swooping for food, and the waves crashed against the shore, the smell of saltwater heavy in the air. It had been so long since I'd been here.

"I didn't know you could smile."

Lost in thoughts of my shiny new car, I jumped a mile at the sound of Caiden's voice close to my ear. He held out his fist, and I bumped it with his, then Weston's.

"I could say the same to you," I said, taking in his grinning face. We looked alike, with the same jet-black hair and similar build. While Weston's hair was the tiniest bit lighter, there was no mistaking that the three of us were related.

We spent a while catching up as we walked down the pier, stopping for greasy, salty chips and drinks. When we headed off the pier and onto the beach, I followed my cousins underneath the pier, where we collapsed onto the bigger rocks that were scattered across the sand.

"How was the lighthouse? We had a fucking epic party there once," Weston said around a mouthful of chips. "Remember that, Cade?"

"I remember Dad giving me shit because I let you drink when you were underage."

"Yeah, he conveniently forgot you were also underage at the time."

"I wasn't the one who threw up on his favourite chesterfield, was I, West?"

They grinned at each other, and then both turned to me at the same time. "So?" Weston prompted when I remained silent. "How was it?"

Memories I'd been suppressing rose to the front of my mind, followed by a wave of guilt that choked me, and all I could do was inhale hard in an attempt to get air into my lungs.

Quinn. The boat. My fucking desperation to get us to safety. Black, black depths, so cold and so unknown, but at the same time, unthreatening. Clambering ashore, pebbles biting into the palms of my hands. Rain lashing at me and then dying away. The chill hitting me all at once, my entire body shaking. Staggering up to the lighthouse. Light and noise, too much after what I'd been through. Unquenchable thirst. Myself, almost delirious, mumbling something incomprehensible. A drink thrust into my hand. Then…nothing.

"I can't remember," I said slowly. "I remember part of the night. Then there was a point where I think someone gave me a drink, although that part's a blur. After that…it's like there's a gap in my memory. I had the worst fucking hangover of my life afterwards. Still do, although this is helping." I tapped the side of the box of chips.

"Blackout drunk. Good job Dad didn't know about this. He might've had second thoughts about giving you a car." West smirked, but Cade frowned.

"You can't remember anything at all? How much did you drink?"

I shrugged. "No idea. Must've been a lot because I don't remember anything after a certain point. And I have the hangover to prove that I must've been wasted."

Caiden placed his box of chips down on the beach, not even seeming to notice the cluster of shrieking seagulls that immediately swooped on it. "Something about this doesn't sound right. You said you thought someone gave you a drink, and then there was a gap in your memory. Do you think that maybe someone could've spiked your drink?"

"Cade. We've all been that drunk—" West began but snapped his mouth shut when Caiden shot him a warning look.

"Yeah. We've all been wasted, but I dunno… Talk us through what you remember."

When I'd gone through the events of the night that I actually remembered, minus the parts that included Quinn, Caiden shook his head.

"I can't put my finger on it. It's more of a gut feeling, but something about all this doesn't seem right." His voice lowered. "Keep your eyes open, Ro."

A shiver went through me despite the warmth of the sun's rays piercing through the cracks in the boardwalk above us.

"Yeah. I will."

11

Quinn

"Oh, poor Quinn. I heard what happened. Have you recovered from being stranded at sea?"

I stopped at the sound of the sweet voice, dripping in honeyed faux sympathy, and gritted my teeth. The stone corridor was almost empty, rain battering against the tall, leaded windows that ran down one side, the sound drowning out any other, more distant noises. Ahead of me, one of the carved columns that Hatherley Hall seemed to have in abundance cast a long, dark shadow across the stone floor.

We were alone.

Slowly turning, I met Freya's gaze directly, refusing to give her the satisfaction of realising that her words had affected me.

"Freya." I gave her a smile just as fake as the one she'd given me. "I'm all recovered. Thank you for your concern."

"It's a shame Roman was more interested in drinking than playing the hero. What were you doing on that boat with him, anyway? You surely didn't think you could hold his interest, did you?"

As much as I hated it, pain lanced through me at her words. Roman had changed so much from the boy I'd once known. Or maybe this had always been his true self, and the side I'd seen had been nothing but a facade.

"Why don't you ask him if you're so interested in what we were doing on the boat? I don't owe you any answers."

"Stay away from Roman," she hissed as I spun on my heel, done with being bitched at for something that hadn't even been my choice to begin with. I stopped dead, seeing Penelope standing right behind me. How long had she been there?

Her eyes flicked to Freya, then back to me. Gently squeezing my arm, she moved past me, mouthing, *Sorry*, as she did so. "Freya, come on. That's enough," she chided gently. "Why don't we go and find Roman? He's been asking where you were."

Of course he had.

Penelope shot me another apologetic look as she led Freya away, and I got it. She was feeling guilty, but she shouldn't. Freya was her friend, as was I, and I wouldn't make her pick between the two of us. I'd even hoped—naively—that Freya and I would be able to put our past behind us and become at least civil, but I guess I should have known better. We were both part of the elite—she always had been, and I'd slotted back into my place when I'd returned to Hatherley Hall—but that wasn't enough to put aside our differences.

Left alone, I did my best to push away all thoughts of what might happen when Freya found Roman, probably "comforting" him, aka using any excuse to drape herself all over him. I shifted my bag higher on my shoulder and continued towards the library, where I'd been heading when Freya had intercepted me. As soon as the heavy doors closed behind me and a blanket of silence descended, I felt like I could breathe again. It was so hard to put on a front. It wasn't something I was used to. Maybe once, but I'd been away from England for so long I'd forgotten what it was like in Hatherley Hall. These students could sense weakness like sharks scenting blood in the water, and just like sharks, they'd bite.

Wandering through the tall stacks, I breathed in the scent of books and polished wood, feeling the rest of my tension drain away. When I'd located the textbook I needed for my history project, I settled at a table in one of the farthest corners of the library. Dust motes swirled in the air, dimly illuminated by the soft golden glow of the lamp in the corner. Outside, the skies were dark and angry, rain still lashing at the windows, but it was warm and cosy inside.

After opening my essay file on my laptop, I set it aside in favour of taking notes in my notepad. For a while, I managed to lose myself in the history and legends of ancient Greece, engrossed in accounts of graffiti found on buildings and statues.

As I turned the page of my textbook to a new chapter, a shadow fell across my notepad, and I glanced up to see a golden head of hair and a face that was uncharacteristically serious.

"Can I have a word?" Tristan didn't wait for a reply, just spun around the chair next to me and straddled it, his eyes on mine. His knees were almost touching the side of my chair.

"Haven't you heard of personal space?"

He grinned. "Not according to your friend Aria, no. How is our little scorpion doing, anyway?"

"Scorpion? Excuse me?"

Tapping the large colour image on the open page of my textbook with his index finger, he nodded. "That. The scorpion was sent to slay Orion, if I remember correctly. Let's see…scorpions scuttle around brandishing their claws, and if you're not careful, they sting the fuck out of you. Suits her, right?"

"*No.* What do you want, Tristan?"

He ignored my question, continuing. "Bet she wished she'd come with us at the weekend."

"Maybe if she had, I wouldn't have been left in a fucking boat all night," I bit out, tearing my gaze away from his and doing my best to focus on my open textbook. The words swam in front of my eyes, and I hated that one of the so-called gods was getting a front-row view of my weakness.

Tristan cleared his throat, and out of the corner of my eye, I saw him shift in his seat. I'd made him uncomfortable. Good. "Quinn. That's what I wanted to talk to you about."

"There's nothing to talk about."

"Roman swears he doesn't remember leaving you on the boat. Not until the next day, when we asked him if he'd seen you. I dunno, he must've got blackout drunk. It's not an excuse, but—"

Anger burned through me, and I welcomed it. I twisted to face him, baring my teeth, taking satisfaction in the way his brows flew up, his eyes widening. "Do you know what? He was one hundred percent fucking sober when he left me on that boat, Tristan. And I spent the whole night panicking that he'd drowned. You don't even want to know what went through my mind, the scenarios I tortured myself with. And yet, he decided to go back to the lighthouse and rejoin the party without a care in the world. That's beyond callous. That…that's hateful. I will never,

ever forgive him for that, nor should I have to. Don't you dare come here making excuses for him. There are no excuses that can ever make what he did okay."

Tristan slumped back in his seat. "Yeah," he said eventually. "Yeah." With a sigh, he rose to his feet. "For what it's worth, I don't condone what he did."

"I don't want to hear it. Please, just leave me alone. All I want to do now is finish up this school year and forget Roman Cavendish ever existed." Picking up my pen, I began scribbling notes down…notes that made no sense, but it gave me something to focus on. I would've fallen apart otherwise. Soft footsteps retreated, and then I was alone again.

12

ROMAN

"Good choice." Tristan paced around my new car, admiring it from all angles. "Copying me and Knox with the matte-black theme, I see."

"Nah, my cousins were doing the matte-black thing before you two could even drive." I smoothed a hand across the sleek lines of the passenger door. "It looks fucking amazing, doesn't it?"

Knox glanced over at Tristan, smirking, and then turned to me. "I prefer to be higher up, but I can't deny it's a fucking gorgeous machine."

I rolled my eyes. "Yeah, we all know you like to overcompensate by having a ridiculously oversized car."

"Fuck you. You know that's a blatant lie. You've seen the size of my dick," Knox said way too loudly, catching the attention of Saunders, our lacrosse coach, who was crossing the car park.

"Enough talk about dicks, Ashcroft. You're supposed to be getting ready for practice. I want you out on the field in five minutes!" he bellowed. We all jumped to do his bidding, Tristan and me laughing at Knox because we were assholes.

By the time practice was over, I was in need of some relaxation before I took my new wheels for a spin. The three of us congregated in the crypts, collapsing back on the sofas. The air was much cooler down here with the ancient stone surrounding us. It was just what I needed, my body still overheated from our gruelling training session, even though I'd showered afterwards.

"Fucking hell, Saunders was on one today. I can't feel my legs," Tristan whined.

"Stop whining," I told him, even though I felt the same.

Knox kicked his legs up on the coffee table. "You need to work on your stamina. I feel fine."

"I get more action than the two of you put together, so don't start with that shit," Tristan said.

"Yeah? I don't think Elena would agree with you…"

I tuned out their bickering. Their words had unlocked a memory, and thoughts I'd been pushing aside poured into my brain unchecked.

Quinn's hot mouth around my cock. That fucking blank spot in my brain. Her total avoidance of me ever since—yeah, she'd been avoiding me before, but this felt different. She'd gone out of her way to make sure we didn't cross paths, and it felt as if Knox and Tristan had been working to keep me away from her at the same time. Add to the fact that the usual wannabe goddesses and elite hangers-on had been surrounding me and my friends all week, and I hadn't managed to get near Quinn since my return to Hatherley Hall.

The truth was, I had no fucking clue what to do or what to even say to her. We hadn't resolved anything before I'd left her on the boat, and then I'd done something that was unforgivable in her eyes. But I couldn't explain my actions because I didn't know why I'd acted the way I had, either. Yeah, she'd hurt me and all that other shit, but I wasn't that much of a callous asshole to leave anyone stranded at sea, let alone a girl who'd meant fucking everything to me once.

Groaning, I rubbed my hand across my face. When I lowered it, I found Knox and Tristan staring at me.

"What?"

They exchanged glances, and I gritted my teeth.

"If you've got something to say, just say it."

Tristan cleared his throat. "Look, man. I saw Quinn yesterday, and she's pissed off. Understandably. I guess… we're having trouble getting our heads around what happened, y'know? How is it you can't remember?"

I let my eyes fall closed, my head thumping back against the sofa. "I don't know what you want me to say. There's no way I would've left her, not on purpose. My cousin Cade asked if my drink had been spiked. It… fucking hell, I brushed it off, but the more I think about it, the more I'm wondering if it's true. It's like there's a fucking black hole in my head."

"Fuck. You really think someone would've spiked your drink? Who and why?"

My fists clenched as I reluctantly opened my eyes to meet Tristan's gaze. "I don't fucking *know*, okay? None of it makes sense."

Knox was frowning, his bottom lip pulled between his teeth. "I don't like this. If, and it's a big if, someone did spike your drink, they must've had a reason. Let me do some digging. Speak to a few people, see if I can pick up any vibes."

"Yeah. I'll do the same," Tristan agreed. "I dunno about the whole spiking thing, but it was way out of character for you. You're an asshole, and you get yourself into shit a lot—"

"A whole fucking lot," Knox added, and I glared at them both.

Tristan continued. "But I don't think you'd go that far. I know you have morals, even if you deny it, and you like Quinn too much for that. You want her, even now."

I gritted my teeth. "I don't fucking like or want her. She burned all her bridges with me."

Knox swung his legs off the coffee table, shifting in his seat. His gaze flicked to Tristan, although he was addressing me. "You sure this wasn't some kind of fucked-up revenge you were taking and your mind just blanked it out?"

"Fucking hell, I can't believe you're even asking me that." I launched myself to my feet, too fucking pissed off to stay in this room with my "friends" for one second longer. "Fuck you both."

Storming up the stairs, ignoring my protesting muscles, I exited the crypts, the heavy wooden door slamming shut behind me.

I was only vaguely aware of going to the room I shared with Tristan, stripping out of my clothes on autopilot and pulling on my Hatherley Hall swim team shorts. The shorts I hadn't been able to bring myself to throw away, even though I'd been kicked off the team. I threw on waterproof clothes over the top, then helped myself to Tristan's heavy raincoat. Grabbing my swim bag, which was already packed, I left everything else behind. I needed some fucking peace. I needed the silence that only being in the water could bring.

The rain lashed against my face as I left Hatherley Hall behind, but I barely even noticed its sting. When I reached the cover of the trees, I took a second to catch my breath before making my way down to the lakeshore.

I wasted no time in stripping down, and then, taking note of the weather, I jogged back to the tree line to leave everything under the shelter of thick, heavy branches. That done, I ran for the lake, diving off the edge of the jetty, submerged in seconds.

The swirling, angry clouds unleashing their vengeance disappeared in the stillness of the deep centre of the lake. Everything around me was dark, the visibility almost non-existent, but I knew this lake well, and I finally felt at peace.

I cut through the water with ease, the methodical strokes calming my mind, and with that calm came a sense of complete fucking clarity.

My cousin's intuition had been right. I *hadn't* been blackout drunk. It didn't fit. If I had been drinking, I would've at least remembered part of the night after those few scrambled moments after my return to the lighthouse.

But after that first drink, I drew a blank. There was no one with the motivation to spike my drink. I was one of the fucking gods of Hatherley Hall. Who would even dare to do that to me?

I swam until my lungs felt as if they were going to burst, and then I emerged from the lake, gulping in air and rainwater while thunder rumbled overhead.

Fuck. *Thunder.* I needed to leave the lake before lightning struck. I loved the water, but I didn't have a death wish. Swimming to the edge of the jetty, I gripped the wooden boards, slippery from the rain, and pulled myself out of the lake. Water sluiced from my body, my hair plastered to my head as I stood there, drenched from head to toe.

It was refreshing. Cleansing. Exactly what I fucking needed.

I took a step towards the shore, the weathered boards creaking underfoot, but stopped dead when I saw the small, huddled figure covered by a huge raincoat standing at the far end of the jetty.

I ran. My feet slipped on the slick surface, but somehow, I kept my balance, reaching Quinn in seconds.

My arms wrapped around her shivering body, pulling her into me. She beat her wrists against my chest, screaming into the wind and rain, and I didn't try to stop her, but I didn't let her go.

Her struggles eventually ceased, and she slumped against me. "I hate you so much," she cried, her tears hot against the chilled skin of my collarbone. "You ruined everything. I can't go anywhere without being reminded of you."

"I know," I murmured, pushing back her hood enough that I could kiss the top of her head.

She trembled, and whether it was in anger or from the cold, I wasn't sure, but I wrapped my arms more tightly around her.

Her head lifted, and the devastation and utter betrayal on her face made me fucking choke on the sudden lump in my throat. "You *left me there*. Why did you leave me, Roman? Why? How could you be so fucking *cruel?*"

"I-I didn't know. I was going to come back for you, I promise. I left to get help."

"But you didn't. You left me," she sobbed. "I'll never forgive you. Never."

My jaw clenched. I fucking hated myself in that moment. "I'll never forgive me, either."

"Roman." Her arms went around my neck, and

suddenly, we were kissing, and I never fucking wanted it to end.

13

Quinn

What was I doing?

Have some self-respect, Quinn.

I tore myself away, breathing hard. Roman's eyes reflected the storm, and his darkened gaze was fixed on me. He was breathing just as hard as I was, his chest rising and falling in time with mine.

"No, you fucking don't, Quinn," he growled, yanking me back into him and covering my mouth with his. The kiss only lasted for a second before a bright flash of light had him springing back, cursing under his breath. Wrapping his fingers around my wrist, he tugged me towards the tree line.

"We need to get away from the water." He stooped to pick up a bundle of fabric, still gripping me tightly, and then moved to my left, still holding on to my wrist and leaving me with no choice but to go wherever he was leading me. The truth was, a part of me *wanted* to go with him, wanted answers for what had happened on the boat. To find out why he'd been so hostile towards me ever since

I'd returned to Hatherley Hall. I wanted to have it out with him once and for all.

I kept my gaze fixed on him, an anchor in the gathering storm. His raven hair, dripping water onto his broad back, his muscles shifting beneath his tanned skin as he moved with purpose, seemingly unaffected by the rain. He came to a stop in front of the boat sheds, pushing open the door, and then he tugged me inside. As soon as the door closed, he was on me again, one hand cupping my throat underneath my jaw, the other wrapped around my back.

"Let's get one thing straight," he rasped. "I'm guilty of leaving you, but you're not innocent, either. We still need to talk, and we will. After."

I swallowed around his grip, my chilled body rapidly heating against his. He stared at me, his lashes inky spikes, his eyes still reflecting the storm clouds outside. Fuck him for being so hot, with his chiselled body and that intense, heated gaze focused on me. He was a god, and no mortal could resist him.

"After what?" I managed.

"This."

He kissed me, hard, making me gasp against his mouth, and then he pulled away. "Fuck you for making my life so difficult," he muttered, dipping down to rummage in the bundle of fabric he'd dropped near our feet.

"I could say the same about you." I wrapped my arms around my body in a futile attempt to warm it.

He didn't reply. Instead, he rose to his feet, tugging my raincoat from my shoulders. Something that looked a lot like guilt flashed in his gaze, and he cleared his throat.

"I can't fucking stand to see you shivering." Before I could reply, he stepped closer. "This is what should have happened after the boat," he murmured, wrapping a soft, fluffy towel around my shoulders.

My shivers stopped, and he smiled. *That smile*. It made me melt inside, gave me butterflies, made my heart race… all the things I'd been suppressing and denying to myself.

It was beautiful, and it was for me.

He gently wiped the towel over the parts of me that had been exposed to the elements, taking extra care with my face. With his brows pulled together, his gaze intent on what he was doing, I had a moment to just study him. What a mess of contradictions this man was. Like the sea in a storm. Restless, churning, wild, but in the hidden depths, far beneath the surface, there was calm. Stillness.

"So beautiful," he whispered, almost inaudibly, and I wasn't sure if he'd even meant to say it aloud. He traced the pad of his finger across my cheekbone, leaving a trail of sparks in its wake. My face was bare of make-up, my hair was a mass of wild tangles from the wind and rain, despite the protection of my hood, and I knew there were dark shadows beneath my eyes from my lack of sleep. But the way he looked at me…it was almost reverential.

Dipping his head, he kissed me again, so softly. "Put this on," he murmured, handing me a navy zip-up hoodie. My breath caught in my throat. It was his lacrosse hoodie, with his surname across the back in royal blue lettering.

I hesitated for too long, and his softness disappeared, his jaw visibly clenching. "Fucking hell, stop being so stubborn. Put it on. Now. You're still cold."

"Fine." I handed him the towel, pulling on his hoodie, and I watched as he roughly dried his hair and body.

A smirk curved over his lips when he caught me staring at him. His fingers teased the waistband of his tight swim shorts. "Might want to turn around unless you want a show."

I spun around instantly, my face heating, and I heard him laugh behind me. We'd had a moment on the boat, but a nude Roman Cavendish was not something I was equipped to deal with.

"You can turn around now," he said.

I turned.

And stopped.

And stared.

And kept staring.

My mouth went dry.

Yes, Roman Cavendish had his back to me, but he was fully naked.

Oh, fuck.

That body.

I couldn't breathe.

"You're a bit quiet, Quinn. Something wrong?"

His faux-innocent tone immediately riled me up. "Shut up." I spun back around, pressing my forehead against the wall, reminding myself of what he'd done. Except it was hard to hold on to the anger and bitterness when I'd just seen him bared to me. When I'd been overcome by that rush of want. To touch, to taste, to have him touch me back.

Strong arms slid around my waist, his voice a low rumble in my ear, making me shiver despite myself. "Fuck. You in my hoodie…"

"Roman, please. Don't. We need to talk."

Releasing me, he turned me to face him. "We will. After."

Then he lifted me into his arms, stalking over to one of the rowing boats moored inside the huge shed. It looked as if it was undergoing maintenance, with the interior completely stripped out, piled on the wooden dock next to it.

The boat bobbed gently in the water as Roman threw his damp towel inside and then lowered me so I was lying along the bottom of the boat. He climbed in after me, making it rock as he lowered himself. Thankfully, for my sanity, he'd pulled on a pair of sweatpants, although he hadn't bothered with a top, his chest still bared to me.

"What are you doing?"

"Returning the favour so we're on more equal footing for this fucking conversation that neither of us wants to have," he said and then pulled off my trainers, throwing them onto the dock. I shrieked, my legs instinctively coming up. "Stay still," he ground out and then tugged down my leggings and underwear in one go.

A shocked gasp tore from my throat as I yanked my hands down to cover myself. "Roman!"

"Quiet." He crawled over me, balancing on his forearms. His head lowered to mine. "Let me make you feel as good as you made me feel."

He kissed me slowly, carefully, until I gave in, opening my mouth to him and letting his tongue slide over mine. My hands gradually came up, circling his back. Somehow, between the shock of him ripping my leggings off and now, my nudity no longer bothered me, even though it probably should've, given the circumstances.

"Good girl," he murmured, kissing down my jaw and onto my throat. Balancing on one arm, he slid the other down my body, stopping right at the edge of my clit. "I know you're wet for me. I know you want me, don't you?"

"It's just a physical reaction. It could happen with any good-looking guy," I lied, my body trembling as I held myself as still as possible rather than rocking up into his touch.

"Liar. You're mine, Quinn, whether you like it or not. Whether *I* like it or not. No one else can make you feel this good. No one else will ever get to touch you the way I do." With those words, he skimmed over my clit with the pad of his thumb. *Fuck.* Trying to stay away from him was a lost cause. My body arched upwards, seeking more friction, and he chuckled darkly against my throat, his teeth scraping over my skin. "Admit it, baby. No one affects you the way I do."

"You're so arrogant." My hands slid into his hair, then down over the back of his head, my palms stroking over the muscles of his shoulders. I moaned as he circled his thumb. "Ro. Please."

Lifting his head, he grinned at me before shifting down the boat, making it rock, his fingers teasing over my wetness, making my hips arch again. He stared up at me with a sinful smirk before he lowered his head, his hot mouth joining his fingers.

"Fuuuuck. Roman." I wound my legs around him, holding him in place, and he laughed against me, the vibrations sending shivers through my body. Then he stopped teasing me with a long, slow swipe of his tongue along my slit while his thumb continued circling, this time with more pressure.

This man knew *exactly* what he was doing. I moaned as his fingers curled around my thigh, lifting my leg over his shoulder and adjusting the angle as he licked inside me.

"*Roman.*" I gasped his name as I shattered around him, my thighs shaking as he held me in place, never letting up, until I had to tug at his hair to move him away. I collapsed back, my eyes closing as I gulped air into my oxygen-deprived lungs. I was wrung out, gone for him, my brain blissfully blank as I lost myself in the haze of pleasure he'd given me.

When I felt him move again, my eyes fluttered open, and I watched as he straddled my thighs. My eyes were drawn to the erection tenting his joggers, but when I lifted my hand, he shook his head.

"No. You lie there and let me do all the work. Don't move." Pushing my—or his—hoodie and top out of the way to expose the entirety of my stomach area, he lowered his joggers, his hard cock coming into view, the head glistening with precum. His tongue swiped across his lips. "Mmm. You taste so good."

My cheeks heated, and he gave me that arrogant, sexy grin again before he began to stroke his length, his hand moving faster as I watched avidly, barely able to breathe as he chased his release while pinning me in place with his powerful thighs.

"Fuck," he groaned, giving his hand a twist, and then his cock pulsed, striping my lower body with his cum. It was *so* hot, and I was so. Fucking. Turned. On.

He slumped forwards, panting, and then he gave his cock one last, slow stroke, groaning again. "Don't move," he warned, his voice hoarse. His finger slid across my lower stomach, smearing his release over my skin. Then he moved it with purpose, and I suddenly realised he was *writing letters on my body with his cum.*

"W-what are you doing?"

His eyes met mine as he sat back, finally finished. "Making something clear. Read the word, and I want you to remember this."

Propping myself up on my elbows, I focused on the lines glistening on my skin. It was difficult to make it out at first, but I eventually got it.

The word he'd written?

Mine.

14

ROMAN

Quinn's fucking phone interrupted what was supposed to be our time to have an uninterrupted conversation.

"Hello?" She listened intently to whoever the intruder was on the other end, biting down on her pouty lower lip as she glanced over at me. "No, it's okay. I can come. I'll be there as quickly as I can." When the call ended, she sighed. "Sorry. That was Pen. There's a committee meeting for the May ball. I forgot."

My brows rose. "You're on the committee?"

"No…well, I guess I am now. Penelope's trying to help me fit back in." Her voice grew quieter. "It's hard, coming back, trying to find a place to fit in again after being away for so long."

My stomach lurched at the implication. Yeah, I hadn't rolled out the welcome mat, and because of that, she'd probably had a harder time than necessary.

She deserved it, remember.

But then I'd done the unforgivable thing.

Maybe it was time to draw a line in the sand and find

out where she stood. "Before you go, I want to know something, and I want you to give me an honest answer. What do you want to happen here? With us?"

She was silent for a long time, and then she sighed. "There is no 'us,' Roman. How can there be? Okay, there's clearly some…attraction between us. I won't deny that. But I can't—it can't happen. Even if there were no external obstacles, can you really see us getting past everything that's happened recently?"

It took everything in me to keep my voice even. "I thought…I thought when we talked, you might understand. You might tell me why you fucking ghosted me and then just strolled back into my life like nothing was wrong. Apart from the whole telling me I wasn't fucking good enough for you and you didn't want me to go anywhere near you. You still haven't even given me an explanation for why you said that."

"So what?" Her voice rose. "Are you going to give me a satisfactory reason for why you left me in the middle of the fucking ocean?"

Fuck. "I don't have a reason! I think my drink was spiked when I got back to the lighthouse—"

She physically recoiled from me as if I'd slapped her, instantly cutting off my words. "Don't give me your fucking excuses. I don't want to hear them. This was a mistake. *You're* a mistake." She covered her mouth with a trembling hand, her eyes filling with tears. "I wish…I really wish things were different. But they're not. Like I said, we need to stay away from each other, and even if that wasn't the case, too much has happened between us. You must see that. You must see why I can't forgive you for the boat."

You're a mistake. I can't forgive you.

She was right. I'd played my part, just as she'd played hers. She'd tainted what had been a fucking rare, special connection between us when she'd ghosted me, and I'd poisoned whatever was left with everything I'd done since she returned to Hatherley Hall.

"Yeah," I said quietly. "Yeah. Okay."

"Please. Listen to me. Let's just stay out of each other's way from now on." She zipped up her raincoat with shaky fingers, and I made no mention of the fact that she was still wearing my hoodie, that she still had my mark branded across her soft skin.

"Yeah." It was all I could say.

She nodded once and then turned to leave. When she reached the door, she paused, her back to me. "Just so you know, I don't hate you. I should, and I've tried, but I can't hate you, Roman."

When the door closed behind her, I bit down on my lip so hard that I tasted blood.

"I can't hate you, either," I said.

A long, hot shower did nothing to improve my dark mood. I was restless, pacing up and down my room, my fists clenched, trying to talk myself out of doing something completely fucking inadvisable. Something destructive. Why shouldn't I? I'd already been kicked off the swimming and diving teams, and they'd been the only things that brought me any fucking joy.

"Uh-oh, I recognise that face."

My pacing ended abruptly when Tristan barged into our shared room, his eyes full of unwarranted concern.

"Fuck off. I'm still not talking to you."

"No can do, my friend." He came right up to me, completely disregarding the hostile "fuck off" vibes I was projecting, and slung his arm across my shoulders. "You need me to steer you away from the dark side. See the light." He gestured dramatically with his free hand. "Here's what you're going to do."

"You don't tell me what to do."

"I thought I heard you say you weren't talking to me. Must've been mistaken." With a grin, he gestured with his hand again, ignoring my warning growl. "You're going to stay here until Knox shows up. Then you're going to listen to him. After that, you're gonna take your new car for a drive instead of fucking with school property and getting yourself suspended or expelled. When you get back, we're having a party in the crypts."

I shrugged his arm off me, crossing the room to the wall and leaning back against it with my arms folded across my chest. I stared silently at him, and he opened his mouth to speak but was interrupted by the door flying open. Knox stepped inside, his gaze sliding to Tristan's. When Tristan gave him a short nod, he came to stand in front of me. Shifting on his feet, he cleared his throat. "Uh. Ro. I'm sorry. I was out of line. I shouldn't have questioned you. I believe you, okay? I'm just struggling to get my head around the fact that someone would actually dare to spike *your* drink."

"You and me both," I muttered.

Tristan came to stand beside Knox, shaking his head. "I don't fucking like this. We need to remind people they can't fuck with us. A show of power, that's what we need." He threw his arm out yet again. "Hence the party."

"Yeah, okay," I agreed. It wasn't as if I had any better ideas. My anger was slowly draining away, the itch to destroy something still there, but I found I could ignore it now.

When Tristan pulled out his phone and began tapping

at it, mumbling something about the party, Knox moved closer, lowering his voice. "We okay?"

I nodded. "Yeah, we're okay." A relieved expression crossed his face, and I realised he'd actually been worried about it. "You were a dick, but I'm over it. Probably would've said the same to you, to be honest."

"Yeah, you would've." We grinned at each other, and I unfolded my arms, shoving my hands into my pockets. Knox took a seat on Tristan's bed, pulling out his phone. "This party. Want me to ask Elena to invite Quinn?"

Just like that, the restless feeling was back. "Invite her, don't invite her. I don't care. We spoke after I left you." Tristan looked up from his phone, and Knox sat forwards, both of them giving me their full attention. "We agreed to stay out of each other's way from now on."

Tristan's brows flew up. "So that's it? You're going to just forget about her?"

"Yes. That's it. So, like I said, I don't care if you invite her or not. She's no longer my concern, and the party will be crowded enough that we can stay out of each other's way."

"Five hundred quid says you can't even stay away from her for the duration of the party." Tristan smirked at me. I knew he was trying to lighten the mood, but everything was too fucking raw, and once again, I needed to escape.

Knox spoke up quietly. "Mate, now isn't the time."

"Yeah. Sorry." Tristan was instantly contrite. "Go. Take your new baby out for a drive. When you get back, come down to the crypts, and we'll make you forget all about Quinn Farrow. Girls, weed, alcohol…it's all there for the taking. We're the fucking gods, and I'm gonna make sure you remember that fact tonight."

15

ROMAN

The drive had taken away some of my restless feelings. As I gripped the leather steering wheel, my Jaguar roaring down the quiet country roads, smoothly navigating the twists and turns, I finally managed to do what I did best. Lock my emotions away. It was easier that way, and I was good at it. Having absent parents had given me enough practice over the years, after all.

My mask was fucking perfect, and tonight, I'd remind everyone of just who Roman Cavendish was.

When I descended the stairs to the crypts, the first person I saw was Harriet, who attempted to thrust a drink into my hand. Ignoring her, I headed for the fridge and helped myself to a beer, popping the cap myself. Whether or not she was trying to be helpful, I wasn't going to accept drinks from anyone unless they happened to be one of my two best mates. There was no one else I trusted at this point, not even my lacrosse teammates.

"Roman." Freya stepped in front of me, eyeing me from beneath abnormally long false lashes. Her blonde hair was curled, cascading over her shoulders, the ends teasing the swell of her tits, which were barely covered by a low-cut green top. Ever since Knox had become unavailable, her attention had been on me. And fuck it, this was what I needed. A distraction. Something meaningless. A bit of normality. We both knew it would be nothing more than me blowing off steam if I took her down to the lower levels.

"Freya." I wrapped my arm around her waist. She was fucking hot, even though her personality grated on me at times. "Want a drink?"

Her hand slid up my chest, and something inside me wanted to recoil. Fuck. I needed more alcohol for this. *No.* That wasn't a good idea, not when I needed to stay alert.

"I'd love a drink," she murmured in my ear, but too bad for her, I'd just changed my mind.

"Forget the drink. Want to shotgun with me?" Ditching my beer, I led her over to the sofas, jerking my head to indicate that the people sitting there needed to move. Now. They scrambled to do my bidding, and I took a seat in the centre of the sofa across from Tristan, who was already getting everything set up. Fuck, yeah. I loved it when we were on the same wavelength.

A thought was pushing at the back of my mind, but I forced myself to focus on what was happening right now. My mask was going to stay in place. I was going to have a good fucking night, and I wasn't going to allow myself to think about the girl who had the power to hurt me more than anyone else.

"Roman, can I have a quick word?"

I glanced up at the new voice, my eyes widening as I took in the sight of head girl Penelope leaning over the back of the sofa. She was biting down on her lip, her straight blonde hair a curtain hiding her expression, but I could hear the concern in her voice.

"Be back in a minute," I said to Freya, dislodging her from my thigh and climbing to my feet. Why the fuck was the head girl singling me out here of all places?

"Somewhere private," Penelope said when I reached her. Okay, that meant taking Hatherley Hall's incorruptible golden girl down to the lower levels of the crypts because the only private room on this level was Knox's bedroom, and the only person allowed in there aside from him was his girlfriend.

"You sure you wanna go down to the lower levels? People might talk."

"Oh. Yes." Her mouth twisted. "I'd rather not. Perhaps we could go upstairs into the cellars? Or even a private corner down here? I just want to make sure we aren't overheard."

I glanced around us. No one was paying us any attention that I could see. No one except for Freya, who was staring daggers at her friend. I smiled to myself. As if she had anything to be jealous about. Penelope was the last person I'd ever do anything with, and she'd never sully her squeaky-clean head girl reputation with me, either. She wasn't a deviant like our head boy was, currently sitting with two girls with their hands all over his body, smirking as he rolled a joint.

"Yeah, we can go here. No one's listening." I led her through the archway to the far corner of the crypt, where we were mostly in the shadows, out of earshot of the other students. "What's up?"

"It's about Quinn."

Of fucking course it was.

"No offence, but I don't want to talk about her."

"Sorry. I just…she seemed upset earlier, and she mentioned she'd seen you. I'm worried about her." Penelope turned pleading blue eyes on me, and to my complete fucking horror, they filled with tears. I froze. What the fuck were you supposed to do with crying girls? Quinn had been different. This, I was not equipped to deal with.

"Uh…"

"Sorry," she sniffed, leaning into me, and oh, fuck, she wanted me to hug her, didn't she? Where was Tristan when I needed him? He was good with this kind of shit. I gingerly wrapped my arms around her, and she collapsed against me with a shaky exhale. Her arms came around me in turn, and she buried her face in my shoulder.

Fucking hell. Even though I was just providing her comfort or whatever, it still felt wrong. Quinn had really fucked with my head, and I didn't like it.

Fucking finally, Penelope raised her head, and I was relieved that her eyes were now dry. "Sorry," she said again. "I suppose I wanted to say that I think you should stay away from her. I…you're a friend, Roman, but she's having a hard time, and I—"

"I get it." Releasing her, I stepped back, dislodging her grip on me.

She blinked and then gave a small laugh. "Sorry. Again. I don't usually make a habit of crying all over people."

"Yeah, bit awkward," I agreed with a cough. I fucking hoped it didn't happen again. With her or with anyone. "Listen, you don't need to worry about me going near her. I'm not planning on it. I have no interest in making her life harder. In fact, I'd prefer to avoid her completely, but that's not gonna happen with us both being in the same location twenty-four seven. But you have my word, I won't go near her if I can help it."

Her shoulders relaxed, and she smiled. "Okay. Good. I

debated whether to say anything, and I hope you don't think I'm interfering. I was just worried about her."

"Don't worry about it. You're just being a friend." Tristan caught my eye over Penelope's shoulder, waving a joint in the air at me. "Are we done here? Because there's a joint with my name on it over there."

Distracted by the prospect of weed, I didn't wait for a reply. The conversation was over. Penelope had done her job, and now she could go running to Quinn, and as for me…

Back in my original place, I stretched out on the sofa, tugging Freya onto my thighs again. It still felt fucking wrong—everything did—but I was going to do everything I could to get back to normal.

"What did Pen want? I saw you hugging her." Freya pouted, and I winced internally. I liked her so much better when she didn't speak.

"Nothing important," I said dismissively, sliding my hand onto her bare thigh. She immediately shut up. Perfect. Now, all I needed was a nice buzz from the weed, and then maybe things would feel right again. "Pass me the joint, will you?"

16

Quinn

This was the first time I'd been in the infamous crypts, and I was only here because everyone else was. Despite knowing Roman would be here, I'd believed him when he said he'd stay away from me, and I had to learn how to handle seeing him around the school, until the sight of him stopped affecting me. I *longed* for the day I'd be indifferent to him.

"I won't let him near you," Aria promised, threading her arm through mine as we descended the stone stairs. I smoothed down the hem of my short dress, glad I'd worn my Converse with it so I could at least attempt to be casual. I didn't want Roman to know how he affected me.

From my vantage point, I could see an archway leading into a large underground chamber far beneath the school. Laid-back beats played from hidden speakers, echoing off the ancient walls, and people were crowded into most of the available floor space, talking, drinking, and chilling. Amidst the haze of smoke clouding the air, I caught a glimpse of raven hair on the cluster of sofas beyond the archway, and my heart beat faster. I immediately averted my gaze, but not before noticing the blonde seated on his lap.

It had taken him less than four hours to move on.

I hadn't been prepared for it to hurt so badly.

Aria stiffened next to me, her sharp gaze taking in the same sight I had. "That motherfucker," she hissed. "Grace, Mira, c'mere. Get our girl a drink, and keep her away from you-know-who while I give that wanker a piece of my mind." Before any of us could reply, she bounded down the final few steps and stormed over to the sofas, pushing through the crowd with ease despite her small stature.

"Oh, shit." I glanced behind me at Gracelyn and Samira.

"Oh, shit is right." Samira grimaced. "Come on. We'd better catch up before anything happens." We followed in Aria's wake as quickly as we could, catching up with her as she rounded the corner of the sofa where Tristan was seated with a girl on either side of him, a joint dangling from his fingers. When he caught sight of the rage on Aria's face, he smirked, his hand shooting out to grab her wrist, stopping her in her tracks. With another jerk of his hand, she lost her balance, falling into his lap with a cry, much to the displeasure of the girls on either side of him.

"Aww, sweetheart, you don't need to throw yourself at me to get my attention," he drawled, banding his arm around her waist to hold her in place. She didn't miss a beat, swinging her body around to straddle his thighs. Their eyes connected, and she raised a disdainful brow.

"What's the matter, head boy? Two girls aren't enough to satisfy you anymore? I hate to disappoint, but I have no interest in joining your little orgy."

He lifted the joint to his lips and inhaled deeply.

"Shame," he breathed on an exhale, smoke curling from his mouth.

Aria leaned in, stealing the smoke while the rest of us watched, wide-eyed. "I seem to remember you calling me a drug user. Bit hypocritical, don't you think?"

Tristan leaned in even closer, murmuring something too low to catch, but one of the girls at his side frowned. Aria leaned in and whispered something in his ear, making him chuckle. "You're right. Up you get, little scorpion. Go and shout at Roman so we can get on with enjoying the party."

"Enjoy your orgy," she said sweetly, swinging herself off his lap and blowing him a kiss with her middle finger. He raised his finger in return with a wide grin on his face, and I was so engrossed in watching their bizarre exchange that it took a moment for Tristan's words to register.

Then everything came flooding back in one sickening rush.

Roman.

"Aria, no," I called, drawing everyone's attention, including the one person I didn't want to notice me. I kept my gaze fixed on my friend, well aware of the two sets of eyes across the table. One set bored holes into my skull—Freya—and the other slid over me before pointedly turning away. Roman's gaze was like a burn, but a burn of ice.

Cold. So very cold.

And the jealousy. How I *hated* it. Hated that I wanted to tear Freya from him, to choose violence, to make sure she never went near him again. That was not me, and the fact that Roman affected me in such a visceral way was just another reason why I needed to forget about him as soon as possible.

Aria glanced at me, and her shoulders slumped.

Twisting her head, she bared her teeth at Roman. "Stay the fuck away from my friend, Cavendish," she ground out before dragging me away. I heard Freya mumbling something about how he'd never go near me, but her words were thankfully lost in the crowd. Aria, Gracelyn, and Samira surrounded me, forcing my focus away from the people clustered on the sofas.

After a quick detour to the makeshift bar, Gracelyn thrust a drink into my hand, and I happily accepted it. Holding up my can, I looked at each of my friends in turn. "Tonight, we forget the gods exist."

We clinked our cans together, and a smile crossed Aria's face. "You know what's even better than a god? A goddess. What do you say?"

Unlike the last time I'd been a student at Hatherley Hall, wanting to be a goddess at the ball and somehow ending up as their youngest ever one, it was at the bottom of my list of priorities. I groaned. "You really want me to be one of the goddesses, don't you?"

"Mostly because I'm petty and it would amuse me to see Freya's face if you were crowned. Elena's definitely gonna be one of the three goddesses—that's pretty much a guarantee now she's Knox's girlfriend—and probably Penelope since she's head girl and she was one of the goddesses last year. You need to be the third."

"I'll let you campaign for me if I can campaign for you." I smirked at her when she pulled a disgusted face. "Don't look at me like that. Out of the two of us, you'd probably end up being the one who gets crowned. Everyone likes you. You're popular, whether you want to be or not."

"Ugh, no. Don't even joke about that. Not everyone likes me, anyway. The wannabe goddesses don't."

"Yeah, because they're jealous that Tristan flirts with

you all the time," Gracelyn interjected, and Samira nodded.

"She's right. He totally does."

Aria blanched. "That's just wrong. *So* wrong. If you knew—" She cut herself off, shaking her head. "Whatever. The point is, not everyone likes me."

"Come on." I batted my lashes at her. "Do it for me? Double the chance to oust Freya."

"You do realise the gods and goddesses have to dance together? In front of the whole fucking school? It's a complete farce," she muttered.

"Yeah, and if you're crowned, you can pick Roman and 'accidentally' knee him in the balls. Or tread on his foot with your heels. Penelope would dance with Tristan, wouldn't she? It makes sense since they're head boy and girl."

"True. Fuck it, okay, I'll let it be known that I'm throwing my hat in the ring. Just for you. But I want it to be known that I'm doing this under duress. And there's no chance I'll get voted in over you, anyway."

"Noted."

We smiled at each other.

A couple of hours later, and the drinks and the atmosphere were beginning to work their magic. I'd made sure I kept my back to Roman, not wanting to witness the point when he invariably took Freya down to the lower level of the crypts, which, as Elena had previously informed me, was where the gods took their girl of the moment when they wanted some privacy. I couldn't deal with that, not yet.

An arm loosely wrapped around my waist, and I turned to see Lincoln, one of the guys from the lacrosse team, grinning down at me. "Tonight is your lucky night, Quinn. You and me—we're gonna get a chance to do what we should've been doing before you left us all behind to move to Switzerland." He paused, his brows pulling together. "Uh, maybe not back then, but whatever, we need a chance to do this now."

"And 'this' is?"

His grin widened. "First, you have to dance with me. Then I'll tell you."

I glanced around us. There were a few people dancing, including Gracelyn and Samira, their thighs sliding together as Samira ran her hands down Gracelyn's back. But most importantly, there was no sign of Roman.

"Go on," Aria whispered from my side. "He's hot and not as much of an asshole as certain team members I could mention."

"Such a glowing character reference," I murmured, amused, but let Lincoln tug me over to the space where the others were dancing. At least he wouldn't ring any alarm bells with my parents—although I hoped I was out of their reach down here. I placed my hands lightly on his shoulders, but he shook his head.

"Nah, that's not how we dance. We dance dirrrty," he said with a smirk, spinning me around and pulling me back against his chest. His hands landed on my hips, moving us to the heady beat of the music thrumming through the stone cavern. Across from me, Knox and Elena were wrapped up in each other, less…dancing and more… grinding. I tore my gaze away from them, but not before Lincoln noticed.

"If I play my cards right, that could be you and me later."

Why did that sentence feel so wrong? He was gorgeous, a lacrosse player, and, from what I knew of him, nowhere near as arrogant as most of the elite were. I should know. I'd been one of them once, back when Roman had been on the fringes. Now, he was in the centre, and I was the one on the outside.

Instead of replying, I kept dancing, gradually losing myself in the music and the feel of a warm body pressed against mine without any expectations…at least, not yet.

Lincoln's head dipped to my ear. "All this dancing is thirsty work. Wanna grab a drink?"

I nodded, and he released his hold on my hips but placed a hand at the small of my back as we pressed through the crowds. It was only when we reached the wall that I realised the direction he'd led us was taking us straight past the sofas where Roman was still sitting. Freya was still in his lap, but now she was straddling his thighs, and he was—he was— *Is he kissing her neck?*

My breath stuttered. Biting down on my lip, I somehow managed to stifle my gasp. I curled my fingers into my palms, the sting of my nails grounding me, and leaned into Lincoln, using his big body to shield me from the sight. He responded instantly, moving his hand from the small of my back to slide his arm around my waist instead. As far as I knew, only Roman's inner circle, my roommates, and Penelope were aware of what had gone down between me and Roman. I'd told my roommates the basics, and Penelope had a general idea based on the small details she'd picked up on and the few things I'd mentioned to her in passing. I mentally crossed my fingers, hoping everyone else was none the wiser, and did my best to act like I was unaffected by the sight. And it turned out that Lincoln was completely unaware because as we passed the sofas, he shoved at Roman's shoulder.

"Get a fucking room, bro."

Roman blinked slowly, lifting his head, and I could see

his pupils were wide and glassy and a little unfocused. Probably high or drunk or both. A lazy smile curled across his lips.

"Thought I'd give you a free show."

"I don't need a show. I've got my girl right here." Lincoln moved suddenly, and then Roman's bleary gaze was on mine.

It was as if someone had thrown a bucket of icy water over him. The haze instantly disappeared, and his jaw clenched so tightly I could hear his teeth grinding together.

"Get the fuck away from her."

Lincoln reeled back at the venom in his tone. "What the fuck, Ro? Why?"

"Because I fucking said so. If you know what's good for you, you'll do it."

Lincoln stiffened. "No. If you've got a claim on Quinn, that's one thing, but from where I'm standing, you already picked your girl for the night."

Roman blinked again, his gaze sliding to Freya. She wound her arms around his neck, kissing the side of his head, and I had to turn my back, which meant that I was facing Lincoln directly. He tilted my chin up gently, lowering his head, and I was frozen in place—

There was a high-pitched shriek from the direction of the sofas, and two seconds later, Lincoln was gone from in front of me, his head swinging to the side as Roman punched him in the face. He roared in pain and anger, lunging for Roman, and then people were diving out of the way—including me—as the two of them went at each other. Tristan leapt to his feet, shouting for Knox, and we were suddenly surrounded by half the lacrosse team, pulling their two teammates apart.

"What the *fuck* is going on?" I'd never seen Tristan so livid. "You don't attack a fucking teammate!"

Roman snarled like an animal, and it really, really shouldn't have been hot. There was something seriously wrong with me. Seeing him standing there, his chest heaving, rage in his eyes, his fists still clenched as he bared his teeth at his best friend…it did something to me.

"Ro." Tristan stepped closer, lowering his voice, and I was only able to hear him because I was pressed against the wall right behind them. That, and the fact that the crypt had gone silent other than the music still playing, with everyone focused on the drama happening between the elite. "You can't afford to get into any more shit, and he's our teammate. How are you gonna explain his black eye to Saunders? What if you'd hurt him and he couldn't play?"

"He fought back—why the fuck am I the one you're having a go at?"

"Because you started it. I saw you."

"Fuck this. I don't need this shit." Roman pushed past him, heading straight for the door that led to the lower level of the crypts, and wrenched it open. As it slammed behind him, the main crypt gradually filled with noise again.

Freya rose from where she'd been sprawled on the side of the sofa, her wide eyes meeting mine. They narrowed when our gazes connected, and she opened her mouth. "I'm going to comfort Roman."

"No, you're not," Tristan and I both said at the same time. He glanced at me, nodding towards the door Roman had just gone through, and I returned his nod. Satisfied, he turned back to Lincoln, directing him to take a seat on the sofa while another of their team members held a makeshift ice pack to his face. Freya shot me a savage glare and went to move, but I raised my palm in a universal "stop" gesture. "Don't even think about it," I hissed. Before she could reply, I turned my back to her. I forgot all about the threats of my parents, about all the reasons why this was a bad idea.

Sucking in a breath and squaring my shoulders, I headed towards the door that led downstairs.

17

Quinn

I crept down the stairs and along a long, dark passageway illuminated by low lighting. Up ahead of me, there was a soft creak, and I caught sight of a door closing at the end of the passageway. *There.* I moved faster, my heart pounding, a shiver going through my body. It was so oppressive down here, buried beneath layers of earth. How Elena and Knox actually enjoyed being down here, I had no idea. I would much rather be out in the open, close to the water, feeling the breeze on my face.

But this was where Roman had gone, and so I had to follow. *Why* I had to follow, I couldn't even explain to myself.

I reached the wooden door, curled my fingers around the handle, and pushed it open.

It took a moment for me to adjust to the dim lighting in the room. The only illumination came from a few sconces set into the walls, throwing the rest of the room into shadow, and a heavy iron pendulum hanging from the crumbling stone ceiling in the centre, casting a soft glow over a large iron bed, with a cracked black leather sofa in front of it. Roman was on the sofa, his legs spread in a lazy sprawl, his arms outstretched and draped along the backrest.

My hands were shaking as I stepped closer, Roman silently watching me with a dark look in his eyes. When the tips of my Converse touched his Nikes, his mouth curled into a sneer, but still, he remained silent.

I licked my lips, my mouth suddenly dry. What the fuck was I supposed to do?

He took the decision away from me, rising to his feet, causing me to take a quick step backwards to avoid our bodies colliding. Even so, I still ended up so close to him that when I inhaled, my breasts were brushing against the fabric of his black T-shirt.

His arms came out, and he spun me, yanking me back against him in an aggressive imitation of the movement Lincoln had used earlier. Unlike Lincoln, he held me tightly in place with one arm securely banded around my waist and his other hand gripping my throat. He lowered his head to my ear.

"Seems familiar, doesn't it? Yeah, I was watching you. All fucking night," he rasped. His lips skimmed across my lobe as he continued. "I was watching you with *him*."

I swallowed around his grip. "I thought you were too busy with Freya to notice anything else."

He laughed darkly. "Guess what, baby. I've tried everything tonight, and nothing has been able to erase the taste of you from my tongue."

"You kissed her?"

There was silence, and I wondered if he was going to ignore the question. "Just her neck," he said eventually. "You fucked me up too much. Felt like fucking cheating, even though there's nothing between you and me."

"I hated seeing you with her." My words came out in a whisper, the truth dragged from me, even though I didn't want to give him any ammunition.

"Yeah? I fucking hated seeing you with him. Look what you made me do. Link's my friend, my fucking teammate, and I saw red when I saw he was going to kiss you."

My hand came up, sliding into his soft hair and tugging. "I didn't do that to you. You don't get to blame that on me."

"I know. But you need to understand. You can't have anyone else. You've got my mark branded on your fucking skin. You're *mine*."

I didn't bother to mention I'd showered since the boat shed, because it was true. He *had* branded me. Once upon a time, I'd fallen for a boy who hid his true self from the world, and I'd been his ever since. As much as we both hated it.

He slid his nose down the side of my face, nipping at my jaw right above the place his fingers were curled around my throat. His hard cock pressed into my back. "You're fucking mine, Quinn Farrow."

"We can't. I thought we agreed—"

"I don't give a fuck what we agreed and what you think we can and can't do. It's clear that it isn't working. How long did it take? A few hours before we both cracked? The fact you followed me down here speaks volumes, baby. What are you gonna be like the next time you see me with another girl? Do you want to be jealous of every fucking person who comes near me? Because I can tell you now, if another guy attempts what Link did tonight, I'll make them regret it. And I don't give a fuck that it could get me expelled."

I exhaled shakily, tilting my head a little. He lowered his hand enough that he could get his mouth on my throat, sucking a mark into my skin, branding me where everyone would be able to see.

"I want you, Quinn, and I've decided I'm going to have you. So you'd better speak up now and tell me exactly what happened when you left and why you think you have to avoid me now. No more secrets."

"Where do I start?" My voice cracked, and I hated it. "The lake. Th-the boat. I—"

"Speak to Tris and Knox. They both believe that my drink was spiked—something you didn't even let me fucking explain before."

I twisted in his grip, and he let me. Our eyes met, his still so dark, stormy seas raging in them. "Can you blame me?" I hissed. "Can you tell me you—"

His mouth came down on mine in a hard, furious kiss, stealing the breath from my lungs.

He held me in place as he kissed me over and over again. I melted into him, moaning into his mouth, and he responded by kissing me harder, collapsing back onto the sofa and pulling me down with him so I was straddling his thighs, never moving his mouth from mine.

I lost myself in him. I couldn't get enough.

His cock was hard beneath me, and I ground down on him, needing the friction, but he stopped my movements, tearing his mouth from mine.

"Wait," he panted. "Need." He kissed me again. "To talk."

I nodded, too breathless to speak, and the corner of his lips curved up. He stroked a hand through the length of my hair over and over while we regained our breaths, and then he drew back a little so we could look into each other's eyes. Being this close to him and holding eye contact when we were about to have a difficult conversation was intimidating, to say the least, but it was now clear to me that we needed to get it all out there. Or I did, at least. I owed him his answers, and then maybe he'd understand why I'd acted the way I had.

Exhaling an unsteady breath, I held his gaze. "Okay. Where do I start?"

"How about starting from the point where you left me? When you ghosted me?"

I could hear the hurt in his voice, even though he was trying to hide it.

"My parents…when we were…friends before, remember how I said they could be a little controlling, and they had connections with some of the staff? They found out about my rebellious phase, as they called it, and the fact I'd been hanging around with you. I guess they were concerned, in their own way, but they completely overreacted. My dad had been offered a secondment to his Swiss office and just…told me I was coming, too, and that was that. They said it would be a clean break, and they cut me off from *everything*. I wasn't even allowed to stay in touch with people they'd previously approved of, like Penelope. After…when I was away, I gradually got my privileges back, but I thought there was no point in trying to contact anyone after so much time had passed. I thought…I thought you'd have forgotten about me, in all honesty." I bit down on my lip, and Roman sighed, shaking his head.

"Baby, I could never forget about you. Believe me, I tried. Didn't work."

I attempted a smile, but against my will, my lips turned down. "I wish… There are so many things I wish had happened differently. But I can't change them. Anyway, I became more and more unhappy, isolated from everything and everyone I knew, far away from home. My parents eventually realised that it was best for me to come back here, so I came back."

Roman cupped my cheek, catching a tear with the pad of his thumb. I hadn't even realised I was crying until then. Despite his gentle movement, his eyes were dark, and I could see the muscle ticking in his jaw.

"No one gets to make you cry," he ground out. "Not even me. Not anymore."

I wrapped my arms around him, burying my face in the crook of his neck, and he held me, a strong, solid presence I could cling to. When I raised my head, I met his gaze again, swallowing hard before I continued.

"There were conditions they placed on me. Conditions I had to meet in order to be allowed back. You were one of those conditions. I wasn't allowed to interact with you. They…they knew you were on your last warning, Ro. They threatened to make sure you were expelled if I—if I —" I broke off with a deep, shuddering breath, and he swore loudly.

I could *see* the moment he understood what I was telling him. His entire expression softened, the visible concern and care in his eyes chasing all the darkness away. "Fucking hell. I get it now. They held that over you so you'd toe the line. Because I'm not good enough for you."

My lip trembled. "You are. You're so good. Too good for me. It killed me to say those things to you. I didn't know how else to protect you. How to make you stay away."

"Baby. Come here." He kissed me so softly, softer than he ever had before. "I understand why you did it. I don't fucking like your methods, and I wish you'd told me why, but I get it. Now, I need you to listen to me and listen carefully. I'm not gonna make your life more difficult with your parents, but I want you to understand that despite whatever power they have or think they have, I have more. Yeah, there is a genuine threat of me getting expelled, but if it came down to it, I'd have Knox's and Tristan's families on my side, as well as my uncle. And believe me, they're way more influential than your parents could ever hope to be. It's not just about the money. We all have plenty of that here. It's about the power. Who you know. There is zero fucking chance of them getting rid of me, not if it was for something I didn't do." He spoke confidently, but I could hear the underlying hesitance in his tone that he was trying to hide, and I knew it wasn't as simple as he was making it out to be.

I shook my head. "I still don't want to risk it. They could…I don't know, frame you or something. I'd like to think they wouldn't go that far, that they actually have some morals, but after they did what they did to me, pulling me out of school…" My fingers stroked through the short hairs on the back of his head. "I just don't know how far they'd go, and I'd never forgive myself if something happened to you because of me."

He stared at me, his eyes wide, before huffing out a disbelieving laugh. "You really mean that, don't you?"

"Yes. I know I hurt you, Roman. But I couldn't live with myself if your life was ruined because of something I did, when I know that by staying away from you, I can keep you safe."

"Fuck, Quinn." Pulling me into him, he kissed the side of my head before drawing back a little to meet my gaze. "I want you to answer one question before we move on to the topic of the boat. Do you want to be with me? Imagine none of this other shit existed. Would you want us to be together?"

"Yes." I didn't have to think about my answer, not even

for a second. "That's all I wanted back then, and it's all I want now."

"Okay," he said, a wide grin spreading across his face, happier than I'd ever seen him before. "Okay. Then we'll make it happen."

18

ROMAN

Quinn lifted her head from my shoulder, staring at me. "How?"

"We can worry about that later. I'll talk to the boys, if you don't mind them knowing."

She shook her head, giving me a small smile. "I don't mind." Pausing, she bit down on her lip. "Do—do you want to be with me?"

How was that even a question? "Fuck yes, I do. There's no question of that. You're a motherfucking goddess, baby, and I'm just here to worship you."

That got me a bigger smile. "You're ridiculous," she huffed.

"Ridiculously into you." I grinned at her, leaning forwards to kiss the tip of her nose. "But seriously, there's no one else I want. Freya…earlier…shit, I don't even know what that was. My fucked-up attempt to get you out of my head. It didn't work."

"Yeah, I could tell by the way you attacked your friend." She smirked, and yeah, she even looked hot with a smirk on her face. Fucking hell, how did I get so lucky to have this girl here in my arms after everything?

"I should probably apologise to him. Speaking of apologies, about the boat… I honestly have no fucking idea what happened. All I remember is getting back to the lighthouse, completely fucking delirious from the swim and the cold water, and panicking about leaving you out there for too long. I think I said something about you, but I don't even know if I was talking to myself or a person. My head was so messed up. It feels like a dream or something. I remember that someone shoved a drink into my hand. My mouth was full of the taste of saltwater, and I was so thirsty I downed it in one go. After that…nothing. It's like my memory is completely blank. Whatever it was gave me a hell of a hangover, like I'd gone on a week-long bender or something."

Her brows pulled together. "I don't like the sound of this. I'm sorry I didn't listen to you when you tried to tell me before. Who would spike your drink, and why? What purpose would it achieve?"

I shrugged, unease creeping down my spine. "No clue. The boys have no idea, either. I'm just being careful, keeping an eye out. We all are. I might have accidentally been targeted, but if it was on purpose, then we need to be on our guard. No more letting anyone hand me drinks. That's why I wasn't drinking tonight, and Tristan took care of the weed. Him and Knox are the only ones I trust. And you. I trust you, Quinn."

Her lip trembled again, and I couldn't have that. I kissed her, and she sighed against me. "How have we gone from you hating me to this?"

"I never hated you. I hated that I wanted you. There's a difference. And yeah, it's no excuse for the way I acted. I can't tell you how fucking sorry I am for the way I treated you. But you were always meant to be mine, Quinn."

Finally, she smiled. "Everything you said goes for me, too. And just so you know, I trust you, too, Roman."

"Good." Now we'd managed to get the difficult conversation out of the way, it was time to do something I'd been wanting to do for-fucking-ever. "Lock the door, baby. I'm gonna show you how a god fucks his goddess."

She stared at me and then burst out laughing. "I'm sorry, but that line was terrible."

"Yeah? You don't want me to make you see stars with my mighty rod?"

"Stop it." She collapsed into me, her shoulders shaking with laughter. "I can't take any more."

"But, baby, I can take you to heaven."

"No more," she gasped, clambering off me, still laughing. I noticed she was pretty fucking quick at getting the door locked, though. Good. I wasn't the only one eager for this. And my girl was a goddess, whether she liked it or not, and I was going to make sure she was treated like one. Beginning with getting her naked and worshipping every inch of her beautiful body.

When she returned, I wasted no time in sweeping her off her feet and carrying her over to the bed, where I lowered her down. Seeing her lying there, ready for me, staring up at me with so much lust in her eyes, made my dick throb. I needed to be inside her. After I'd made her feel good.

I tugged off my shirt and kicked off my shoes, fucking loving the way her gaze went all heavy-lidded, dragging down my body and stopping at the bulge in my jeans.

"Roman."

"Yeah? Like what you see?"

"More," she moaned. Fucking hell, this girl was so fucking sexy.

"You want more? You know what to do."

She licked her lips and then kicked off her shoes. I raised a brow, and so she took her socks off. Fine. If she was going to be a little tease, two could play that game.

I took my socks off, wincing at the freezing temperature of the flagstones beneath my feet.

"More," she demanded.

"You first."

Moving into a seated position, she tossed her hair over her shoulder. Her hands disappeared behind her back, and then the next thing I knew, she was pulling her bra out from under her short dress. Fuuuck. Just one layer of fabric separated me from those delicious tits I couldn't wait to play with.

Sliding her hand down her body, she lay back down. I palmed my aching cock through my jeans, staring at her with my mouth open. Yeah, I was aware I probably looked like a dickhead, but I couldn't quite get my head around the fact that she was here and all the shit we'd been dealing with since she'd come back was over. Okay, not over, but there was a reason. I knew why she'd been acting the way she had. She accepted that I'd had my drink spiked. And now? Now, I finally got a proper second chance with the only girl I'd ever really wanted. And I wasn't going to fuck it up.

"Roman. More." I could see her nipples through the fabric of her dress, and it was fucking mouthwatering.

"More?" My fingers drifted to the button of my jeans. As she stared at me, I divested myself of both my jeans and underwear in one go, and I groaned in relief as my cock was finally freed from its confines.

A breathy moan fell from her throat, and my cock

jerked. Stepping up to the bed, I lowered my head, nipping at her lip as I slid my hand up her thigh. "Your turn. I want it all off."

Thankfully for both my dick and my sanity, she complied instantly, pulling off her dress and treating me to the sight of her gorgeous breasts, leaving just a tiny scrap of material covering the final part of her that I really fucking wanted to see. Placing my free hand on her other thigh, I pushed her legs apart and then traced a single finger over her underwear, already wet with her arousal.

I spoke against her lips. "All. Off."

She took a deep, shuddering breath and then fell backwards onto the bed, sliding her underwear off her body.

I stilled, taking in the sight of this beautiful woman who was about to become mine in every single way.

"Fuck," I rasped. "If you could see yourself now…"

Her lashes lowered, her cheeks flushing as she curled her fingers into the sheets. "Roman. I need you. Please."

"Condoms. Need—"

"I haven't been—I had a full set of tests for everything when I came back to England. And I'm on the pill."

Fucking hell. Was she saying what I thought she was saying?

"I get tested regularly. If you want to go without…"

"*Please.*"

There was no way I could wait another second. I climbed onto the bed, covering her with my body. "I've never been with anyone without a condom before." *I've never been with anyone I felt so fucking much for.*

"Me neither." Her eyes met mine, and it was like we could read each other perfectly as I slowly pressed inside her tight, wet heat. I'd imagined this so many times, but it had mostly been hate fucking in my head because I hadn't been able to see a way past our animosity. I'd thought I would want it hard and fast, and yeah, I did still want that, but this…this was everything I hadn't known I needed. It was pure fucking perfection. Quinn wrapped her arms and legs around me, moving beneath me like we'd done this a hundred times before, meeting me thrust for thrust. Bracing myself, I switched up positions, kissing and licking her breasts, then up to her collarbone, and finally marking her throat with my lips and teeth. Her breaths grew rapid beneath me, her nails pressing into my skin as she gasped out a litany of swear words interspersed with my name, and I knew she was close.

Angling my body, I got my fingers on her clit, and it was game over. She cried out my name, fucking shattering around me, and there was no possible way I could even attempt to hold back. I followed her over the edge, my cum filling her as she gripped me so fucking tightly, milking my cock until we were both completely spent.

I rolled us over, pulling her on top of me as my dick slowly recovered and we stopped breathing like we'd just run a marathon. Stroking my fingers through her hair, I smiled to myself.

"You know how you're my goddess and I'm a god?"

Lifting her head, she raised her brows. "I'm not sure I want to hear whatever you're about to say."

My smile widened into a grin. "All I was going to tell you was that you can finally be in on the secret."

"What secret?" Amusement danced in her eyes.

"You've just experienced the real nectar of the gods. I filled you with—"

"No. No more!" She slammed her hand over my mouth, muffling my words as she bit back her own smile. "If you mention gods or goddesses or god-related innuendos one more time, I'm leaving."

I palmed the soft curves of her ass, and when she shivered and removed her hand from my mouth, I angled my head for a kiss.

"No more. Want to hear another secret? A real one?"

"Yes." Laying her head on my chest, she stroked up my arm.

"Remember our first kiss? I couldn't stop thinking about it—about you. I was gonna text you in the summer and see if we could meet up somehow, so I could ask you to be my girlfriend."

Her breath hitched. "Really?" she whispered.

"Yeah. I thought at first that you were just fucking around with me, y'know, rebelling or whatever, but the more we talked, the more I realised you saw me. The real me."

She pressed the softest kiss to my skin. "I did see you, and I *do* see you. You saw me, too. You saw beneath the surface, and you were the only one I felt I could be myself with."

"We'll get that back." It was a promise that I wouldn't break. "We knew everything about each other back then, and all we need to do now is catch up. We both want the same thing, Quinn. You're fucking mine, and I'm yours, okay?"

"Okay." Her hand found mine, squeezing it gently. "It's a deal."

19

Quinn

"No one will disturb us," Roman promised me, clearly having seen the look I'd darted towards the locked door. Wrapping his arms around my body, he pulled me into him. I pressed my face into the crook of his neck, breathing him in. He was so warm. So real. I couldn't believe just how quickly everything had turned on its head. For the first time since my return, I had hope. Hope that somehow, we could be together. That he'd be mine.

But beneath the hope, there was unease. Who could have spiked Roman's drink, and why?

"The drink thing. Do you think it was a case of mistaken identity?"

He sighed, kissing the top of my head as he brushed my hair aside so he could run his hand up and down my bare back. "Fuck knows. I'd like to think so, but I remember the drink being thrust into my hand, so it seems pretty deliberate to me. I just wish I could remember more about it. I didn't even see who did it. Not even their hand. Fuck," he muttered. "Every time I think about it, it makes me so fucking angry. Not even the fact that someone did that to me. The fact you got caught up in it, left alone on the boat. It's—"

Raising my head, I kissed the scowl from his face until he was smiling at me. "It's okay. I mean, it's not okay, but I don't hold it against you, Roman. I think I always knew, deep down, that you wouldn't have done that to me. That was why I could never be as angry with you as I wanted to be. Why I let what happened in the boat shed happen."

His smile curved into a sexy smirk that I wanted to kiss from his face. "Yeah. I seem to remember you enjoyed that *very* much. We're definitely gonna have a repeat of that— the good parts."

"It's a deal." I let him pull me into his kiss, our naked bodies entwined, and I'd never felt so close to anyone before. Had never been so physically close, but this was more than that. I'd been Roman's ever since that first day we'd spoken, the day he'd taken me to the lake. *His* lake.

"In the morning, we'll speak to the others and work out what to do about your parents. Is there anyone you want to bring into this?"

I lay my head back down on his shoulder, idly caressing the defined lines of his stomach. "Aria, I guess, because she'd never forgive me if I left her out. I don't really want to involve Penelope because I don't want her to get caught between me and Freya any more than she already is. Other than that…Elena, maybe? I don't know her all that well yet, but she's Knox's girlfriend, and it's not really fair to ask him to hide this from her."

He shook his head. "Baby, if you're not comfortable, he'd understand. Fuck, I mean, we don't even need to involve him at all. Not if you don't want to."

"No, it's okay. You trust him, and that's enough for me.

I get good vibes from Elena, anyway. So, Tristan, Knox, Aria, and Elena. And you and me."

"You and me." I could hear the smile in his voice, and then he laughed. "I can't wait to see Tristan's face when he finds out he's got to spend more time with Aria."

"Yeah, what's all that about, anyway? Aria always changes the subject whenever I bring him up. Or says something uncomplimentary."

"Yeah? Tristan does the same. Fuck if I know what's going on there. There must be some history between them, but if neither of them is willing to volunteer the information…"

"I guess it'll have to remain a mystery. For now."

Roman suddenly rolled us so I was lying underneath him, grinding his hardening length into me. "We've got far more important things to do. I've got the woman of my dreams in my bed and a lot of lost time to make up for."

The look in his darkened eyes made the breath catch in my throat. And then I registered his words. "Woman of your dreams?"

"Fuck, yes. You're mine, Quinn. In and out of my dreams. All. Fucking. Mine." He punctuated the words with rolls of his hips, sliding his erection along the length of my pussy, and I moaned.

"*Roman.*"

"Yeah. Say my name, baby," he growled into my throat. "I'm gonna make you fucking scream it by the end of the night."

I raked my nails down his back, and he hissed, then bit down on my throat as his fingers pinched my nipple, a pleasure-pain combination that made me so fucking wet.

"Roman. Oh. Fuck. More," I gasped out as he continued to torment me with little bites and touches and teases until I was writhing beneath him, desperate to feel him inside me. "Please. Need you."

Holding himself up on one elbow, his hard cock taunting me with just the glistening tip dragging across my stomach, his fingertips traced circles on my breasts. "I don't think you're ready to scream my name yet."

"I am. *Please*." This had to be torturing him as well as me, surely? His cock was jerking and dripping precum, and his entire body was taut, his muscles straining, riding that knife edge of self-control when I knew without a shadow of a doubt that he wanted to sink inside me.

"So fucking impatient," he rasped, lowering his head to flick his tongue over my nipple before lightly biting down. "You want my dick inside you?"

This man was the biggest tease, and I couldn't stand it anymore. "Roman." I dragged my nails down his chest. "I'm so wet for you. All for you. Ready for you to fill me with your big—"

I didn't even get to finish the sentence, but it had the desired effect. He flipped me, dragging me into a kneeling position with my back bowed and my face in the pillow. Gathering my hair into a ponytail, he wound it around his hand, the other gripping my hip. A groan fell from his throat. "So fucking hot and all fucking *mine*."

As soon as he said "mine," he thrust inside me with one powerful movement that stole the breath from my lungs.

He fucked me hard and fast, pounding into me, tugging at my hair, his body so hot and hard against me. I braced my elbows on the bed, pushing back into him, needing this just as badly as he did. I wanted to still be able to feel him tomorrow. To have a reminder of his claiming of me.

As if he could read my thoughts, he gripped me harder. "You're fucking mine."

Then, he released my hair, his hand sliding under my body. One, two, three strokes of his fingers across my clit, and my orgasm hit me out of nowhere, sudden and so powerful that I couldn't breathe, couldn't see, consumed with this overwhelming wave crashing over me and dragging me under.

"Fuck. *Quinn*." He thrust again, his cock pulsing inside me, filling me with his hot cum, marking me as his inside and out. I gasped for breath, collapsing down with him on top of me. "Quinn," he breathed into my nape, his voice unsteady as we both struggled to get air into our lungs. He carefully rolled off me, easing out of me as he did so. I could feel his cum dripping out of me, and I rubbed my thighs together.

"What are you doing?"

I buried my face in the pillow, my cheeks heating. "I wanted to keep your cum inside me," I whispered into the soft fabric. Because he was so close, his breath skating across my ear, he heard every word.

"Fuck, baby. That's so hot. I've got a better idea, though. Roll onto your back for me."

When I instantly complied, he gave me a slow, dirty smile. "Good girl. Lie back and relax. I'm gonna make you feel so good."

Then, he used his fingers to fuck the cum back into me while he played with my oversensitive clit and got his hot mouth all over my breasts until I was coming again, falling apart on his fingers.

After that, there was nothing.

"Morning."

I blinked until the figure leaning over me came into focus, amusement dancing in those deep blue eyes.

"Morning. What time is it?" I croaked.

"Early. Almost eleven."

My eyes widened. "Eleven? That's not early. How did I sleep so late?"

"I fucked you so good you needed a long recovery period, I guess. Remember how you passed out after I gave you your best orgasm of the night?"

I half-heartedly punched Roman's bicep, and he laughed. "You can't deny it, Quinn."

"Okay, okay." Rising into a seated position, I glanced down at my body, gasping as I took in the marks he'd left on me. "Roman. Look."

His gaze went dark and hot. "Mmm. Yeah. I left my marks on you. Just like you left yours on me." He pointed at his torso and then twisted so I could see his back.

"I did that?" I whispered, staring at the red scratches on his smooth skin.

"Yep, and I like it. Feel free to do it anytime you like. Do you like my marks on you?"

Did I like his marks on me? Yes, I did. I loved them. I wanted him to mark me up all the time so everyone knew I was his. But— "I love them, but how am I going to explain them? If anyone finds out that you gave me these and it gets back to my parents—"

He leaned forwards, pressing a soft kiss to my lips. "Don't worry about it now. We're going to sort this out, I promise. Let's go upstairs, shower, and get the others rounded up, and we'll come up with a plan. It's gonna be okay, Quinn. I'm not letting you go, no matter what."

20

ROMAN

"It's the only thing that makes sense."

I glared at Tristan, aka my former best friend, my fists clenching and unclenching at my sides.

"As much as I hate to agree with the head boy, he has a point." Aria shot Tristan a look of distaste that would've amused me if I wasn't so fucking pissed off with what he'd just proposed. "You don't want anyone outside of this room to find out about this situation. As far as I know, Knox and Elena don't have an open relationship. Me and Quinn are both straight, and it can't be you, Roman, because you're trying to keep your whatever you have going on with Quinn under the radar. So that leaves one person."

A hand slid over my clenched fist, and I turned to meet Quinn's gaze. Her mouth twisted. "I don't like it, either, but they're right."

Tristan cleared his throat. "Maybe if you'd been a bit more discreet with where you put your mouth, I wouldn't have to pretend I'd had an all-night fuck-fest with your girlfriend."

I growled under my breath, and he rolled his eyes. "So fucking possessive." He jabbed his finger at Knox, who was sprawled on the other sofa with Elena in his lap. "You too. Possessive as fuck. I don't get it."

"Maybe when you find someone who puts up with your arrogant self, you'll know what it's like to be protective of them," Aria spoke up.

"Aww, little scorpion. Life's too short for that. I know it upsets you to hear it, but I have no intention of following in the ways of my besties."

"Yeah, just keep spreading those STDs around, why don't you?"

"Will do." He did his usual thing of blowing her a kiss with his middle finger, which she returned. I slumped back on the sofa, rubbing my hand over my face. Tristan was right, the bastard. He was the only option. I'd marked Quinn up too obviously. Part of me fucking loved it—okay, all of me fucking loved it. What I did *not* love was the fact that everyone would think that Tristan was the one who'd done it.

"Fine. Fuck. If there's no other option," I muttered.

"You're lucky this is even an option. If I hadn't ended up getting so high last night, I would've had my own all-night fuck-fest with two girls at once."

Aria made a gagging sound, and Tristan smirked at her before turning serious.

"Okay, one obstacle down. We have two remaining. Quinn's parents and our mystery drink spiker. I think that between us, we could put enough pressure on the school to avoid you getting expelled, Ro, but it's a big risk with all the shit that's happened already. I'd recommend keeping this quiet, if you're planning on continuing it?"

"We are," I said instantly and then glanced at Quinn. Fuck. I hoped we were still on the same page.

"We are," she confirmed with a shy smile, and I had to kiss her. I gave my friends the middle finger as I did so because the fuckers started cheering and whistling. It ended up with Quinn laughing against my mouth, so I pulled her into me, seating her on my thighs and wrapping an arm around her waist, before pressing a kiss to one of the marks I'd left on her throat.

"Okay, then I think you need to be discreet. No more marks where other people can see them. Be careful in the communal showers," Tristan cautioned Quinn. "I'm happy to help. It's not like it's a hardship—I mean, have you seen you?—but I don't want other girls to think I'm not available. As far as everyone knows, this was a one-time thing. No cockblocking, please."

My girl rolled her eyes at him. "Believe me, I have no interest in people thinking I'm in a relationship with you, of all people."

"What's that supposed to mean?" His voice went high and indignant, and I snorted.

"I'm sure you can work it out. Back to the drink spiker. I think the only thing we can do is keep an eye out and watch for anyone acting weirdly around me or us. Like I said before, it's possible I wasn't even the target, or it was a spontaneous thing. Fuck knows."

The others were all in agreement, and with that, I swore everyone to secrecy, and we were done. Except for the one thing which I really fucking hated the thought of, but it was a necessary evil. Even though it made me want to stab my own eyeballs and possibly stab Tristan as well.

"Let's get this over with," I muttered when Quinn, Tristan, Knox, and I were assembled in the lower level of the crypts. Tristan glanced at me, his eyes sparkling with amusement, and I wanted to punch the smirk from his face.

"He's doing this for you and Quinn," Knox reminded me in an undertone, and I acknowledged his words with a jerky nod. Yeah, he was, but it didn't mean I had to like it.

"Bed," Tristan decided. Eyeing the sheets dubiously, he pulled a face. "On second thoughts, I don't wanna risk getting near anyone's bodily fluids. Ro, strip the bed. We'll dump this in the laundry room and have it decontaminated."

"Fuck you." I did as he said, though, Quinn helping me without a word, and surprise of all surprises, my boys made the bed up with clean bedding.

"Quinn, lie here," Tristan instructed, dropping all signs of his usual teasing, flirty persona. "We're gonna make it look like you just woke up. I'll lie here and take a selfie."

She arranged herself on the bed, Tristan keeping his hands to himself as he directed her to his liking. When he was satisfied, he climbed onto the bed, glancing back over at me. "I'm gonna put my arm around your girl now. Try to remember that, yeah, she's hot, but I'm not attracted to her, okay?"

"Just get it over with," I gritted out, shaking off Knox's hand on my arm. "I'm not gonna punch you or anything. I just don't like seeing Quinn with anyone else."

"I know. I'll make it quick. Quinn. You good?" She nodded, and he carefully brushed her hair away from her neck, exposing the marks I'd left on the side of her throat. He slid one arm beneath her shoulders and held out his phone, angling it so that both of their heads and the marks on Quinn's neck were visible on-screen. Holding his thumb over the shutter button, he grinned at the camera. Quinn blinked up at the screen, a soft smile curving over her lips, and something inside me twisted because that was a smile that Tristan had no business seeing, let alone anyone else, but once he posted it to our Hatherley Hall group chat, all the elite were going to see that smile. And even worse, they'd think Tristan was the one to put it on her face.

"All done, so you can drop that murderous look from your face," Tristan announced, and I wasted no time in sweeping Quinn off the bed and into my arms. I didn't fucking care what my friends thought of me—the only thing I was concerned with was having my girl back with me, where she belonged.

"Hey. Roman." Quinn's words were breathed into my throat. "Do you want to know how I found it so easy to smile when Tristan took that photo? It was because I was looking at the marks you left me. A reminder that last night really happened, that somehow, we've made it past all the bad things that happened between us. And…even though it's going to be hard, I know things are going to get better from here."

I raised my head from where I'd had it buried in her hair to find that Knox and Tristan had left us, giving us the privacy we needed. Meeting Quinn's gaze, I smiled. "Yeah, they are."

ROMAN

"Nice save," I panted as I passed Tristan, running down the field. He shot me a grin from beneath his helmet, raising his hand in acknowledgement. Dodging around the guy marking me, I flung my body in the direction of the ball, which had landed two feet away from me, swiping it into my scoop and then wasting no time in flinging it towards a stone-faced Lincoln.

Lincoln. I still owed him an apology. I'd muted the elite group chat for the past week because there was no fucking way I was going to torture myself with whatever people were saying about the photo. As far as everyone knew, my best mate had spent the night with Quinn, and that thought was enough to make me want to rage.

But there was no time to get into that now, not when our defence was swamped, with the players from Stowe School throwing everything they had at us in an attempt to get possession of the ball. The score was tied, and we were almost at the end of the game. Both schools needed the points, and there was everything to play for.

Keeping my eyes peeled for any chance of getting the ball and sending it towards the Stowe goalie, I made sure to block the guy that was on my heels. He was determined that I wouldn't get the ball, but too bad for him, I was faster and better, my skills honed from the endless drills Saunders had made us practice over and over until we could do them without even thinking. It was muscle memory at this point.

I knew Quinn was there in the stands, watching me, ostensibly cheering the whole team on…but we both knew I was her full focus. That knowledge made me push my body harder, faster, sweat making my lacrosse jersey stick to my back as the sun beat down on us relentlessly. Despite the heat, adrenaline thrummed through my veins, and if it hadn't been for the guy on my heels all the fucking time, way too close for comfort, I'd have been on a high.

The ball shot past me, and the guy marking me dived for it at the same time I did. My height gave me an advantage as I swung my stick, the scoop catching the ball in midair and sending it soaring towards Tristan.

A second later, the Stowe player was crashing into my side, sending us both flying, falling onto the grass and rolling. The stick fell from my grip. "Fucking dickhead!" I shouted, punching him in the ribs with my gloved hand.

"Fuck you," he hissed, his fists flailing. In the back of my mind, I registered the blow of a whistle, and I shoved him away, climbing to my feet and bending over with my hands on my knees, breathing hard.

Knox was instantly there, his hand ghosting over my arm before he moved away. "Ro. Cool it. You're gonna get kicked out, and you know none of our subs are on your level."

"Yeah. I know. Okay. Fuck." Retrieving my stick from the grass, I turned to face the wrath of the ref. He awarded me a two-minute suspension and possession to Stowe. Pacing up and down, I concentrated on regulating my breathing while I counted down the seconds until I could get back on the field.

Two minutes left on the clock, and the score was still tied, 11–11. From my vantage point, I saw the moment it happened in slow motion. Link got possession of the ball within our box, right next to the crease and way too close to our goal for comfort. He ran, a blue streak down the field, dodging Stowe players left and right. When he had a clear shot, he flung the ball towards Knox, who caught it in his scoop effortlessly and, without missing a beat, darted around the player marking him, his stick outstretched. A powerful flick sent the ball arching towards the goal, skating over the tip of the goalie's stick and straight into the net.

"Yes!" I punched the air and then ran towards my teammates, the whistle sounding as the Hatherley Hall students went wild, all of us on the field and in the stands celebrating our win.

Pulling myself out of the huddle of cheering teammates, I glanced over to where Quinn was in the stands, her arm around Aria and a bright smile on her face. I shot her a grin that could've technically been directed at anyone, but she knew it was just for her. Her smile widened, and fucking hell, I was either getting butterflies or indigestion, and I hadn't eaten anything since this morning.

A large shadow blocked my view of Quinn, passing in front of me, unclasping his helmet as he strode across the field in the direction of the changing rooms. *Lincoln.* Quickly removing my own helmet, I jogged across the grass to catch up with him, stopping him in his tracks with a hand on his shoulder.

He gave me a wary look, and I winced internally at the faint yellow bruising that remained on his face. I cleared my throat. "Uh, good game today." Fucking hell, I hated doing this kind of shit. I didn't do this kind of shit. But then again, I'd never outright attacked one of my friends before. "Sorry for, uh, y'know. Punching you or whatever."

His lips thinned as he shook his head. "What the fuck is going on with you, bro? You come at me for being with Quinn, who, by the way, I didn't even fucking know you were into, and yet Tristan posts that picture of her and tells us all they spent the night together. I don't see any evidence of bruising on his skin like mine." He jabbed his finger towards his face. "So what the fuck is that all about? You share her with him or something?"

"Uh, yeah. Something like that," I muttered, shifting on my feet as I stared down at the ground. "I was out of line, and I don't want—" With a frustrated breath, I forced my head up to meet his gaze again. "Look, I'm sorry, okay? That's the last time I'm gonna say it. Accept it or don't; it's up to you."

I resumed walking, and after a second of hesitation, Lincoln fell into step next to me. "No hard feelings. I appreciate the apology."

"Good." We grinned at each other. Look at me, acting all responsible. This was weird. Maybe I'd turned over a new leaf and hadn't realised it.

"You throw one hell of a punch." He elbowed me in the side. "I don't want to get on your bad side again."

"Stay away from Qu— Oh, shit." So much for keeping my interest in her a secret. But he didn't know the extent of it, and hopefully, he wouldn't think anything of it.

A loud laugh fell from his throat. "I don't even wanna know what's going on there. You have my word I'll stay away from her, though. But if you're trying to be discreet, I suggest keeping the dirty looks and eye fucking to a minimum."

"I'll keep that in mind." We pushed inside the changing rooms and split off towards our lockers. All I wanted now was to get out of my sweaty uniform, shower, and then celebrate our win with my teammates and friends.

And if I was lucky, I'd be able to get Quinn alone for our own celebrations.

22

Quinn

After three days of sunshine, the weather had turned cold and grey. I curled up on my bed, snuggled into Roman's lacrosse team hoodie, my laptop open in front of me and music playing softly through my earbuds. Scrolling through the notes for my history extra-credit assignment, I made minor adjustments here and there before sitting back, satisfied that it was as good as I was going to get it for now. After saving my file and emailing myself a copy as a backup, I stopped the music and removed my earbuds.

Across the room, Aria raised her head. "Done?"

"So far, it's just a collection of notes, but I've finished for now. Have you?"

She stretched, yawning. "Yeah, I've done as much as I want to for today. Do you want to do something before your committee meeting? The common room will probably be quiet. We might be able to commandeer the TV for a bit."

As she spoke, rain began pattering against the windowpanes, and I felt the chill emanating through the stone walls. I shivered, pulling Roman's hoodie more tightly around me, completely on board with Aria's suggestion. The common room was always warm and cosy. And since I didn't have Roman to warm me up, it would have to do.

"Sounds good to me. I'll just clear this stuff away, and then we can go."

Aria had been right. The common room was almost empty when we entered. The only occupants were Katy and Will, two of Hatherley Hall's prefects and good friends of Elena's. They were tucked into the corner of the room, deep into a game of chess, and after greeting Aria and me, they returned to their game.

Grabbing the TV remote, Aria dropped onto one of the large sofas. After scrolling aimlessly for a while, she threw the remote down. "There's nothing good on. Want to play *Mario Kart?*"

"Okay."

As she was setting up the game, my phone vibrated with a message notification. When I unlocked the screen, I smiled.

ROMAN:

Why aren't we studying the same A-level subjects? Knox isn't as pretty to look at as you

ME:

Don't tell him that

ROMAN:

It would crush him. It can be another one of our secrets

Speaking of secrets. I can't wait until we get out of here. No more school. No more parental demands. Just you and me baby

ME:

I can't wait either

I couldn't help but wonder what a future between me and Roman looked like. The way he spoke with so much certainty, referring to the future like there was no doubt that we'd be together, made something inside me ache. I wanted that more than anything.

My phone vibrated again, and I glanced back down at the screen with a smile, which was wiped away when I saw who the message was from.

DAD:

> Your mother and I received word of your latest assignment results. Keep up the good work. We're pleased with your progress. However, it has been brought to our attention that you've been fraternising with the Cavendish boy. Remember our agreement, darling. This is for your benefit.

Fuck. I blew out a breath, my mind racing. And then, I prepared to lie to one of my parents.

ME:

> Thanks, Dad. I've only been in a group situation with him. I haven't sought him out at all, as per your rules. In fact, I've only really been speaking to his friend, Tristan Smith-Chamberlain

DAD:

> I see. The Smith-Chamberlains are a prestigious family, and Tristan is the head boy. Your mother and I certainly won't discourage you from gently pursuing something with someone of his standing when your studies are over, but your focus must be on your schoolwork now. I don't want to hear any hint of a scandal.

"Gently pursuing" was parental speak for keeping things strictly PG. Little did they know that Tristan was the last person to keep things PG with someone he was interested in. Not that they'd ever find out. And if they wanted to think I was interested in him in the meantime, that would keep the focus away from Roman.

I sent one final reply.

ME:

> I understand. I have to go now. I have a committee meeting for the ball soon. Give my love to Mum

DAD:

> I will. Remember, we only want what's best for you. Keep up the good work, darling.

Throwing my phone down next to me, I groaned. "Parents."

Aria's mouth twisted. "What now?"

"They apparently found out that I've been speaking to Roman. My dad didn't seem too concerned, not after I insinuated that Tristan was the one I was interested in, so whoever gave them the information couldn't know very much about the situation. I just need to be really careful."

A throat cleared next to my ear, and then a head dipped down, a swift kiss brushing over my cheek. My gaze flew to Katy and Will, but they were thankfully oblivious, too engrossed in their game of chess. Relaxing, I turned to smile at Roman, who was sinking down next to me, and then Knox, who threw himself down onto the rug, stretching his legs in front of him with a groan.

"Nice hoodie," Roman murmured with a smirk. I glanced down at myself.

"Someone lent it to me and never took it back."

"Someone thinks you should wear it all the time."

If only. I probably shouldn't even wear it around the school in case it gave anyone ideas, but it was probably safe enough in here. I was feeling a little better after the text conversation with my dad, and I was sure Tristan wouldn't mind being used as an excuse if necessary. He'd surprised me—there was more to him than appeared on the surface.

"Mmm. It is very comfortable." I shifted closer, Roman eyeing me with amusement. "What are you doing here, anyway?"

"We got out of our class early, so we thought we'd come and—" He glanced at the TV screen. "—beat you at *Mario Kart.*"

"I didn't think this through," Aria cut in as she threw controllers to Knox and Roman. She pointed between me and Roman. "You and him means me having to spend more time around the gods. At least the head boy isn't here this time."

"We'll wear you down." Roman shot her a wink. "We'll even let you win this game."

She snorted. "I don't need any help to kick your ass. Let's do this."

Aria was in the middle of getting our third game set up when everything went wrong.

"Whose hoodie is that?"

I squeezed my controller, the hard plastic digging into

my palm, refusing to look at the three girls who had just entered the common room.

"She was cold. I lent it to her. What's the problem?" Knox drawled from his position on the floor, his expression icy as he stared Freya down. Next to her, Penelope's lips were pursed, her eyes closing as if she could wish herself away. I knew the feeling.

Freya placed her hands on her hips. "Why did you give her Roman's hoodie? Why not yours?"

He rolled his eyes. "None of your fucking business. Move, please. You're blocking my view of the TV."

She huffed, moving to stand at the side of the sofa next to Roman. "Roman. Why?"

"She was cold, and he helped himself to my shit. You think his girlfriend wants to see another girl wearing his hoodie? Me? I don't give a fuck. Don't read anything into it." Roman's words were dismissive, and if I hadn't known how he really felt about me, I might've believed them myself.

Freya had no response to that, taking a seat on one of the other sofas, along with Penelope and Harriet. I sighed. There was no point in me staying here now. I rose to my feet, throwing the controller to Freya, who caught it, her eyes wide.

"Your turn to play. I have homework to do." Roman and Knox both ignored me as I lifted my hand in a wave and then escaped the common room. But when I got back to my dorm, throwing the hoodie down on the end of my bed, I received a text.

ROMAN:

You look fucking hot in my clothes but even hotter out of them

Can't believe you left me here with Freya.
Now I have to play nice so she doesn't get
suspicious

I know what you're thinking and I'm not
flirting or doing anything to lead her on.
You're the only one I want

ME:

I know. This whole situation is so messed
up. Sorry

ROMAN:

Not your fault and you're worth it

ME:

Thank you *heart emoji*

ROMAN:

heart emoji *heart emoji*

I smiled down at the little emojis. How could a tiny collection of pixels lift my mood so much?

Since Aria had been forced into remaining in the common room and I was alone, I decided to make the most of my free time and return my library books, then get back to my extra-credit assignment for my history class. Only five of us in the class had taken on the project, and while it didn't count towards our A-level results, our final papers would be submitted for potential publication in *The Historical Review*, a prestigious academic research journal. It was an amazing opportunity, especially for someone who had hopes of becoming a historian one day, which Penelope and I both did. We'd been discussing ideas for our papers, and I'd been researching my chosen discipline, but I had yet to narrow down the final subject of my paper.

I lost track of time, buried in the library stacks, until

my phone beeped softly with the reminder I'd set for today's ball committee meeting. Gathering up my notebook and the new books I'd borrowed, I made my way back to the dorm room.

Stopping dead in the centre of the room, I stared at my bed, at the place I'd thrown Roman's hoodie.

It was gone.

23

Quinn

"The committee meeting will come to order." Penelope banged a gavel on the desk. Where she'd managed to get an actual gavel from, I had no idea, but she seemed to be overly enthusiastic about bashing it on the wooden surface. The members of the ball committee were seated in one of the classrooms, Penelope at the front as the head of the committee, and the rest of us spread out across several of the desks. Freya and Harriet occupied the desk to my right, and behind them were Katy and Will. The rest of the committee members were other A-level students who I knew but didn't particularly spend time with.

The door flew open with a crash, and Tristan strutted inside, throwing himself down into the seat next to me. He ignored Penelope's huff of annoyance at being interrupted, shooting her a wink as he rocked back in his chair.

"Your latest committee member, reporting for duty. Anyone want to catch me up on what I've missed?"

"What are you doing here?" Penelope's brows were

raised. "I thought you said you didn't want to be involved with the organisation of the ball."

He sighed. "I don't, but Professor Donnelly made me. Said it was part of my head boy duties. So here I am, gracing you all with my presence."

Penelope nodded, accepting his words. "If that's all, let's get on with today's agenda. I thought we could have staff circulating with canapés through the evening…"

Tristan dipped his head to my ear. "I'm actually here because Roman's a paranoid bastard, and he wants me to keep an eye on you to make sure no one gives you any shit. He told me about the text you sent him about the hoodie, and I have my suspicions." His gaze slid to Freya and then back. "Doesn't really help with the rumours that things are going on between us, does it?"

"No, but I'm glad you're here," I said honestly. "I can't believe—"

"Quinn." Penelope spoke loudly. Her brows pulled together, her expression instantly contrite. "Sorry, but this is important."

I nodded. "Of course. Sorry. I'm listening."

She smiled and continued her rundown of the plans, but my mind wandered. Would Freya really take the hoodie? I didn't think she was that petty. My roommates hadn't seen any sign of it, so it hadn't been accidentally tidied away. I couldn't shake the uneasy feeling inside me, sitting heavy in my stomach.

"This is fucking boring, isn't it?" Tristan whispered to me.

"Hmm." Tapping my pen against my lips, I pretended to think. "Maybe you should contribute to the discussion. Make some suggestions."

"Oh, I have suggestions." He smirked at me.

"Tristan. As you're the head boy, could you join me at

the front?" Penelope said sharply, and I grimaced when I realised everyone was staring at us.

"I'd love to," he replied, drawing his chair back with a loud screech, and then sauntered up to the front of the classroom. "I have some ideas. Let's get into this ancient Greece theme. Dress the staff in togas. Our gods—of which I will be one—should receive crowns of laurel wreaths made from actual laurels, and each will be served by a harem of women."

"Absolutely no to a harem. Yes, to the togas, no to the laurel wreaths. My parents are contributing a generous amount towards the budget, and so I'd like us to have laurels of gold, as we usually do."

"I guess that works. What would you do without me?" Tristan winked at Penelope, and her cheeks flushed. It seemed that even the head girl wasn't immune to his charms. Clearing his throat loudly, he continued. "I had an idea for the name. How about the Olympus ball? Like Mount Olympus, the home of the gods."

"I like that," Harriet spoke up, and I could see several other nodding heads. I had no preference either way, so I kept my mouth shut. As far as I knew, there had always been a gods-and-goddesses theme, so it made sense to name the ball after the mythical gathering place of the gods.

"I had a couple of names jotted down, but I like yours. Olympus it is," Penelope decided, shuffling through her huge binder and making a note.

The conversation turned to food and drink, with Tristan proclaiming that we needed to have a separate alcohol table for those of us who could legally drink, in order to keep it historically accurate. He and Penelope went back and forth for a while, but eventually, they got the food and drink options locked down. Most of the other details had already been worked out, so all that was left to do was to book a DJ and decorator for the main hall, where the ball would take place. Then we could officially kick off the gods-and-goddesses campaign, which I wasn't looking forward to. Having to try to get people to vote for me when I'd rather not be involved at all…

When the meeting was over, Tristan quickly disappeared, shooting me a quick grin as he left, and I slumped back in my seat, rubbing at my head. The room emptied out until only Penelope was left, and when she'd gathered all her things together, she came to stand in front of me.

"Quinn, are you okay? I can't help but feel as if you're putting too much pressure on yourself." She bit down on her lip. "I'm worried about you. Maybe it would be better if you took off some of the pressure."

"How?"

"Well, you're taking on all these extra-credit things. The history project, for one. It's not going to count towards your final grade, so why not drop it and ease up some of your time? Or…ugh, I can't even believe I'm saying this, because I selfishly want you up there with me, but what about *not* campaigning to be one of the Olympus ball goddesses? You don't have anything to prove to these people."

If only. But I'd made an agreement about the goddesses with Aria, and I *wanted* to do the project.

"I know I have nothing to prove. I…I'll be okay. Thanks, though. I really appreciate your friendship and your concern."

She gave me a soft smile. "If you're sure. But just consider it. I'll help out on your project; you know I will. We'll pool our resources, and that should help to ease some of your workload."

"Thanks. That sounds good."

"Okay." Shifting her heavy binder in her arms, she laughed. "Maybe not tonight, though. We've covered a lot today, and I don't think my brain can take any more. I need an early night, and so do you. I can see you haven't been sleeping properly."

"You're right." Rising to my feet, I followed her out of the classroom, and we made our way in the direction of the Epicurus common room and the dorms.

We parted ways when I reached my dorm, and I threw myself onto my bed, burying my face in my pillow with a groan.

The bed dipped. "That bad, huh? I know just what you need. How about a little late-night trip to the tower? I have it on good authority that a certain person might be there."

I twisted around until I could see Aria. "I was going to have an early night, but…"

"But nothing. Grace? Mira? Are you two in?"

"Nope. We'll amuse ourselves while you two are up in the tower," Samira said, and Gracelyn laughed.

"I'm sure we can find something to do."

"It's a deal." Aria climbed off my bed. "I'll get all the shit together. Quinn, if you want to nap or anything, I'll wake you when it's time to go."

"Mmm. Okay," I murmured, my eyes already closed. The bed was soft beneath me, and in no time at all, I was falling into blissful oblivion.

24

ROMAN

"Y ou owe me. A lot. Like a whole fucking lot," Tristan hissed as I helped him push his car down the gravel driveway to the open gates. We'd worked our magic with the Cerberus security system…or, more truthfully, we'd used our status and money to make it happen, and if the dozing security guard happened to glance at the entrance camera, he'd see the same feed playing on a loop. Still, it didn't hurt to be cautious, and that was why we were pushing our cars down the long driveway. The long, *long* driveway.

"I know I do. I wish things were different, mate, I really do, but how the fuck else am I supposed to spend time with my girl?"

"I still think the tower was a better plan." His car rolled to a stop next to mine, and he applied the brake, tipping his head back with a sigh.

"It's cold up there, and it gives me fucking vertigo. How am I supposed to impress Quinn there?"

"Aww, is bad boy Roman Cavendish scared of heights?" he taunted with a smirk.

I gave him my middle finger. "Fuck off. I'm not scared of heights, and you know it. You're the one with a death wish, hanging out in a crumbling tower with half the wall missing."

"That's an exaggeration."

"Whatever. We're going for a drive, whether you like it or not. And I know you love any excuse to show off your wheels, so don't pretend you don't."

"Yeah, yeah." He glanced back down the long driveway. "Where are they? Did you text them with the change of plans?"

"I—" I began and then cut myself off as two figures came into view, skulking down the side of the driveway, keeping to the soft grass. A grin spread across my face as Quinn's eyes met mine, her face slightly obscured by a hoodie—unfortunately, not *my* hoodie—but I could see the smile curving over her pretty mouth. The second she reached me, I kissed that smile right off her lips until she was breathless against me.

"Hi," I said. "Ready to take a ride?"

"Hey—" From the other side of my car, Tristan's words were abruptly cut off by Aria slapping her hand over his mouth.

"No, I do not want to do anything with you that involves riding, or shafts, or big sticks, or whatever line you were going to come out with."

He tutted at her. "You have a dirty mind, little scorpion. Don't worry, I wasn't about to proposition you. I know you couldn't handle me or my stick."

She rolled her eyes. "You're the one who can't handle me. I'm here for one reason and one reason only. The same reason you're here."

"Oh, so we *are* gonna fuck?" When the three of us glared at him, he held up his hands. "Bloody hell, none of you have a sense of humour. It was a joke. Believe me, my dick sees enough action with girls who actually want it. I don't need to go chasing after the one who doesn't." He paused and then added, "And I don't want to fuck her, anyway."

"Sure," Quinn muttered sarcastically under her breath, and I bit back a laugh.

"Come on, baby. Check out my wheels, and act impressed, even if you're not. Tris, see you at the viewpoint in an hour, yeah?" I tugged Quinn around to the passenger door of my F-Type and opened it for her. With a smile, she slid inside. After closing the door behind her, I saluted Tristan and Aria, unable to keep the smirk from my face, and my best mate mouthed, *Fuck you, bastard*, throwing up his middle finger.

When I was inside the car, I ripped off my hoodie, leaving me in my T-shirt. Placing one hand on the wheel, I turned to my girl. "What do you think?"

"Hmm." She trailed her fingertips across the dashboard. "Very nice. I don't know much about cars, but I like it. Really like it." Ducking her head, she added, "Especially because you're inside it."

"Mmm. Having us inside it makes it a hundred times hotter," I agreed as I started the engine. The smooth, rumbling purr of the car was like a shot of dopamine to my system, and I couldn't help wondering whether I'd have been less destructive if I'd had it earlier. Too late to worry about it now, though.

I navigated onto the road, and as we left Hatherley Hall in the rear-view mirror, my entire body relaxed. Fuck, yeah, this was what I needed. My girl, my car, and an empty road. Keeping one hand on the wheel, I slid the other onto Quinn's thigh. She exhaled sharply, and then her legs shifted, widening slightly. I stroked my palm higher up her thigh, fucking wishing she wasn't wearing leggings. Her thigh was so smooth and warm, and the higher my fingers travelled, the more my dick reacted, lengthening inside my sweatpants.

"Fuck," I muttered, stopping right at the top of her thigh, so close to the place I knew she wanted me to touch.

"*Roman.*"

"I know. I fucking know. I've got to—" I had to cut myself off, my hand lifting from her thigh to grip the wheel with both hands as the car drifted round a sharp bend. After what had happened to Knox's dad and Elena…yeah, they'd been run off the road, but even so, I had a new respect for these sharp corners, and I wasn't going to take any chances when I had the most precious cargo on board. When we hit the straight, open stretch of road, though… that was when I'd be able to showcase the true power of my car. There were no speed cameras and never any police at night in this part of the Cotswolds, and both Tristan and I were going to make the most of it.

I felt Quinn's gaze on the side of my face. "Ro?"

"Yeah?" I spun the wheel to the right, throwing us into another corner. This one was an easy curve, and the car leaned into it, sending us closer to the open stretch where we could really let go.

"Do you think Freya took your hoodie?"

Good question, and one I didn't have the answer for. Freya…she was bitchy at times, and yeah, she could be petty, but she was harmless for the most part. Status mattered to her, but I wasn't the only single person available. There was Tristan, for a start, and even if none of the three so-called gods were interested, there were plenty of other guys who were single and also part of the elite. Guys she'd been with before.

Would she have taken my hoodie? I thought back

through the interactions I'd witnessed between her and Quinn, and I shrugged.

"Honestly? I have no fucking clue. It's not like she could wear it anywhere because people would know it was my hoodie, and it would get back to me."

"It makes no sense."

"Spiking my drink made no sense, either."

Quinn sucked in a breath, her hand flying to her mouth. "Fuck, Roman, I didn't even think of that. What if the two things are connected? What if you're being targeted?"

An icy tendril of unease snaked its way down my spine.

"I don't know what's happening, and I don't know what they hope to achieve, but if someone's after me, they need to stop being so fucking cowardly and come after me in person. Whatever it is, whoever it is, whatever their reason…they won't get the better of me. They'll regret ever crossing Roman Cavendish." I knew she could hear the dark promise in my voice.

"Good. I just…I don't want you to get hurt. And…and I can't help but feel a bit responsible. Both of those things are connected to me. What if…" Her voice dropped to a shaky whisper. "What if I'm making it worse for you? What if something bad happens because of me? I couldn't live with myself."

Fucking finally, we shot out of the bends onto the straight, wide A417 road. The Cotswolds stretched out before us, shadows in the darkness, thrown into relief by the faint glow of the shrouded moon. Two lanes of wide, smooth tarmac stretched out ahead as far as I could see, with no other traffic other than a lorry rumbling along in the slow lane in the opposite direction.

"We'll discuss this in a minute when I can concentrate

properly, but I want you to know that none of this is your fault, okay? Nothing that happens is because of you. I don't want you to feel bad or guilty or any-fucking-thing except happy that you're mine."

"O-okay."

I could tell she was unconvinced, but I'd just keep reminding her of the facts until she believed them. In the meantime, I had the perfect way to make her forget.

I swung the car into the fast lane. "Hold on. I'm gonna show you what this car can do."

Then, I floored it. The engine roared, responding to me instantly, and we fucking *flew*.

Quinn gasped, and then she laughed out loud. "This is amazing!"

A wide grin stretched across my face. This was everything. The rush of adrenaline and the girl who appreciated it just as much as me. The headlights cut through the darkness, illuminating our way, the bass of the music thrumming in time with my pounding heart.

Quinn's hand slid onto my leg, and I groaned. My dick was so fucking hard, mostly because of her, and maybe a sliver of it was because of this pure fucking rush I was experiencing.

"I want you," she murmured, and I allowed a sideways glance to see her other hand down between her legs.

Fuuuuck.

"Almost there," I ground out. Gripping the steering wheel harder than I ever had, forcing every bit of my concentration towards my driving, I eased off on the accelerator, allowing the car to slow as we drifted towards the roundabout. When we reached it, I took the exit that led to our first destination. We ended up on a narrow road flanked by Cotswold stone walls, and I scanned them carefully until I saw my destination. When I turned off the road and came to a stop, Quinn stared around us. It was impossible to see much with the moon being obscured by clouds, and I knew she was probably wondering why the fuck we'd stopped in the middle of nowhere.

Talking was overrated, and I'd had enough.

I unsnapped my seat belt, then hers, and then leaned over to her, sliding my fingers into her hair as my other hand landed back on her thigh. I pulled her into a kiss, moving my hand up her thigh. Kissing down to her throat, I nipped at her soft skin, wishing I could leave a mark where everyone would see it. "You were touching yourself. Couldn't wait for me, could you?"

She moaned. "You would've done the same if you hadn't been driving. You looked… *Ohhhh*." Another moan fell from her throat as I placed my hand where hers had been, right between her legs, so fucking hot and soft. "You looked so hot driving, holding the steering wheel like that. Your arms…"

I glanced up at her flushed cheeks and smirked. "My arms? You like my arms?"

"They were flexing. Ah, don't make me explain." Twisting her body, she buried her head in the crook of my neck. "You're so hot, Roman. Everything about you is just…"

"Yeah?" I began moving my fingers up and down, stroking over her fabric-covered pussy. "Funny, because I feel the same way about you. Touch me. See what you do to me."

She ran her hand up the muscle of my thigh and onto the massive bulge in my sweatpants. My cock jerked beneath her grip as she curved her fingers around my length.

Biting back a groan, I thrust up into her hand. "Fuck,

yeah. Feel that? It's all for you." I applied more pressure between her legs, and she gasped.

"More."

"You want more? Hoodie off, seat back, hands on those gorgeous breasts," I instructed hoarsely. My dick was fucking throbbing, but the need to make sure she was satisfied took priority.

When her hoodie was off and she was reclined back in her seat, I practically drooled at the sight of her tits spilling out of her tiny sports crop top. I had to have a taste. Tugging her top down, I lowered my head, kissing and sucking and laving my tongue over her breasts until her nipples were hardened, sensitive points and she was moaning, reaching for my hand to get it back down between her legs.

"Keep touching yourself. I want to watch while I make you come on my fingers."

"Fuck," she whispered, her mouth falling open, a tremble in her hands as she palmed her tits. So fucking sexy.

I ran my fingers down her stomach to the top of her leggings and dipped them beneath the waistband. I dragged them over her hot, silky skin and down inside her underwear until I was sliding them through her wetness. I wasted no time—she was so on edge already—easing two fingers inside her while I pressed down on her clit with the heel of my hand.

"Roman. *Roman.*"

"Yeah. You're gonna come for me. Make a mess all over my fingers." I stroked inside her, stimulating her inside and out, while she took shallow, shuddering breaths, her eyes falling closed as she arched her body upwards.

She fucking shattered around me, tightening on my fingers, gasping out a moan as I finger fucked her through it until she was whimpering against me and stilling my hand.

I withdrew from her, and when she opened her eyes, I gave her a dirty grin and took my time licking the evidence of her arousal from my fingers while she tracked my movements through blown-out, glassy pupils.

"Your turn," she whispered, her hand going to my sweatpants, where the head of my dick was straining against the fabric, a fucking wet patch there showing just how ruined I was by her already. Her thumb rubbed against it.

My breath caught in my throat. "Don't fucking tease me. You've got me so fucking worked up. It's not gonna take much."

Biting down on her lip, unsuccessfully trying to hide just how pleased she was by my words, she curled her fingers around the band of my sweatpants. Together, we tugged them down. I hadn't bothered with underwear—there was no point when I knew, or hoped, exactly how this night was going to play out—and I groaned with relief as my dick was freed from its confines, rock hard and erect, foreskin rolled back, precum fucking everywhere from how turned on I was by her.

Because my girl liked to make me suffer, she danced her fingers down my length, cupping my balls and gently tugging them. My dick jerked, dripping precum, and I clenched my fists, taking deep, deliberate breaths. I was not going to come from fucking nothing. I had stamina, for fuck's sake.

Except Quinn curled her fingers around the base of my erection with a much firmer grip, playing with my balls with her other hand, and then she stroked up my cock. Once. When her hand was at the top, she twisted it over my sensitive, exposed head and at the same time pressed a finger against my perineum. I shot like a fucking rocket. No joke.

"Holy fuck," I breathed as she stroked me through it, my dick pulsing in her hand, my cum decorating the formerly pristine interior of my car. When I remembered how to breathe again, I yanked her into me, slamming my mouth down on hers. "You. Are. Fucking. Incredible," I ground out between kisses, and she kissed me back just as roughly, none of us caring about the mess, just needing this connection between us.

After we'd managed to disentangle our bodies and clean ourselves up, I glanced over at her kiss-swollen lips and blissed-out expression and smiled.

"I can tell you now, hand on heart, that I've never been that turned on from a hand job. If you ever tell anyone I came that fast, I'll… Fuck, just don't tell anyone. It's embarrassing."

Quinn laughed, leaning over to kiss my cheek. "It's not embarrassing. I liked it. Anyway, you made me come almost as quickly, and you were on the edge for a lot longer than I was."

"Yeah, I guess so," I said as I started up the engine. "Still, no one else needs to know about it."

"They never will. So. Are you going to tell me why we stopped here?"

The car swung back onto the main road, and I glanced both ways before directing it back the way we'd originally come. "It's nowhere special. Tristan's relatives own the land. They own a lot of it around here. We come here in the summer sometimes when we want to get away from everyone without any risk of someone showing up. There's a stream with a rope swing farther down and a big hollow oak tree. Tristan used to play here as a kid, and he said I could use it tonight. It's… I know it's not much, just a dark field, but I wanted to stop somewhere I knew we'd be properly alone. I don't want to risk fucking anything up for you, Quinn. I couldn't live with myself."

"I trust you." She placed her hand on my leg, squeezing lightly. "It might be nice to come back here in the daylight sometime."

"We can do that." I slowed for the roundabout again and then headed in the direction of the lookout point where we were meeting Tristan and Aria. The roads were still silent and empty for the most part, and it gave me the chance to relax and enjoy the feel of my powerful machine effortlessly eating up the miles. "Going back to the discussion we were having before we stopped, I don't want you to have to worry about anything, okay? Whatever happens, we'll deal with it. No one can fuck with us and expect to escape unscathed. It's all gonna work out. Even if it does mean you have to be seen with Tristan once or twice." My jaw clenched. I still hated the thought of anyone else touching her, even if it was for show.

"Okay. I'm sorry to keep bringing it up. I'll...I'll stay positive. Or try to."

"That's my girl." Shooting her a grin, I flipped on the indicator, turning into the entrance of the lookout point. "Keep an eye out for Tristan's car. He should be parked up here somewhere."

"Why did Tristan come, anyway?" she asked, scanning the tree line.

"You'd arranged to do something with Aria. Then we were joining you—I dunno if she told you that part. My car's only a two-seater, and I didn't want you to miss out on quality time with your friend, so Tristan got to play chauffeur."

"It's a bit risky for the head boy, isn't it?"

I laughed. "Believe me, if he really thought there was a

risk, he would've done his best to talk me out of this. Deep down, he likes the sense of adventure. And getting to spend quality time with Aria." Smirking, I thought of just how pissed off he'd be after forty minutes stuck alone with her.

"Oh, I bet they both loved it." Quinn smirked as well, rubbing her hands together like a little evil villain, and yeah, that was one of the reasons right there that I lov— liked her.

Liked her.

Yeah.

Not the other thing.

It was too soon to be thinking about that, wasn't it?

25

Quinn

I'd forgotten what the whole gods-and-goddesses campaign was like. When I'd campaigned the first time when I was younger, it had been something new and exciting. Now, though, it seemed like it was taking up precious time that I needed to spend studying or even hanging out with my friends…not to mention my stolen moments with Roman. So many stolen moments. We'd become even closer than we had been the first time around. I couldn't believe how quickly it had happened, but at the same time, it felt inevitable. He'd always known me so well. Our connection now was solid, growing deeper and stronger every day.

The campaign itself had officially begun with posters of the potential candidates being plastered all around the school, as well as on the school intranet and our various group chats. We'd all had to submit a campaign video—non-negotiable. Some people—Freya, Penelope, Tristan, and a few of the others—had actually booked professional videographers to put together aesthetic montage videos of themselves, complete with music and slo-mo clips. I'd been with Elena when the first one was revealed, and her jaw had dropped, complete with disbelieving head shaking. I couldn't blame her. People here went over the top. Very over the top.

As for my video…I'd gone for a more laid-back approach and put together a slideshow of selfies, photos with my friends, images I'd dug out from my younger days, back when I had no cares and no idea of what awaited me. A few of the other candidates had created videos along the same lines as me, too.

Roman, on the other hand, had gone for a different approach to everyone else. His video was mostly footage alluding to his various pranks, some of which had been serious enough for him to be suspended or even expelled, if he hadn't been lucky. Everything was hinted at, so there was nothing actually incriminating, but everyone in the school knew his reputation and had at least a general idea of the things he'd done. Interspersed with the footage were clips of him on the swim and dive teams, his powerful body so at home in the water, so strong and sexy and…well. It was impossible that people wouldn't vote for him after seeing that, whether he'd been one of the elite or not.

Unreasonable jealousy rushed through me. I didn't want to feel this way. I knew he wanted me, but…it was hard. Hard when I couldn't touch him in public. Hard when I couldn't tell the world I was his and he belonged to me.

Straightening my shoulders as I entered the library, I told myself to forget about everything. The only thing that mattered right now was completing my history assignment so I could give my hoped-for future career the best chance possible.

I lost myself deep in the stacks, the dust motes dancing around me as I carefully paged through old books, some written before my great-grandparents had been born. Yellowed pages, faded with age, bound within cracked leather covers. Most of my research had been compiled via more modern books, but now I'd selected my final subject and had it approved, I wanted to be able to compare and contrast it with this older view of history, before modern technology was able to uncover so many of the things we now knew. I'd had to get special permission from my history teacher to be here because some of the books were so valuable and so fragile I had to wear protective gloves to handle them. The oldest books were kept in a locked glass cabinet with special lighting. It was amazing to think I was looking at words that were written so long ago, and it gave me a thrill. There was no doubt in my mind that this was what I wanted to do with my future.

But before I could think about that, I needed to get this project done.

When I'd replaced the books, I headed back into the main library. I could make out the low hum of conversation from a distance, but there was no one around me. It was out of hours, so that was most likely why, and I was thankful for my more comfortable and casual jeans and sports top instead of my perfectly pressed uniform. Somehow, when I was out of my uniform, I felt less pressured. Less stressed.

Placing my things down on a small table, I made my way back into the stacks to gather up a few copies of *The Historical Review* so I could see how the research papers were presented. This could be the key to ensuring the academics looked more closely at my work, and maybe…if I were incredibly lucky, I'd even be published. If not with this paper, then maybe with another, one day.

Turning a corner, my mind focused on the journals I needed, I ran straight into a firm torso. With a cry, I jerked backwards, but an arm came out to steady me. I looked up, seeing tousled raven hair, deep blue eyes sparkling down at me, and a mouth curving into an amused smile.

"You should watch where you're going, Quinn." Roman backed me into the stacks with his body, caging me in with his arms.

"Should I?" I ran my hand up his chest, watching his eyes darken. His tongue swiped across his lips, his gaze fixed on my mouth, and when he lowered his head, we were both on the same page. I wrapped my arms around his neck, pulling him closer, swept away in the feeling of his hot mouth on mine and his body, so strong, holding me securely in place. Protecting me.

"Fuck, Quinn," he muttered, kissing down the side of my throat. "We shouldn't be doing this here."

"I know."

Neither of us stopped.

I lost track of time, my whole world narrowed down to this tiny corner of the library, where we were the only two people to exist.

Until we weren't.

The distinct sound of a sharp intake of breath, immediately stifled, had me shoving Roman backwards, panicked. From the side of the stacks, there was a flash of movement.

"Stay here," Roman growled, stalking to the end of the aisle. He glanced around him, tense and alert, listening. Eventually, though, his shoulders lowered, and he shook his head as he returned to where I was slumped against the stacks, my heart still racing. He spoke in a whisper. "I don't see anything. Whoever was here is gone, but you should leave."

"I...I can't. I need to look at some journals. We're not

allowed to take them out of the library, and I have to submit the first draft of my assignment tomorrow."

He shook his head again, his eyes hard and his jaw clenched. "No. We can't be seen alone together, and I'm not leaving you alone in here. Fuck the rules—take the journals with you and bring them back tomorrow, early. It's late now, and no one's gonna notice they're gone. Keeping you safe is the most important thing."

"Do you really think anything would happen to me in here?" Even as I said the words, doubt crept into my mind. Suddenly, the warm, welcoming library seemed ominous, full of dark shadows and hidden corners where anyone could— "Ugh. Shut up, brain," I hissed.

"I'm not taking any risks, not when it comes to you. I shouldn't have even kissed you, not here, but…" His lips curved into a wry smile. "You're impossible to resist, Quinn Farrow."

I melted. "Likewise." With a sigh, I straightened up. Turning to face the shelves, I hesitated. "Um. I…I'll take a couple with me, only because I really want to produce the best paper I possibly can. I never really understood why the research journals weren't allowed to be taken out of the library. I'll take good care of them."

"It sounds like you're trying to convince yourself," Roman commented. He dipped his head to my ear. "Don't change, Quinn. Your conscience is one of the things I lo— like about you. But in this instance, you don't need to feel guilty. You're only borrowing them for a few hours, for a good cause."

"When you put it like that…" I *did* need to submit the first draft of my paper in the morning. Swallowing down my guilt, I quickly scanned the shelves, pulling out the journals I needed before I could change my mind. Roman remained in the stacks as I made my way back to the table where I'd left my things. I wished things were different, but they weren't, and there was nothing I could do about it. Patience. That was what I needed. One day, we wouldn't have to hide. One day, I could love Roman Cavendish in the way he deserved.

When I reached the library doors, the borrowed journals sitting heavy in my bag, I saw Roman lounging around the small sports section, talking to one of the lacrosse team guys. As I pushed the doors open, he shot me a wink, and I ducked my head to hide my smile.

Quinn

"Miss Farrow." Professor Fitzgerald came to a stop in front of me, his brows lowered and his mouth set in a flat line. "See me after class."

My eyes widened.

He knows about the journals.

Swallowing hard, I managed to nod. "Y-yes, sir."

Turning on his heel, he swept away from me, back to the front of the classroom. I blinked rapidly, attempting to get myself under control as I unpacked my bag with shaking hands.

Tristan slid into Penelope's usual seat next to me. Before I could ask him what he was doing, he leaned over to me, speaking low in my ear. "What's he done now?"

My head shot around to face him. "Who?"

"My best mate, who else? Or— Shit, has something else happened?" He was immediately on alert.

I shook my head violently, my ponytail swinging. "No. Nothing. It's Professor Fitzgerald. He asked me to see him after class. I...I took some journals from the library. I just…I wanted to make sure my paper was as good as it could be." My lip trembled. "He…he must've found out."

Cocking his head, he stared at me. "Journals? What's the problem?"

"We're not allowed to remove them from the library."

His brows pulled together. "We're not? I've always taken them."

Of course he has. "Well…okay. But you're you, and I'm me, and removing them from the library isn't allowed."

"Quinn, honestly, I think you're making a big deal about it. You borrowed some books, so what? You put them back, yeah? You didn't damage them?"

"Of course I put them back. I borrowed them the night before last and put them back first thing in the morning, before breakfast. I was really careful with them. I wouldn't do anything to damage them."

His expression cleared. "Then you have nothing to worry about. He probably just wants to talk to you about your paper. You submitted the first draft, right?"

"Do you really think that?" I wanted so badly to believe him.

"I know that, Miss Extra Credit. He probably has a boner over your paper and wants to tell you all about it."

"That's gross!" I shoved at his shoulder, and he laughed, rising to his feet.

"I bet it's true, though. Stop worrying. It's gonna be fine." Flashing me a grin, he went to take his usual seat, and a moment later, Penelope appeared.

"What did Tristan want?"

I shook my head. "Nothing, really. Just Tristan being Tristan."

"He—"

"Miss Byron-Chopard, please take your seat. This is not gossip hour. Do that on your own time, not mine."

Her body stiffened, and she took her seat without another word, her cheeks flushing. I grimaced—it was almost unheard of for the head girl to be berated for anything. When Professor Fitzgerald turned his attention to the screen at the front of the classroom, I discreetly reached out and squeezed her arm. Some of her tension seemed to melt away, although she didn't look at me, her gaze fixating on the screen.

The class passed far too quickly, and before I knew it, the bell was sounding. As everyone gathered up their things, ready to leave, I remained where I was, a ball of anxiety sitting heavy in my stomach.

"Are you coming?" Penelope glanced down at me as she swung her bag over her shoulder.

Doing my best not to let my emotions show on my face, I mustered up a small smile. "No. Professor Fitzgerald wants to speak to me about something. I'll catch up with you later."

"Okay." She took my word for it, thankfully, disappearing with a wave. When the classroom was finally empty, I gathered up my courage and made my way to the front of the classroom.

"Take a seat, Miss Farrow." Professor Fitzgerald indicated towards the chair he'd placed opposite his desk. When I was seated, he cleared his throat. His stern expression faded away as his mouth turned down. "I'm very disappointed, Quinn. Of all my students, you're the one who has shown the most promise. The most integrity. And yet—" He threw his hand out, his finger jabbing at his laptop screen. "—it appears I was wrong."

I licked my dry lips. "I-I know it was wrong to take the journals from the library. I only borrowed them overnight. I just wanted—"

"If it had only been a case of you borrowing the

journals, then maybe—" Cutting himself off, he jabbed at the screen again. "That doesn't even matter. What matters is the fact that you not only removed those books from the library without permission, but you plagiarised several of those journal sources." His voice rose. "Did you think I wouldn't notice? Did you think *The Historical Review* wouldn't notice when you submitted your paper?"

I stared at him in horror. "*Plagiarised?*"

"Yes. I expected so much more from you, Quinn. To stoop so low as to cheat—"

"I didn't cheat! I didn't—I didn't plagiarise anyone! The only reason I wanted those journals was to make sure I could structure my essay properly! I would never—" My voice cracked, tears filling my eyes. "Please. You have to believe me!"

"Enough!" His hand came down on the desk, hard. "I am looking at your draft right now, and I can see the evidence in front of me."

"*What?*"

Spinning the laptop to face me, he scrolled past highlighted passages scattered throughout my paper, furiously clicking the mouse. "Here. Here. Here."

I rubbed my eyes, trying to make sense of what I was seeing on the screen. Leaning forwards, I blinked back my tears, focusing on the words.

The words.

Those weren't my words.

"This isn't my paper," I gasped.

"Don't give me that. We'd already signed off on your chosen research subject, and the paper came from your email address. I suppose I should thank Mr. Cavendish for bringing your misdemeanours to my attention. Without the knowledge that you'd taken the journals, I might not have inspected it so closely. You were clever, I'll give you that.

Rewording it just enough that it wasn't obvious at a casual glance."

"I-I-I—" Roman. *He wouldn't.* A hot lash of betrayal sliced through me. "Roman told you?"

"Emailed me, yes. Even gave me the names of the journals you'd taken."

"No. There's no way—" That wasn't the most important thing right now. "Please. You have to believe me. This isn't my work. I swear it. I'd never, ever steal someone else's hard work and try to claim it as my own."

Professor Fitzgerald pinched his brow. "You mean to say this isn't your opening paragraph?" Scrolling back up to the top, he began to read aloud, and nausea rose in my throat as I heard the words I'd carefully crafted over hours and hours of notes, research, deliberation, and countless rough drafts.

"Y-yes." The tears fell, and this time, I didn't bother wiping them away. How could I refute what was so plain to him? How could I defend myself when those were the words I'd written? "I-I didn't plagiarise, though. I didn't. I would *never*. S-someone must've tampered with it. I have backups. I can show you."

"Quinn." His gaze softened fractionally. "I'm sorry. I have to disqualify you from the extra-credit project, and I'll be keeping a careful eye on all your future work."

I couldn't breathe. It hurt so much. "P-please."

"I'm sorry."

The consequences hit me all at once. This was really happening. "Please don't tell my parents. I-I'll do anything."

He sighed heavily. "Plagiarism is a serious offence. I have no choice in the matter. Your head of house will also be informed. As far as I'm concerned, detention for the rest of the term will be a suitable punishment. You can serve it in the library, returning books to the shelf. It seems fitting."

"M-my future…"

"You did this to yourself, Miss Farrow. Cheating has consequences. Please remember that."

I was sobbing now, unable to see through my tears. Professor Fitzgerald cleared his throat, and then he rose to his feet. Coming around the desk, he placed his hand on my shoulder. "Against my better judgement, I'll keep it to myself until after the ball. I know you've been campaigning to be one of the goddesses, and, well…I won't take that away from you."

"Th-thank you," I said brokenly. It hurt even more that he thought he was showing me a small kindness, which, if I *had* cheated, I most definitely wouldn't have deserved.

"I hope you'll learn your lesson from this." Removing his hand from my shoulder, he sighed again. "I'll give you a minute."

When he'd left me alone, I buried my face in my hands and cried and cried and cried.

27

ROMAN

*D*evastated.

That was the only word I could come up with to describe the look on my girl's face. Complete and utter devastation.

She didn't even turn to look at me as I approached her, remaining statue-still, sitting with her legs dangling off the side of the pier, her feet and ankles dipping into the water. She'd placed her socks and shoes next to her, and ignoring the tempting bare length of her legs was surprisingly easy to do for once because I was so fucking worried. The breeze lifted the strands of hair that had come loose from her ponytail, sending them across her face, but she didn't even appear to notice, staring straight ahead with her bottom lip trembling.

I tugged off my own shoes and socks, rolling up my trousers so I could sit next to her, mimicking her position and dipping my feet into the lake. Lifting my hand, I gently cupped her chin, turning her head to mine. I swallowed hard when I saw her red-rimmed eyes and the tear tracks down her face.

"Who did this to you?" My voice was soft but so fucking deadly, rage fizzing through my veins.

"You did." It was a whisper, carried away by the breeze.

"*The fuck?*" There was— I hadn't—

"No." Finally, she looked at me. "It was supposed to be you, but I don't…" Leaving the sentence unfinished, she let her head fall forwards, burying it in the crook of my neck as she pressed her shaking body into mine. Instantly, I wrapped my arms around her, tugging her into my lap. My mind spun with a thousand questions, my heart fucking hurting as she fell apart in my arms, but I forced myself to stay silent until she was ready to speak.

When she lifted her head, she told me what had happened and how almost as soon as her professor had told her I was the one who'd thrown her under the bus, she'd dismissed it, knowing that my feelings for her were completely genuine and I'd never knowingly hurt her. Regardless of her words, guilt rolled through me, making me choke on my own breaths. If I hadn't encouraged her to take the journals… Fuck. I needed to make it up to her, and fast. Even if I hadn't been partly to blame, I would still do everything I could to fix it. I didn't even care that someone had tried to frame me—I wasn't the important one here. Whatever my future would bring, I'd deal with it. I didn't need plans. I knew I'd be fine, no matter what. But Quinn—she had a dream. A whole plan for the things she wanted.

Someone had tried to take that away from her today.

Whoever that person was, I'd find them, and then they'd face the wrath of a fucking god.

"Don't lose your head," Tristan cautioned as I paced up and down Knox's dressing room. Yeah, the flash fucker had an actual dressing room in his parents' house. Over a week had passed since everything had gone down with Quinn and whoever the fuck was trying to ruin her or mine or both of our lives, and I was still just as fucking agitated as I was then. Just as helpless, and I *hated* feeling helpless. How was I supposed to make things right if I had no clue where to start?

"I'm trying not to," I ground out, tugging at my tie. Everything was happening too fast, and now I was here at the Ashcroft mansion instead of back at Hatherley Hall with Quinn, where I could protect her. Only the knowledge that Aria was with her—and the fact that she'd sworn to me she wouldn't let Quinn out of her sight—kept me from losing it. The girl was petite, but she was vicious. And I knew she'd call me the second there was any sign of trouble. If it had been up to me, I wouldn't have left the school grounds at all, but Knox's mum had insisted we should all get ready for the ball at their mansion, as was tradition. Or so Knox said. I had a suspicion that my friends were trying to protect me in their own way, keeping me apart from Quinn so that neither of us got into any more trouble. Their loyalty was to me, but I knew they had a soft spot for Quinn. Tristan did, especially, and I was torn between feeling happy about that fact and wanting to rip out his throat for daring to go near her.

Yeah, I had issues.

I came to a stop in front of Knox. "How long until we can leave?"

He rolled his eyes. "Two minutes less than the last time you asked me. Will you fucking relax?"

"Would you relax if Elena was the one in this situation?"

That shut him up. "Fine," he muttered. "You might have a point." He glanced at Tristan. "C'mon. Let's go and find my parents and get these photos and shit over with, then we can reunite Roman with the love of his life."

"Oooh, the love of his life." Tristan elbowed Knox, grinning widely. We both stared at him in silence, and gradually, the smile melted from his face. "*Oh*. It's like that, is it? What am I saying? Of fucking course it's like that. You—" He thrust his finger in my face. "—are just as bad as Knox, if not worse. Obsessed."

"Yeah, yeah, we're obsessed. Get over it." Knox strode over to the door, yanking it open. "Coming?"

We followed him downstairs to where Elena was waiting, and fucking hell, she looked incredible. I only had eyes for Quinn, but damn, Knox had amazing taste in women. We'd all gone for black suits with black shirts, but our ties and the linings of our suits were different. Knox had gone for a deep red that reminded me of blood, and Elena's long, flowing dress matched the colour exactly. She had no jewellery except for the diamond choker Knox had bought her, and if the rumours were to be believed, they got up to some kinky shit involving that choker and ropes and tombs... I shuddered. I did *not* want to imagine my best mate and his girlfriend in any kind of compromising position, let alone—

"You okay?" Tristan's face was suddenly right up in mine, peering into my eyes.

"Fuck off with your garlic breath in my face." I pushed him away.

"Hey! I cleaned my teeth! I used Knox's toothbrush and everything!"

"What did you say?" Knox stared at him suspiciously.

"Uh, nothing. Right, Ro?"

So unhygienic. You're disgusting, I mouthed to Tristan before glancing at Knox. "Yeah, nothing. Just saying you and Elena look good together."

His frown disappeared when he realised I was being sincere. Because they did look good together, there was no denying it. "I'm a lucky man," he said softly, smiling down at his girlfriend, and the fact he was actually letting Tristan and me see this side of him just showed how far gone he was for Elena.

Before Quinn came back to Hatherley Hall, I might not have understood, but I got it now.

"We look good, too." Tristan nudged me, reminding me of his presence.

"I know." It was a fact. Like I'd said before, the three of us were dressed in black but with different colour ties and suit jacket linings. Mine was a deep blue, almost like the ocean, and as for Tristan…no one could say he was subtle. His chosen colour? Gold. Okay, it was more like black with a gold shimmer, but I knew he'd chosen the gold tones specifically to match the laurel wreaths that he couldn't stop fucking talking about. I guess it suited him, with his blond hair, but it wasn't to my personal taste.

Knox's parents took several photos of us, and then his mum took a million pictures of Knox and Elena while Knox's dad brought out a bottle of Scotch for a toast. I was still mostly avoiding alcohol after the lighthouse, but a quick toast wouldn't hurt. Knox, Tristan, and I gathered in the corner of the expansive living room, glasses in hand. I held up my phone as I raised my glass, the three of us posing for a selfie. I captioned it "the gods" and posted it to my social media, tagging Knox and Tristan.

About two minutes after I'd posted it, I had a DM from my cousin Caiden in reply to the photo.

CAIDEN:

Nice pose little cousin. We did it better

He'd attached a picture of himself smirking into the camera alongside Weston and their best friends, Cassius and Zayde, all dressed in black suits.

I sent him back a middle-finger emoji.

CAIDEN:

Disrespecting your elders?

ME:

Seems like you're jealous of how good we look. No you're jealous of how good I look right?

CAIDEN:

eye-roll emoji Why would I be jealous of you? We look alike according to most people

ME:

Is this your roundabout way of complimenting me or are you complimenting yourself? I'm confused

CAIDEN:

Both? Seriously though. Have a good night. Z's girlfriend Fallon was telling us about the ball. Sounds like a big deal

ME:

Yeah I guess it is to some people

CAIDEN:

Not to you?

Scrubbing my hand over my face, I thought for a minute and then came to a decision. I needed the opinion of someone on the outside of this situation, and my cousins already knew about the drink spiking.

"Be back in a minute," I said to Tristan. Not giving him time to reply, I left the room, heading down the hallway to the empty kitchen. Leaning up against the island, I sent another text.

ME:

Are you free to talk?

In response, my phone buzzed in my hand, my cousin's name flashing up on the screen with a video call. I swiped to answer. "Alright?"

Caiden came into view, a figure in a black hoodie with the hood pulled up. "Alright? What's up?" He eyed me cautiously through the screen. Behind him, I could see a crumbling stone wall and, beyond that, the blue-grey line of the horizon. The sounds of seagulls and crashing waves sounded faintly through the speaker.

"Where are you?"

"Alstone Castle. Our girls are having a knife-throwing bonding session, so we're bonding over fire." Flipping to the back camera, he swung it from left to right to show three other hooded figures a little way from him, seated in what looked like the remains of a courtyard, with a fire in the centre. "We're testing how flammable—never mind. That's not important. Tell me what's up." The camera switched back to Cade, his face filling the screen.

I gave him a rundown of everything that had happened, sticking to the facts, even though I wanted to fucking rage, remembering how Quinn had been dragged into one shit situation after another since her return to Hatherley Hall. Half of them had been my fault, too, and I felt so fucking helpless in the face of the latest problem she was having to deal with. I told Caiden about our pact to stay quiet, how her parents had threatened her, and how she didn't want me to be at risk because I was already on my last warning.

When I was done, I placed my phone on the island, propping it up against the fruit bowl, and then slumped forwards, groaning as I lowered my head to my folded arms. Caiden was silent for a while, processing everything I'd told him, and I waited, hoping that somehow, he'd have the answers for me, even though I knew there was no possible way he would.

"I didn't like this when you told me about what happened at Chaceley Rock, and I didn't even have the full story then. Fuck, mate, I hate to say it, but it sounds like someone's got it in for you or Quinn or both of you."

Raising my head, I nodded. "I know. I thought it was me, but this shit didn't start until she came back to Hatherley Hall. No, not even then. The lighthouse was the first time anything happened. Before that, it was—" I cut myself off.

"It was what?" Caiden's brows lifted. "I need all the information so I can help you."

"Fucking fine," I muttered. "Before that, it was me giving Quinn shit because I thought she'd ghosted me, and I dunno, I convinced myself I hated her or something. Fuck even knows what was going on in my brain."

The last thing I expected was for him to laugh. "We really are alike, aren't we?"

"What's that supposed to mean?"

"That's a story for another day. Right now, we need to get to the bottom of this shit. You know West's side hustle?"

Glancing around me to make sure I was still alone in the kitchen, I lowered my voice. "The hacking, you mean?"

"Yeah. He helped out your friend Knox, didn't he?"

"He did."

"Alright." Caiden cleared his throat. "Here's what we're gonna do. You had no solid leads before, but now we have a potential digital lead. Send me everything you have about your email system. How you log in, your email address, Quinn's email address, anything that you have on the system Hatherley Hall uses. I'll speak to Fallon, see what she can remember from her time at your school, and we'll get West on the case. If anyone can get into the system, it's him. If we're lucky, we might be able to find out who actually sent those emails."

I exhaled a long, heavy breath. "Thanks. Really. Thanks. I didn't…I don't fucking know what to do, and I don't want to make anything worse for Quinn."

"You're family. It's what we do," he stated, like it was a fact, and for maybe the first time ever, I truly believed it.

"Yeah. If I can ever repay the favour, y'know…" With a shrug, I attempted a smile. There was a stubborn lump in my throat that wouldn't go away.

"No need, but I'll keep it in mind. We'll work on what we can on our end, and in the meantime, I want you to stay alert. Keep an eye out. And have a good time, yeah? Win the crown of the gods or whatever the fuck it is."

"I'll try."

"You won't try. You will. You know why?" A smirk curved over my cousin's lips, and for a second, it was like looking into a mirror.

"Why?"

"Because you're a motherfucking Cavendish, that's why. And we always come out on top. No matter what. Don't forget it."

With that, he ended the call, leaving me blinking at the screen.

"Dramatic bastard." I swiped my phone from the island, already feeling lighter. It was time to rejoin my friends and get them up to date with the latest developments, and then… Then, it was time to party.

I needed to learn how to fake being happy about this shit very fucking fast. If anyone was after me or Quinn, I couldn't let my mask slip. Not for a second.

28

Quinn

The hall had been transformed, with sheer, billowing white fabric draped everywhere. Strings of white and gold lights wrapped around the columns, and yet more white lights swept across the room, briefly illuminating the shadows before sweeping away again. Waitstaff clad in togas and golden sandals circulated with trays of canapés and alcohol-free champagne, and there was actual champagne at the bar at the side of the room, presided over by Professor Donnelly, head of Epicurus house. He was there to ensure only those of us who were over eighteen could drink and to regulate our drinks, at that. Little did he know—or he turned a blind eye—that there'd be a lot more drinking going on after the ball at the after-party in the crypts.

At the front of the hall, the lectern had been cleared away from the stage, and in front of the stage, a DJ booth was set up, music echoing from the speakers, bouncing off the heavy stone walls and vaulted ceiling. Everywhere I looked, students were talking, dancing, milling around the huge space, clad in outfits that probably cost more than the average person made in a month. At least.

Aria leaned into me. "Remind me why I agreed to do this again?"

"It was your idea, if I remember correctly."

"It was a moment of temporary insanity. Come on. I need some of that champagne if I'm going to make it through the evening." She slipped her hand into mine and began weaving through the crowd towards the bar. When we reached it, she dropped my hand and greeted our head of house, swiping two glasses of champagne as she did so.

"There's a maximum of two glasses of champagne per person tonight, Miss Harper. Make them last," he told her.

"Don't worry, sir. One of these is for Quinn. I'll be back for my other glass later." She blew him a kiss and then tugged me away, leaving me stifling a laugh.

"Only you can get away with acting like that towards the teachers. Actually, no. Only you and Tristan can."

"Don't mention the T-word to me," she hissed before taking a large gulp of her champagne. "Ugh. Why do people drink this stuff?"

I laughed again. "It helps if you sip it rather than swig it like a pint." Taking a sip of my own drink, I demonstrated, and she rolled her eyes at me.

"No, thanks." Her gaze flicked down my body. "Change of subject. Did I mention how hot you look tonight? If I were into girls, I totally would."

"Same." I eyed my friend appreciatively. She'd decided to wear black, clad in a short, slinky dress that dipped dangerously low in both the front and the back. Her dress was paired with the highest, spikiest heels I'd ever seen, adding about six inches to her height. I had no idea how she was managing to walk so easily on the uneven flagstones, but she made it look effortless. Her hair was pulled back into a gleaming, poker-straight high ponytail, wrapped in a gold metal band—her only concession to colour, other than the golden snake cuff wrapped around her upper arm. With all of that, topped off with black eyeliner and dark lipstick, her nails pointed and painted in the same inky colour as her dress, she looked fucking hot and fucking dangerous.

As for me… My mum had taken me dress shopping the previous weekend…

"Remember how important this is. I was one of the goddesses, and I'd love for my only daughter to follow in my footsteps," my mum said as we entered the small, high-end boutique in the local town of Nottswood.

"I know." There was no point in my reiterating that I'd already been a goddess, nor the fact that she'd told me a million times that she'd been one of the goddesses. I'd only be wasting my breath. And I did understand where she was coming from. The ball and everything it stood for might not have been high on my list of priorities anymore, but it was important to her, and I did want her to be happy. We had our differences, and although her rules were stopping me from being with the person I wanted to be with, her heart was in the right place. Even if she was going about it the wrong way.

Not only that, but she'd be hearing from my history professor after the ball, and if I could keep her happy in the meantime, maybe the consequences wouldn't be so bad…

Who was I kidding? I had no defence. None that she'd believe, at least. How could I defend myself without any evidence?

"Good girl." She gave me a small smile. "Right. Let's find the dress that'll ensure you stand out. How about…"

I tuned her out as she drifted off to one of the racks, smoothing her hand over chiffon and satin and silk, every now and then pulling a hanger aside to inspect a dress more closely. My attention was drawn to the back of the boutique, to shimmery material that went from a light sky-blue to a blue so deep it was almost black.

"Ah. I was hoping that might catch your eye."

I jumped at the voice close to my ear, spinning to see a woman eyeing me with amusement. She had a discreet silver badge with the boutique logo and the name Julia engraved below it.

"I…yes. I'd like to look at it more closely." I moved towards the dress, the saleswoman coming with me.

"It's new in today. As soon as you entered the shop, I could see you wearing it." Pulling it from the rack, she draped it over her arm and then directed me towards a pedestal, swiping a small box from a table on the way.

"My mum. I'm not sure…" I trailed off, glancing over to where my mum had an armful of dresses, mostly in pastel colours.

"Leave her to me." Julia lowered her voice, giving me a conspiratorial grin. "Did you notice the shop next door? That's our bridal boutique. I'm used to persuading mothers of the bride to love the dress the bride really wants. Yours will be a piece of cake in comparison."

As promised, she had persuaded my mother…despite the dress being everything she wouldn't have wanted for me. The flowing, shimmering material in shades of blue dipped between my breasts, held in place by strategically placed tape. The back reached the floor, kissing my heels, but the front…the front was a minidress, exposing my lower legs as well as most of my thighs. It was daring, and it was beautiful, and it was mine. All thanks to Julia, who had turned out to be a master in persuasion, throwing out phrases like "most sought-after British designer" and "couture" and "Paris runways." Of course, most of the phrases were meaningless, spoken only to persuade, but her words had worked their magic, and now, here I was.

My hair was curled in loose waves that tumbled down my back, and Aria had done my make-up to match, with subtle sweeps of gold across my lids and cheekbones. I'd completed the look with dangling gold earrings.

Aria touched my arm, breaking me out of my thoughts. "Grace and Mira are on the dance floor. Let's go."

We began making our way towards the area designated as a dance floor, but we'd only taken a few steps when a hush fell over the crowd. Aria and I exchanged glances and then turned as one towards the entrance, where everyone's attention was directed.

I forgot how to breathe.

Standing in the entryway, or more accurately, lounging in the entryway, framed by the huge wooden doors that had been left open for the event, were the three gods. Knox was the first to step into the room, Elena on his arm clad in a gorgeous red dress, both of them looking fucking *incredible*. Knox smirked at the attention they were getting, but then his head dipped to Elena's ear, and I caught the flash of concern in his dark gaze. I still found it difficult to reconcile the arrogant boy I'd once known with this man who very clearly cared deeply for his girlfriend, no matter how much he tried to hide it from everyone else.

Elena nodded and said something back to him, and a small smile flickered over his lips before it disappeared. Slowly and deliberately, he lowered his head again, his hand coming up to cradle Elena's chin, tilting her head to meet his. It was a public claiming, an acknowledgement that they were together and, more importantly, that she had the protection of the elite. I hadn't been at Hatherley Hall when she'd first arrived, but from what Elena and Aria had told me, it sounded like she'd had a rocky start. But here they were, together and unshakeable, and something inside me ached at their display of unity. I wanted that. And I wanted that with one man and one man only. A man I hadn't even dared to take more than a fleeting look at because there was no way on earth that I'd be able to hide the way I felt about him. We were too exposed here. Too many eyes were on the gods. And maybe someone out there in the crowd was watching me, too.

An icy shiver snaked down my spine.

"How dare he," Aria hissed under her breath, and my gaze flew to her, seeing her glaring across the room at… Tristan? Of course it was Tristan. My eyes widened, though, when I saw the way he was *staring* at her. It was— I didn't even know how to describe it.

"Aria?" I whispered.

"No." Holding up her hand, she spun on her heel, her ponytail whipping out behind her as she stalked away.

I debated going after her, but I had the feeling she wanted to be alone, and I wasn't about to overstep any boundaries. So, instead, I forced myself to step forwards and greet Knox and Elena.

"You look beautiful," I told Elena, hugging her carefully so I didn't mess up her hair or make-up.

"So do you." Her mouth moved to my ear. "Roman hasn't taken his eyes off you since we came in."

A smile curved over my lips, even as my heart raced at the thought that someone might notice him looking at me.

"You match."

I glanced up at Knox, my brows pulling together. "Match?"

"You and him. I suggest you go and find a dark corner and make the most of it." Smirking, Knox angled his head towards where I knew Roman was still standing in the entryway.

"Match?" I repeated. Almost unwillingly, my gaze was drawn towards Roman.

I took my first proper look at him, and I lost my breath all over again.

Roman Cavendish in a suit should be illegal.

Fuck. The way his broad shoulders filled it out, that divine body all wrapped up in perfectly tailored material, clinging in just the right places to highlight his powerful muscles. The suit was paired with a tie in the deepest blue that matched the darker hues of my dress, and I instantly understood what Knox had been referring to. His hair was a tousled mess of inky black that shouldn't have worked with the suit, but oh, it did. It really, really did. There was a light dusting of stubble on his jaw, and his lips were shining like he'd just run his tongue across them. So. Gorgeous.

But his eyes. *His eyes.* Deep blue, fringed with those black lashes, and laser-focused on me. The force of his gaze was like a bolt of lightning, shocking and powerful, and I gasped, my heart stuttering in my chest.

"Elena." I sucked in a shuddering breath. "People are going to *see*."

Knox swore under his breath, and he and Elena both moved at the same time, almost as if they'd rehearsed it, stepping between me and Roman and instantly cutting off my view of him. My whole body was shaky, whether from the intensity of Roman's focus or from the sight of him, or even the adrenaline that had burned through me with the knowledge that people could see him looking at me; me looking at him.

Elena instantly placed a hand to my back, steering me to Knox's side. "Knox."

He glanced down at her and nodded once and then held out his arm. "Allow me to escort you, my lady."

"Oh, you do have manners," Elena commented. "I thought that was a myth."

We each took his arm as he muttered something about punishing Elena later, something I tuned out because I was happy to remain ignorant about their sex life. We headed towards the bar, where I finished up my drink, attempting to forget about the fact that Roman was the hottest man in the entire universe, while they helped themselves to brimming flutes of champagne.

Glancing around me for a distraction, I spotted Penelope in the crowd, dressed in a stunning flowing gold dress, and waved her over.

"You already look like a goddess," I told her when she reached me. "Beautiful."

"Thank you." She gave me an approximation of a hug, as careful as I was not to mess up my hair or make-up. "I love your dress. Yours, too, Elena."

Elena smiled at her. "Thanks. You guys did a great job organising all this. I still can't believe it's our school. It feels like…not like a school."

"Penelope." Knox didn't even bother to attempt a smile. I'd come to learn that he didn't really have time for many women these days other than Elena, and I guess me, purely for the fact I was Roman's…whatever I was.

She nodded to acknowledge him and then turned back to me. "I'll catch up with you later. I need to check that we have everything in place for the crowning ceremony."

"Do you need any help? I don't mind."

"No. Relax and enjoy yourself. I'll see you later on." With a wave, she melted into the crowd.

"Alright, mate?" Warmth radiated from a presence directly behind me, and my heart stuttered all over again.

"Roman." Knox directed a smirk over my shoulder. "Couldn't stay away, could you?"

"What can I say? I missed you," Roman drawled. I felt the brush of one of his fingers across my lower back, sparking goosebumps all over my skin.

"How sweet."

"I can be sweet when I want to be." The finger trailed lower. I shivered.

Glancing up at Knox, I noticed that he seemed to be having a silent conversation over my head. Holding my breath, I waited, and then—

"It seems to me like you're struggling to keep your hands off her." Roman's voice lowered to a soft rasp. "Like she looks so fucking good that you want to worship her, to fucking claim her in front of everyone, so there's no doubt that she's mi—yours."

"Fucking hell," Knox muttered. He downed the rest of his champagne in one go. "Yeah. Don't worry. I'll be doing some worshipping later. But we'll be somewhere far less public."

Elena was staring between them both and biting down on her lip, clearly trying to hold back laughter. Me? I was melting into a puddle of want and need because there was no doubt that Roman was talking to me…through Knox. Which was bizarre but wonderful. Maybe I should return the favour.

"Um." I licked my lips. "Elena. Do you feel like the luckiest person here tonight? To know that this gorgeous, hot, amazing man wants you and you want him back? That you can't believe how he looks tonight because—"

"Tone it down," she warned. There was a low chuckle

in my ear, and the finger returned, circling over the small of my back.

"You're a fucking goddess," Roman murmured, too low for anyone else to hear, and then he was gone.

"I'm never doing that again. I don't give a fuck that he's one of my best mates. Give me that champagne." Knox grabbed another flute from the bar, downing the contents in one swift movement, and then slammed the glass back down with a grimace. He picked up another, bringing it to his lips, but he was interrupted by a loud, pointed clearing of someone's throat.

"Mr. Ashcroft. The limit is two glasses per student," Professor Donnelly informed him.

"Is that so?" Knox eyed him over the top of his glass and then deliberately tipped it to his lips.

Professor Donnelly shook his head. "Ashcroft. Don't push me."

Elena nudged her boyfriend, and he sighed. "Fine."

"You may as well take that one. It has your germs all over it."

"Cheers, sir." Knox lifted the glass, and our head of house rolled his eyes.

"Get out of my sight. And that's your last one, so don't even think about another."

Elena dragged him away before he could reply, and I decided to go and find Aria or my roommates. From memory, the crowning ceremony happened around ninety minutes or so after the ball's start time, and although I didn't have my phone with me, I guesstimated it had been going for around forty-five minutes, maybe longer, so there should be plenty of time to dance before the ceremony. I'd said that I didn't want to be one of the goddesses, but right now, after seeing Roman, I really, really did. It would be my only chance to dance with him, and it could all be explained away if my parents ever found out. Tristan and Penelope would dance together as head boy and girl—and they even matched with Penelope's dress and Tristan's gold accents. Knox would be with Elena, and I'd have no choice but to dance with Roman.

But there was no guarantee I'd win. In fact, it was most likely that Freya or Aria would win. The thought of Freya dancing with Roman sent hot prickles of jealousy through me. She'd have her hands all over *my* man, and I'd have to stand there and do fucking nothing.

"You look like you're contemplating murder. Who are we unaliving?"

I blinked, Mira's face coming into focus. Forcing out a laugh, I shook my head. "It's nothing. Hey, have you seen Aria?"

"She's with us. Come on." Samira led me to the centre of the dance floor, where Aria, Gracelyn, and several of our other classmates were dancing in a big group. I spotted Katy and Will in the crowd of bodies, wrapped up in each other, and beyond them, several of the lacrosse team appeared to be trying to impress their dates with loosely synchronised dance moves.

A smile spread across my face. No matter what was to come, both later tonight and beyond—when my parents found out about my paper—I had this. Time with my friends, just having fun. And that was something I'd really, really missed when I'd been away.

I spent a while dancing with everyone, losing myself in the music. Aria appeared a little while later, giving me a nod when I mouthed, *Are you okay?* to her, and then gave me a bright, genuine smile.

"Let's party!" she shouted, and as if she was in sync with the DJ, the music changed to a faster, headier beat, and loud cheers and shouts sounded through the hall. We grinned at each other and began to move, lost to the music once again.

Until it suddenly came to a screeching halt.

"Students of Hatherley Hall," a loud voice boomed, and our headmaster, Professor Lexington, strode onto the stage, a spotlight illuminating him as he walked. "It's the moment you've all been waiting for. Time to crown your gods and goddesses!"

29

Quinn

The cheers were deafening.

Professor Lexington lifted his hand. "Silence."

He stared towards the back of the hall, raising his hand higher, to the huge projector screen behind him. "Robin, if you would."

The spotlight swept to the side of the stage and dimmed, and the screen lit up with a series of images of all the contenders for the gods and goddesses. More cheers sounded again, and again when the photos faded away and were replaced with a video montage spliced together from pieces of footage from the campaign videos. As the montage played, there was movement to the side of the stage as the school secretary and two of the teachers carried six black cases onto the stage, placing them in two rows on a table next to the headmaster. They opened the cases before leaving the stage, and I caught the gleam of gold inside.

As the video finished, Professor Lexington spoke up again. "Your votes have been cast and counted." The screen lit up with an image of six empty gilt frames, which

I knew would fill with the headshots of the chosen gods and goddesses, with their names below. As I watched, a photo began to appear on the screen, accompanied by a name. "Our first god…Tristan Smith-Chamberlain!"

Above the cheers, a loud whoop came from somewhere behind me, and the crowd parted to allow Tristan to strut his way through the hall and up onto the stage. He bowed theatrically and gave a regal wave, and Aria mumbled something next to me, which sounded suspiciously like "dickhead."

"Mr. Smith-Chamberlain."

Tristan shot our headmaster a grin and took his place on the stage, marked out by an X taped on the surface. There had never been any doubt who the gods would be—there was no contest.

Another name, another photo. "Our second god… Knox Ashcroft!"

When Knox had joined Tristan onstage, the headmaster waited for the noise to die away. When the hall was silent again, he continued. "Our third and final god… Roman Cavendish!" There was a small frown on his face as he announced Roman's name, probably due to the fact that despite Roman's overwhelming popularity with the student body, the same couldn't be said for a large percentage of the teachers. Our headmaster in particular, given how close his Bugatti had apparently come to going up in flames thanks to Roman's arson incident, not to mention all the fuel he'd been storing in the outbuildings.

As Roman sauntered up onto the stage, I drank him in, regret sitting heavy in my stomach as I realised that my lacklustre campaign efforts had probably cost me the chance of being there with him.

When he'd taken his place, his gaze scanned the crowd and found mine. The corner of his mouth curved into a tiny smile, just for me, and my anxiety melted away. Whatever happened, even if Freya did get her hands on him, he would never be hers. I trusted him, and that meant I could deal with whatever came next.

Another photo faded into view. "Our first goddess… Penelope Byron-Chopard!" I clapped loudly for my friend as she swept onto the stage, her head held high and her posture perfectly straight. She smiled out at the crowd, acknowledging them with a lift of her hand, before stepping over to her marked spot.

"Our second goddess—" I held my breath. "—Elena Greenwood!"

"Yes!" Aria punched the air as I cheered, clapping so hard my palms were stinging. We watched as Elena made her way onto the stage, her movements hesitant and her eyes wide. Had she really thought she wouldn't be crowned as one of the goddesses? Even if she hadn't been Knox's girlfriend, she deserved to be up there.

The headmaster cleared his throat again. "Finally… our third goddess is…"

"*No fucking way*," Aria ground out as the image in the sixth frame began to appear. "What the actual fuck?"

"…Aria Harper!"

My head spun, disappointment and relief and excitement for my friend combining in a swirl that left me feeling faintly nauseous. Gritting my teeth through it, I nudged Aria, hard. "Get up there!"

"This has to be a joke," she hissed.

"Miss Harper?"

"Go," I said again, and she finally moved, stalking through the crowd and up to join the others, her eyes flashing with fire and her jaw set. She glared at the students below her, shock and disbelief clear in her gaze, and I couldn't help the laugh that fell from my throat.

Maybe she really didn't have any idea just how popular she actually was.

The crowning ceremony began, the headmaster placing the gold laurel wreaths on the heads of the gods and the goddesses one by one. When they were all crowned, they bowed in unison to yet more cheers and applause. Roman's gaze kept finding mine, and every time, he gave me that tiny, secretive smile that warmed me from the inside out.

"Clear the dance floor for your gods-and-goddesses dance," Professor Lexington boomed. We all shuffled back to make a space as the gods and goddesses descended the stairs, and then several things happened in quick succession.

Knox swept Elena into his arms.

Aria started towards Roman.

Roman stepped towards her.

Tristan held out his hand to Penelope.

And then…Penelope moved, cutting in front of Aria, and slid her arms around Roman's neck…at the same time as a hand gripped my wrist tightly and yanked me backwards.

30

ROMAN

What the fuck was happening? I blinked, trying to make sense of everything. One minute, I'd been ready to dance with Aria, and now I had a different, taller body pressing against me, way too fucking close for comfort, with a heavy, flowery perfume that made me want to sneeze. I moved back, but Penelope moved with me, and again, what the fuck was happening?

"Pen, back up," I murmured, attempting politeness, even though it was the last thing I felt like. I was all too aware of the eyes on us, though, so I wasn't going to cause a scene.

"Sorry." Immediately unwinding her arms from around my neck, she placed one hand on my shoulder and slid our fingers together. She stepped away fractionally and gave me a hesitant smile. "I didn't mean to…I just wanted to make sure we could dance together. If you want to, that is. Dance with me?"

"Don't you want to dance with Tristan?" I'd assumed she would—their colours even fucking matched, and surely it was a given that the head boy and girl would dance together.

The music started up as she shook her head. "Honestly, no. I've spent enough time with Tristan. He's on the ball committee, not to mention our duties together. It feels like I've spent more time with him than my own friends lately." Her voice lowered. "And don't tell him I said so, but you're a much better dancer than he is. You'd be doing me a favour."

I glanced over at my friend, who was having a silent stare-off with Aria, and smirked. Yeah, maybe this was a good thing. Plus, Penelope was Quinn's friend, so it wasn't like I had to worry about wandering hands.

"In that case, yeah. Let's dance." We began to move, my body on autopilot as I scanned the crowd surrounding us for Quinn. Fuck. What must she be feeling right now? I honestly thought she would end up being one of the goddesses, and when Aria's name was read out, it had taken everything in me to keep my face impassive. My mask had been in place all fucking night, in fact, from the second I'd seen my girl across the room, looking so beautiful that I was completely lost for words. I never thought I'd even be capable of the depth of feelings I had for her, but when I'd seen her tonight, I'd found myself submerged, drowning in everything I felt for Quinn Farrow. And I didn't resist. On the outside, I was untouchable, but inside…

The realisation hit me like a fucking sledgehammer to the face. That four-letter word I'd told myself it was too early for?

I couldn't lie to myself anymore.

"Is everything okay?"

"Huh?" My gaze focused on Penelope before darting

away again, back to scanning the surrounding faces. Where was Quinn?

"I just asked if everything was okay. Sorry if I'm overstepping. You just looked like you were deep in thought."

"Yeah, fine." I spun her so I could scan the crowds on my other side. How fucking long was this dance? Shouldn't it be over by now?

My phone buzzed in my pocket, temporarily stealing my focus. Now what? Whoever it was, it couldn't be important. All my friends were here. Quinn was here somewhere, and I knew for a fact she didn't have a phone with her because she'd already told me she was leaving it in her room tonight because she hadn't wanted to carry a bag. I smirked to myself, remembering the fact that Knox's pockets were stuffed with Elena's phone and make-up shit, as well as his own phone.

My phone buzzed again, and I let go of Penelope's waist and shoved my hand into my pocket, attempting to switch it to silent instead of vibrate mode. The buzzing stopped, so I guessed I'd been successful.

"Roman? Are you sure everything's okay?"

"Don't worry about it. Just putting my phone on silent," I told Penelope, placing my hand on her waist again. She smiled, and I spun her again, scanning the new faces that came into view. Still no Quinn.

A sense of unease crept through my body.

Surely I would've spotted her by now?

My unease grew. I shouldn't have left her. Or got someone to keep an eye on her…except everyone who knew about the shit that had gone down was right here on the dance floor with me and Penelope.

This dance needed to fucking end. Now.

At last, it did. I released Penelope, stepping away. She

smiled. "Thanks for the dance, Roman." Leaning in, she pressed a kiss to my cheek and then left me. I was barely aware of her leaving, too busy looking for Quinn.

"Ro." Tristan tapped my arm. "Photos."

"Oh, for fuck's sake." Penelope hadn't left at all, no— she'd gone to stand next to Knox and Elena because the fucking photographer wanted to take our photos. My hand went to my crown, my fingers brushing the cool metal, wishing I could rip it from my head. I *needed* to find my girl.

"Have you seen Quinn?" I hissed to Aria as the photographer arranged us to his liking. She glared at Tristan when he tried to put his arm around her waist before turning to me.

"No, but that's not surprising. She probably didn't want to watch that farce of a dance. I don't blame her."

"You wound me, little scorpion. Anyone would be happy to dance with me," Tristan interjected.

She arched a brow. "Were *you* happy to dance with *me*?"

Tristan's grin faded, his expression shuttering, and without another word, he stepped behind Aria, putting an arm around her waist as he'd been instructed by the photographer. I stared at him, but he just shook his head and plastered on a smile for the camera. Giving it up as a lost cause for now, I took my place behind Penelope, lightly gripping her waist and plastering on my own fake smile. The photographer must've been able to sense my impatience because she wrapped it up quickly, snapping a few quick photos before instructing us to separate into two groups—one with the gods and one with the goddesses. This time, my smile didn't need to be faked. I was here with my two best mates, and Aria was probably right. Quinn wouldn't have wanted to watch the dance. If our positions had been reversed, I wouldn't have wanted to watch her, either. In fact, I wouldn't have been able to control myself, and it would have ended with a black eye or two and probably a suspension or worse.

"Mate. Selfie." Tristan nudged me out of my thoughts.

"Yeah." I grinned into his camera. Out of the corner of my eye, I noticed the girls separating, Penelope disappearing into the crowd and Aria and Elena heading towards Katy and Will. Still no Quinn.

We posed for a few photos, alternating between a range of poses, generally fucking around and acting like kids despite the fact that we were all technically adults. When we were done, Tristan scrolled through the selfies, his brows pulling together. "No, wait. I need to be in the middle. You two have dark hair. We need a better aesthetic." He moved in between me and Knox, slinging his arms around our shoulders. "Ro, you do the honours. I don't have any free hands."

"Alright. But I'm taking it with my phone. Yours is shit," I said, just to wind him up, and he cuffed me around the back of the neck.

"He's right," Knox added, just to be an asshole, and got a cuff of his own. The three of us grinned at each other. I tugged my phone from my pocket, lifting it in front of us.

"Someone's popular," Tristan commented, staring at my screen.

"Huh?" I followed his glance, and my stomach dropped. Four messages and three missed calls. Swiping my screen, I saw they were all from my cousin Caiden.

"Oh, fuck," I whispered. "Fuck."

"Ro? You okay? What's going on?"

"Roman? What is it?"

I ignored Tristan and Knox, backing away with my phone gripped tightly in my hand. I needed to get out of here. It was too fucking loud, too many people. If Cade had contacted me this many times in such a short period, it wasn't a social call.

I was jogging by the time I reached the entryway, speeding up to a run as my feet pounded against the flagstones, the sound echoing through the emptying corridor. Coming to a stop at the sweeping staircase that led to our dorms, I hit my cousin's number, pacing up and down while I waited for it to connect.

"Cade?"

He got straight to the point. "We traced the digital footprint. A bit more than that, in fact. I don't know how it all links up, but I'll send you everything, and hopefully, you'll be able to make sense of it. If there's anything more we can do, let me know. We've got your back."

"What are you saying?" I couldn't make sense of his words.

"It's probably best if you read the info. I'm sending it through now."

Switching him to speaker, I sank down onto the bottom step of the staircase, opening the message. My brows pulled together as I read the words on the screen.

"This makes no sense. Both the emails relating to Quinn's paper came from one of the administrators' computers? And what? How? Fuck. I don't understand."

Cade sighed. "Yeah. I dunno, West said it originated from there, but the sender had been able to spoof your email addresses so it looked like they came from you and Quinn. Uh…you know how they can do a 'send as' thing, so it looks like it comes from another address? It's mostly used if an admin assistant wants to send an email as their boss, y'know, shit like that, but in this case…it was used on you. West found the deleted email that contained Quinn's original paper, too. Someone had managed to get into her history professor's email and erase it before he had a chance to look at it."

"What the fuck? How could the school staff be behind this?"

"It's not them. I mean, I can't say for sure, but I'd put money on the fact that it was someone else. Someone who was able to access that computer and wanted to cover their tracks."

I slumped back, rubbing my hand over my face. "So we still don't know who it was?"

"Look at the rest of the shit I sent you. I have an idea, but I don't know these people. You do. Do you think it could be connected? Do you think they'd have a reason to do all this?"

"What?" I swiped down the screen, my mouth falling open as I took in the information in front of me. "The ball votes, too? What the fuck? Who?"

31

Quinn

"You need to come with me. Right now." The grip on my wrist tightened, the person forcibly dragging me away from the dance floor.

"What are you doing? Let go of me!"

"No. You need to see this." Freya's expression was grim. "Seriously, Quinn. I wouldn't be here if it wasn't important."

"Fine," I bit out. It wasn't like I wanted to stand there and torture myself watching Roman dance with someone else, anyway. Even if it was with Penelope. Penelope? Not Aria? Everything had happened so fast I still wasn't sure what exactly *had* happened.

Freya's grip loosened on my wrist once she realised I was coming with her willingly. She led me out of the main hall, down the corridor, and up the stairs in the direction of our dorms.

"Freya? What are we doing?"

"I need to show you something."

I looked at her. Really looked at her. Normally so cool and put together, she was jittery and chewing on her nails, which was a definite sign that something was wrong. The Freya I knew wouldn't ever do anything to mess up her perfect manicure. Maybe it was stupid of me to go with her when I knew how much she disliked me, but it didn't feel like anything to do with the petty, one-sided rivalry that had been going on since Roman had started showing interest in me. It felt bigger, and that… That scared me.

We reached the room she shared with Penelope, and she paused, her eyes briefly closing as she took a deep breath and then pushed the door open.

"You didn't get to be a goddess," was the first thing she said, entering the room and heading over to her desk, where her laptop was open.

"I know, neither did you," I snapped reflexively, regretting it as soon as the words fell from my mouth. "Sorry. I didn't mean to— What does that have to do with anything?"

She huffed impatiently. "I'm getting to that. Look at this. I was…curious yesterday. I wanted to know how to ask my stylist to style my hair for the ball, and…well, I knew the third goddess place would be between you and me. Pen and Elena were a given, and so I thought the final spot would be between us."

"Except Aria won."

"She did." Freya nodded. "But here's the weird thing. I borrowed Pen's key card so I could sneak into the admin office after hours, because the admin computers are the only ones where you can see the voting results as they come in, right?"

"You stole her key card? What key card?"

"Please, like you can take the moral high ground." She rolled her eyes. "I heard about your plagiarism. Anyway, yes, the key card. The one the head boy and girl have? Or maybe just the head girl? I don't know. Pen's allowed access for the ball things. You know, sorting out the bookings and invoices or whatever. Soooo, I used it to get into the office. How was I supposed to know how to ask my stylist to do my hair if I didn't know if I'd be getting a crown?" Running her fingers through her glossy curls, she shook her head. "I looked at the votes. I calculated that ninety-six percent had been cast by that point, so there was no possible way the outcome would have changed between last night and tonight. The votes weren't close enough."

I sank down into her desk chair, staring at her. "So, what are you saying?"

"I'm saying it should've been you up there tonight. You…you were way ahead."

"Of Aria?"

"No." She swallowed hard and turned to meet my gaze. "Of Penelope."

"Penelope?" I whispered. "I don't understand."

"Look." Tapping on the trackpad, she woke up her screen. "Look at this. This is how the votes looked last night."

I stared at the image for a long time, my thoughts racing as I struggled to get my head around everything. "I was ahead of Penelope."

"By quite a long way. You were slightly ahead of Aria, even. There was no way Pen could have been one of the goddesses. Look at the numbers. Even if every single one of the remaining four percent of students voted for her, she wouldn't have been able to catch up."

"I don't understand," I said again. "Did someone tamper with the results? Did someone want me out of the way that badly? Wait." A thought came into my mind. "Did *you* do this?" As soon as I said it, I realised how ridiculous that was. Why would Freya switch me with Penelope rather than herself?

Her lip curled. "Like I'd do that. If anything, I'd put myself up there. Anyway, I wouldn't cheat. I'd rather people voted for me fairly. Clearly, the students here have no taste." She flicked her hair over her shoulder.

"So who did it?"

"I thought…maybe I'd made a mistake. Maybe the votes hadn't been counted properly or something. Maybe I hadn't read the information properly. In the end, I decided to wait and see what happened tonight, but I couldn't get it out of my mind. Pen was out first thing this morning, having her nails done, and my hair appointment wasn't until a bit later. I thought I'd look around a bit." Her gaze shifted to the large wardrobe at the end of Penelope's bed. "Remember when we came into the common room that day when you were playing *Mario Kart* and you were wearing Roman's hoodie?"

"Yeah…"

"Did he… Do you know if he gave a hoodie to any other girls? Did you give the one you were wearing back to him?"

I stared at her. "It went missing, actually. Missing from my room, where I'd left it."

She nodded as if I'd confirmed something for her. Crossing over to Penelope's wardrobe, she flung the door open. Sweeping aside a pile of neatly folded clothes, she reached inside and drew out a bundle of fabric. Shaking it out, she revealed a familiar navy hoodie with royal blue lettering. "That day, I remembered catching a glimpse of navy in Pen's wardrobe, all balled up in the corner. I didn't think much of it at the time because, you know, it's our school colours. But then I thought about it later, and it struck me as weird because you know how neat Penelope is. She'd never treat her clothing with this much disrespect. Yesterday morning, like I said, I looked around a bit, and…it was hidden behind her other clothes, but it was still there, as you can see."

My hands shook. "Why would she take it? I don't get it."

"Don't you?" Freya's brows rose. She threw the hoodie onto Penelope's bed. "It's obvious to me."

My mind flashed to the ball. To the way Penelope had gone straight for Roman instead of Tristan, wrapping her arms around his neck.

"She's interested in Roman?"

"Bloody hell, how can you be so fucking dense!" Freya threw up her hands. "It's not about Roman! It's you! She's always been jealous of you. When you came back, you took her place without even trying. You—"

"Wait a minute. Jealous of *me*? No. That doesn't… What do you know about Chaceley Rock? About Roman?"

Her brows rose even higher. "Chaceley Rock? The bank holiday weekend? What do you mean? What happened?" She paused, a smirk curving over her lips. "I don't know about you, but I had an unforgettable night there with two members of the rugby team."

"Never mind that. I—*hold on*." Another thought hit me out of nowhere. "Freya. You said you heard about my plagiarism. As far as I know, the only person who knows outside of the select few I trust with my life is my history professor. Who told you?"

The smirk disappeared, her eyes widening as the realisation dawned on her face. "Penelope told me."

My mind raced.

Penelope had been my friend from the day we'd started this school.

Penelope had accepted me again when I'd returned, no questions asked, no making me feel guilty for ghosting her, unlike Roman. She hadn't even commented on my time away, other than to say she'd missed me. All she'd done was try to make me feel comfortable.

Penelope had warned me to stay away from Roman.

Penelope had told Freya something about me that not only wasn't true, but was something she shouldn't have been aware of in the first place.

Penelope had Roman's hoodie in her wardrobe.

Penelope had a key card that gave her access to the staff admin computers.

Penelope had been crowned as one of the goddesses instead of me.

"Fuck. I think...I need to...I need Roman."

I took a step, stumbled on the uneven floor, and glared down at my heels.

"You're not great in heels, are you?" Freya commented. "Maybe you should switch to flats."

"Maybe you should stop talking," I bit out and instantly regretted it. Freya owed me nothing, and yet she'd shared her suspicions with me. "Sorry. Really, I am. Look. I honestly appreciate you telling me all this. You don't owe me anything, so...thank you. If you see Penelope, can you keep it quiet? Just until I've had a chance to get to the bottom of this."

"Yeah, yeah. Do what you need to." She waved her hand in the air again. Standing, she headed over to her dresser and began reapplying her lipstick in a small hand mirror. "I've got more important things to do with my time, anyway. I have a date tonight with my two hot rugby players, and I don't want to be late."

"Rugby players?"

"Yes. Despite what Knox, Roman, and Tristan might think, they're not the only hot guys at Hatherley Hall, and the lacrosse team isn't the only elite team. They don't even have the biggest dicks, either." Pausing, she shrugged.

"Okay, maybe they do—it's not like I whip out a ruler each time. Point is, I'm over all that. You're welcome to Roman. It's obvious to anyone with eyes that he's completely obsessed with you."

"It is?"

A laugh fell from her throat. "Did you actually think you were being discreet? Babe, you're eye fucking each other *constantly*. Let's not forget the moment where he started a fight with his own teammate in front of everyone. I was there that night, remember? He was supposed to be with me, and you stole his attention without even trying."

"I—"

"I'm over it. Whatever. Like I said, plenty more fish in the sea. Now, you go get your man, and I'll get my men. If I see Pen in the meantime, my lips are sealed."

"Okay. Yes. Okay. Thanks." I finally got my feet to work, and I made my way to the door as quickly as I could, cursing my heels all the way. "Thanks," I said again and left.

Detouring to my room, I ditched my heels, switching them out for my Converse, and then grabbed the running belt I rarely used, tucking my phone into it. It ruined the whole aesthetic of my dress—not that I cared. No, the *only* thing I cared about right now was finding Roman and getting to the bottom of whatever was going on.

As I raced through the school, I pulled my phone back out. Bypassing the messages from my parents, asking me if I'd been crowned as one of the goddesses, I tapped out a message to Roman, telling him I had my phone and needed to speak with him urgently. It was most likely that he was still at the ball, celebrating, so that was my first destination. I didn't allow myself to think about what I'd do or say if I ran into Penelope first. I couldn't.

I more or less skidded into the hall, drawing the

attention of several students, but I ignored whatever comments they were making, pushing through the crowds, searching for a head of tousled black hair topped with a golden laurel wreath.

"Quinn!" Someone touched my arm. My heart pounding, I spun to see Tristan, his usual grin nowhere to be seen. "Have you seen Roman?"

"I'm looking for him. Why, what's happened?" Panic bled through in my tone, and I took several deep breaths, desperately trying to get air into my lungs.

Tristan glanced around us and lowered his voice. "Let's go somewhere quieter. Knox. Get Elena, quick."

"And me. You're not leaving me out of this." Aria appeared in front of us, her arms folded across her chest. "Don't even think about it."

Tristan rolled his eyes but tipped his head towards the door, and the three of us made our way out of the hall, closely followed by Knox and Elena. He led us in the opposite direction to where I'd come from, to the double doors that led outside. There were a few groups of students milling around on the gravel, but he kept walking, heading around the side of the building and coming to a stop in a shadowy corner.

Leaning back against the wall, he looked down at me, that uncharacteristically serious expression still on his face. "Talk. What's going on?"

"First of all, what happened to Roman?" My panic wasn't going to go away until I knew he was okay.

Tristan exchanged glances with Knox and then shrugged. "We don't know. We were taking selfies, and he pulled out his phone. There were, uh, a lot of notifications on it. When he saw, it was like—not to be a cliché—but it was like he'd seen a ghost. He ran out of the ball before we could ask him what the fuck was going on, and we haven't seen him since. We've both tried calling and texting him, but nothing. I didn't think it was that serious until you came running into the ball with the same expression on your face. What happened, Quinn?"

As quickly as I could, I gave them a rundown of everything Freya had told me. As I spoke, the tension grew until I could physically feel it, thick and suffocating in the night air.

"That fucking bitch," Aria growled. "I'm going to kill her. I'm actually going to commit murder."

"Calm down, little scorpion." Tristan gave her shoulder a condescending pat. She stamped her spike heel on his loafer, and he screeched, yanking his foot out of her reach. "Fuck you!"

"Gladly." She gave him the middle finger.

"Can you two give it a rest for five fucking minutes?" Knox ground out. "We need to get to the bottom of whatever's going on. I guarantee that whatever those notifications on Roman's phone were about, they were to do with what's happening with you. It's all been to do with you, hasn't it?" There was accusation in his tone, and I couldn't blame him.

"Yes. I think so. I think…if it has something to do with the plagiarism accusations, then maybe it is about me and not about him. But what about the boat and the lighthouse? Penelope wouldn't have anything to do with that, surely? That can't be connected."

"It can't be." Tristan shook his head. "I don't…I mean, fuck. We've all known her for years. *I've* been working with her all year, doing all the head boy and girl shit and all that. And our work on the ball committee… She doesn't seem like someone who would do all this, does she?"

Before tonight, before Freya had shown me the evidence, I would've thought the same. But now… Now, I didn't trust anyone. Anyone who wasn't a part of this small group of people in front of me. Even so, I couldn't even imagine how or why she'd have been involved in that incident.

"Maybe…" I thought as I was speaking. "Maybe you guys should look for Roman, and I'll look for Pen. I need to get to the bottom of this. We need answers."

"There's no way you're confronting her on your own," Elena said, and next to her, Aria gave me a hard look.

"Don't even think about it," Knox added. "And you—" His next comment was directed towards his girlfriend. "—aren't going anywhere near her, either. I won't let you put yourself in danger."

Elena laughed without humour. "Knox, do you remember what I told you about the place I used to live? And, oh, remember how my mum basically tried to have your dad killed? And my uncle is in prison? I'm quite capable of dealing with some rich bitch on a power trip or whatever she's doing."

"What?" I said faintly, staring at her with wide eyes. She blinked, seeming to remember the rest of us were there, and gave me a wry smile.

"Um. I guess there are a few things I forgot to mention. I'll tell you later, after we get through tonight."

Knox was staring at his girlfriend like he wanted to rip her clothes off there and then, and I'd had enough of us getting derailed from the only thing that mattered. Turning on my heel, I marched back towards the doors. "I'm going to find Penelope. Please, find Roman, and let him know what's going on, okay?" I threw over my shoulder. From behind me came the sound of various people swearing, followed by the scrape of shoes on gravel, and my mouth curved into a grim smile.

It was time to locate Penelope and find out the truth.

By any means necessary.

A hand wrapping around my wrist stopped me in my tracks.

"Quinn. Look."

The urgency in Tristan's voice had me spinning around.

He held up his phone.

"Roman sent me this. We need to make a plan. Now."

32

ROMAN

"This makes no fucking sense." I clenched and unclenched my fist, my other hand clasping my phone so tightly I could feel the metal straining beneath my grip. "Who would replace Quinn with Penelope? Yeah, she's the head girl, but it's just a fucking ball. Why would the teachers interfere with the voting?"

Caiden cleared his throat. "That's where it gets interesting. When I spoke to West after I'd spoken to you earlier, he set up a scan of the computers, and his system flagged activity on one of the computers. West was watching the votes changing in real time. All he could see was the computer they were being changed from."

"How does that help us?"

"I'm getting to that. He hacked into the security feeds—by the way, he says your school security systems are shit—and although there aren't many cameras inside the building, he collated the footage from around that time. We don't know where the admin computers are based, but you do, and if you tell me, we should be able to work out which CCTV footage to focus on."

"Okay. Yeah. Makes sense." I rubbed my hand across my jaw. Whoever was behind this, they'd made a big fucking mistake by targeting Quinn.

"I'm gonna…hold on. Switch to video." I did as instructed, turning on my camera, and caught sight of Caiden's face for a second before his camera switched to show several computer screens, with Weston tapping away on a keyboard.

He held the phone in front of one of the screens, which held a still from a CCTV feed—I recognised it as the visitors' entrance to Hatherley Hall. "West's gonna flip through these stills. Say 'stop' when you recognise the location of the admin computers."

"Okay." The image changed, showing the main hall. Then, the entrance to the student computer lab. Then, the doorway to the science labs. Then— "There. The admin office is inside that door."

"Got it," West said, and the image disappeared, quickly replaced by an active video feed. West did something on the keyboard, and the timestamp changed. "This is fifteen minutes before the votes were changed. Be on the lookout for any activity." The timestamp began changing again. One minute passed. Then two. Then three— "There!"

The image froze, and I stared through my phone camera at the instantly recognisable figure dressed in a gold ball gown. "That's the head girl. She wouldn't— She's Quinn's friend. She never gets into trouble, not for anything."

West nodded. "I'll keep going." The timestamp began changing again, but when we'd reached the fifteen-minute mark and no one else had appeared, I had to face the truth.

"Want me to keep going? I'll go until just after the votes were changed, see if she comes back out." West tapped at the keyboard again. The three of us saw Penelope exit the room and disappear from the feed.

"Well, fuck," Caiden said. "The head girl…"

"Yeah, the fucking head girl." Rage cut through my shock. "Thanks for the info. I—fuck, I don't know how I can repay you. I'll catch you up with everything later, yeah?" Ending the call, knowing they'd understand, I shoved my phone in my pocket and took off for the hall at a run.

When I rounded the corner, though, I saw a flash of gold slipping around another corner, away from the ball. Slowing my pace, I followed Penelope at a distance, keeping as quiet as possible on the stone floors. Penelope's heels made a clicking sound that echoed off the walls, so it was easy enough to keep track of her movements, especially when we left the sound of the ball behind.

As I walked, I sent a text to Tristan, outlining all my suspicions, and attached copies of the information my cousin had sent me. Out of everyone, he'd be the most likely to check his phone, what with his love of selfies. That done, I placed my phone back in my pocket and continued tracking Penelope, doing my best to avoid the students I passed.

When I judged we were finally alone, I made my move, acting on instinct and hoping it would be enough. I switched my phone to my jacket pocket and set it to recording mode, so all I'd need to do was tap the button to start recording. Then, I called her name.

"Pen."

She spun around, shock flashing in her gaze before she forced herself to laugh. "Roman. What are you doing here?"

I gave her a lazy smile. "Taking a walk. I needed a break. You?"

Her gaze darted around us as she nodded. "The same, I suppose."

"Walk with me? A god and a goddess, together."

"Okay."

I held out my arm, thinking only of Quinn as she took my elbow. I would not let my mask crack. I would not fuck up what might be my only chance to get answers. "This is nice."

Penelope's gaze flew to mine, her eyes narrowing. "It is? What about Quinn? She wouldn't like you to do this, would she?"

I laughed. "Quinn? Whatever rumours you've heard, they're not true. You know me. I wouldn't let myself get tied down to a girl." My mouth curved into a suggestive smile. "Not unless the right one came along."

Her brows pulled together. "Tonight...I saw you looking at her..."

Fuck. I was going to have to step up my game.

Making a big show of looking around us, I lowered my voice. "What you saw was me looking at her with hate. She did something completely fuc—completely unforgivable." Now I knew Penelope was at least behind the ball votes, and probably the rest of it, it was easy to see the gleam of joy in her eyes as she took in my words. How the fuck could I have been so blind? Okay, yeah, there had never been any reason to suspect her of anything, and even now, I couldn't understand it, but her reactions to my words were obvious, written all over her face.

"Oh, Roman." Her grip on my arm tightened as she leaned into me. It took everything I had to remain in place rather than recoil from her touch. "What happened?"

"We need to go somewhere private for this conversation. I don't want anyone else to hear," I said. I needed to get her to let her guard down, to trust me.

Tapping her bottom lip, she thought for a moment, and then her face brightened as she caught sight of the door up ahead. "The library? I'm allowed in there at any time. Head girl privileges. Just don't tell anyone I let you in."

"Your secret's safe with me." I surreptitiously hit the Record button as I entered next to her. Flipping a couple of switches that caused a few dim wall lights to turn on, she led me through the main foyer, into the stacks, and eventually came to a stop next to one of the alcove study tables. She released my arm, turning to face me as I leaned back against the edge of the table, affecting a casual pose.

"Want to talk about it?"

"Yeah," I said, seething beneath my skin. "I could do with speaking to someone who might understand. Please don't tell anyone, though."

"Of course not." She came and stood right in front of me, the fabric of her dress brushing my suit trousers. Too. Fucking. Close.

"Quinn's extra-credit paper, uh, was plagiarised. I can't believe anyone would stoop so low, and I know how that sounds coming from someone with my reputation."

"Oh." Penelope's mouth turned down. "The history paper? I can't believe she would cheat just to win. That's awful." Her hand landed on my arm, and I couldn't stop my body jerking at her touch. It was obvious now. I'd had my suspicions after everything Caiden had told me, but seeing her here and now, I *knew*. The fucking fake sympathy on her face had rage building inside me all over again. How could she stand there and lie to my face? "I see now why you were looking at her like that. I…it's not my place to say anything, but, Roman, you're better off without her. She's my friend, but she doesn't deserve to be with one of the gods."

"Yeah."

"She isn't even one of the goddesses." Penelope's hand went to her laurel wreath. "But you have other options." Her arm slid up my arm to my shoulder, and she leaned in. "I'm the one wearing a crown."

Fuck. This. I lifted my hand, ready to push her away, and then—

"Penelope!"

The cracked, teary shout from behind Penelope had the very welcome effect of making her jump and move away from me. I stared in horror as Quinn came into view, her face streaked with tears, her arms wrapped around her shaking body. What the fuck? I took a step towards her, but she stopped me in my tracks with a savage glare.

"Quinn. I'm a little busy with Roman at the moment," Penelope said.

"Please. It's important." She sniffed, and I wanted to commit murder all over again.

"Fine. Roman, can you wait outside for me, please?" Penelope batted her lashes at me, and all I could manage was a curt nod.

As I passed Quinn, her glare intensified. "I hate you," she spat. "You didn't believe that I hadn't plagiarised my essay, and now I see you cosying up with Penelope? I *knew* you had a thing for her, even though you tried to deny it."

What? My heart fucking stopped. "Quinn—"

"*Get out of my sight.*" Her expression was so fierce, so harsh, that I stumbled backwards, rubbing at my chest. My vision was getting weirdly cloudy, like there was water in my eyes. Oh. Water.

Fucking hell.

I spun on my heel and dived into the stacks, my momentum abruptly halted by an arm yanking me backwards, a palm slamming down over my mouth.

"Shhh," Knox's voice sounded low in my ear. "Don't lose your head. We've got it all in hand." He released his grip on me, and I let my body relax against the bookshelves. When I met his gaze, he mouthed, *Phone. Record*, with a subtle nod towards where I'd left Quinn and Penelope.

My heart rate slowed, seeing the conviction on his face. He had a plan. Following his instructions, I took out my phone, exited out of the voice recording app, and switched to my camera. Carefully pushing aside a couple of books, I inserted my phone into the newly created gap, pointing at Quinn and Penelope. I zoomed in on their faces and hit Record.

33

Quinn

"What do you want?" Penelope stared at me, her expression fluctuating between faux sympathy and irritation. Now I knew what to look for, it was easy to see.

This girl had been my friend.

How could she have betrayed me like this?

"What do I want? Let's talk about what you want first. It looks like you got it, doesn't it? You got the boy, the crown, and next week, you'll get the internship. But how did you manage everything?" Lifting my hand, I began ticking off points on my fingers. "Let's see…you stole Roman's hoodie from my room and hid it in your room." I watched the colour drain from her face, her mouth falling open. "But no, wait. That one wasn't to do with the other points, was it? Why did you take it, Pen?"

I could see the moment when she decided to stop lying to me. Her veneer dropped away, and she straightened up, her mouth set in a harsh line. "You didn't deserve it. You didn't deserve the attention of the elites. You especially didn't deserve something so personal."

"Maybe, maybe not." I began to pace up and down in the way I'd seen detectives do in the whodunnit movies my mum liked to watch. "Let's go back earlier than that. The party at Chaceley Rock. Why did you spike Roman's drink?"

It was a complete gamble because I genuinely had no idea how or why she would even be involved.

But. It paid off.

I stilled, hardly daring to breathe as she spat the words.

"I saw you with him. I saw him taking you to the boat. It was clear you were getting close again. Too close. I thought you would've learnt your lesson after last time. Wasn't leaving Hatherley Hall enough?" Her fists clenched. "When he returned to the lighthouse in a panic, mumbling something about you being left on the boat, it was easy enough to slip something into his drink, just to ensure he'd pass out and forget all about you."

"What? How?"

Her hand sliced through the air impatiently. "Confiscating drugs from one of the stupid boys in year twelve. I wasn't sure exactly how it would affect Roman, because I didn't know what the drugs were, but it worked to my advantage."

My mind was reeling. "It was never about Roman, was it?"

"Of course not." She laughed bitterly. "I warned him to stay away from you. Why should you get everything? Why should you get to be with one of the gods? Why should you show back up at Hatherley Hall after all this time and take everything I wanted? You didn't even have to try. You just stole it like it was your right!"

"You didn't want him, though."

"No. But I didn't want *you* to have him. You two being

together would have cemented your status as queen bee." Huffing out a breath, she shook her head. "Look. It wasn't all bad, was it? I didn't breathe a word of it to your parents, even though I could have. It would have only taken one well-placed call from me, and your parents would have been on your case about him, and he would've been expelled in the process."

Now, my pacing was giving me precious seconds to think, events arranging and rearranging themselves in my head. "Why didn't you do that, then?"

"It would have been my last resort." This time, she smiled, and it wasn't a nice smile. "If Roman had been expelled and word had managed to get out that I'd had anything to do with it, then my life would've been over. The elite would've crucified me, and I couldn't let that happen. Instead, I did everything I could to make both of you see that you shouldn't be together. Then tonight… well…I'd been sowing the seeds for a while now, but when I was crowned and Roman danced with me and allowed me to kiss him, then get him alone…I'm sorry, Quinn, but you'd only ever be a meaningless fling for someone like Roman Cavendish."

I had never been so angry in my life, and it took everything I had to push it down. The *only* thing that mattered was following through with the plan.

I sniffed, hanging my head. "Maybe you're right. Maybe I was only a meaningless fling. What about my history paper? H-how did he fit into that?"

"The paper. That was a bit of a genius move. Restore his damaged reputation by turning you in for plagiarism and at the same time ending things between the two of you for once and for all." She indicated her head towards the part of the library that housed the research journals I'd borrowed. "I saw you both, you know. Heard your little plan of taking the journals, and it was easy enough to come up with a way to remove my competition."

"I worked so hard on that paper, Penelope. Hours and hours of research, endless drafts, trying my hardest to make it the very best paper I possibly could, *without* resorting to cheating. That could have made a difference to my future. And now—" My breath caught in my throat as it hit me all over again. "Now, you've probably ruined every chance I have at the future I want. You *know* I'd never plagiarise anything."

"I know that, but the people that count don't, do they? And you know you're not the only one with a dream to become a historian, Quinn. Only one of us could win, and I couldn't let it be you."

"How did you do it?" There was a long pause, and I realised I'd have to goad her into confessing. "How on earth did you, of all people, manage to achieve that?"

"There are advantages to being the head girl," she said, examining her gold-painted nails as if she was bored with the whole conversation. "All it took was accessing Professor Fitzgerald's email, downloading your essay and making a few changes to make it seem as if you'd plagiarised parts, deleting your previous email, and sending the new version from what would appear to be your email. Then all I had to do was to send another email that appeared to be from Roman, and voilà. You lose all chances of winning."

"You really do hate me that much, don't you?"

She laughed. "I don't have enough energy to spare to hate you. No, what I hate is the fact that someone would try to take my rightful place on top during the most important time in my life."

"Okay." I held up my hand again, ticking off the points on my fingers. "You took the hoodie. You spiked Roman's drink with an illegal substance, causing him to black out and for me to remain at sea for an entire night, where anything could've happened. You edited my paper to make it look like I'd plagiarised it, and then you falsified an email from Roman saying I'd plagiarised my own work. Am I missing anything?"

Penelope's gaze was boring into me, and despite what she'd said, her expression was full of pure, unadulterated hate. Her lip curled, and she opened her mouth to speak, but I wasn't finished.

"The ball tonight. You changed the votes, didn't you?"

"What are you talking about?"

I came to a stop right in front of her, looking her dead in the eye. "Don't play dumb with me. I know what the votes were last night, and I know the percentage of students left to vote at that point. The only way you could have been crowned was by tampering with the votes. You did, didn't you?"

Her entire face flushed a deep red, and then she *snapped*. I was completely unprepared when she lunged for me, sending us both crashing to the floor. She was screaming in my ear, yanking at my hair and scratching at me like someone possessed, her nails raking down my bare arm as I struggled to push her off me. "You didn't deserve to win! The crown was mine! You already had a crown, and you never should have had it!"

Her weight suddenly disappeared, and I blinked up to see Knox holding her struggling body back while Elena held up a phone, angling it towards her face. "Say hi to the students of Hatherley Hall," Knox said with an evil grin.

Elena was obscuring my view of Penelope's face, but the gasp of horror that tore from her throat was unmissable. Elena said something to her, but I missed it because arms were reaching out to me, helping me to my feet and wrapping me up in them.

Safe. Secure.

"I'm so fucking proud of you, baby," Roman murmured, his hands gently stroking up and down my back as everything hit me all at once. The nightmare was over. It was truly over. A sob caught in my throat, and I squeezed my eyes shut, biting down on my lip. Roman kissed my temple so softly. "It's okay. You're okay. I've got you."

I cried into his shirt as he held me, murmuring soft words into my ear, holding me like he'd never let me go. When I finally managed to compose myself, I looked up at him, and he smiled, brushing his thumbs under my eyes, chasing away the last of my tears.

"There's my girl."

"Roman." It was all I could say.

A throat cleared next to us. "I believe this is yours."

I turned to see Elena holding out a golden laurel wreath with a small smile on her face.

"I can't take that. I didn't—"

"It's yours, Quinn. You won it fair and square. It should have always been yours." Her smile widened. "Put it on, and let's get back to the ball and show everyone the goddess you are."

"But I look…" I trailed off. I'd been more or less attacked and then had a prolonged crying fit.

"Baby." Roman smoothed my hair down. "You look beautiful."

"And I have a few things here that might help," Elena interjected, directing my attention to the table where a small selection of make-up was arranged on the edge—a powder compact, eyeliner, and lipstick.

My brows rose. "Where did all that come from?"

"Knox's pockets." She grinned at me. "I didn't want to bring a bag, and my boyfriend was nice enough to help me out."

It was then that I realised Knox and Penelope had disappeared. "Where is Knox, anyway?"

"Dealing with Penelope." Elena led me to the table, where she fixed my make-up and finger-combed my waves. When that was done, she picked up the laurel wreath. "Roman?"

Roman remained silent, and when I glanced over at him, he was staring at my arm with his jaw clenched and his brows pulled together. I took a step towards him, and he raised his hand, carefully tracing his finger down my arm.

"She hurt you."

Following his gaze, I noticed the red lines where Penelope had scraped her nails down my skin. "They'll fade. She hurt me a lot worse than that, even though the rest wasn't physical," I said honestly, and he growled under his breath, a muscle ticking in his jaw.

"I'm going to do every-fucking-thing I can to make sure she pays for all the ways she hurt you. Every single one."

"I know you will." Reaching up, I slid my hand around the nape of his neck, pressing a kiss to his jaw.

"Starting with going back to the ball and taking your rightful place as one of the goddesses." Elena held the laurel wreath out, and this time, Roman took it.

"What about your parents?"

I shook my head. "I've made my peace with the fact they'll see the video or, at the very least, hear about it. It's been broadcast to the entire school, after all. I think we can spin the narrative so they decide not to take action against you, at the very least. Especially when I tell them how you discovered the evidence of what Penelope was up to. Not to mention the fact that the entire time everything was happening, you were constantly looking out for me and making sure I was okay."

Roman stared at me. "What do you mean, broadcast to the entire school?"

"That was Tristan's idea. Actually, the whole plan was mostly his idea. If he managed to succeed in his part of the plan, which I'm sure he did, he and Aria were going to commandeer the projector and broadcast my confrontation with Penelope to the entire ball as it happened."

"That devious fucker." Roman shook his head, a disbelieving smile curving over his lips. "Fucking hell, Quinn, the pressure you must've been under to get her to confess."

"I know. I didn't even know if I'd be able to pull it off or if she was even involved with the drink spiking, but I had to try. And it worked. It really worked." As Roman lifted the wreath, carefully placing it on my head, I smiled. "I'm not going to rub it in my parents' faces, and I'm not going to purposely piss them off, but I am going to explain what I've been dealing with, and I'm going to make sure they understand just how amazing you are."

His throat worked as his lashes lowered, his gaze meeting mine. Tugging me into his arms, he pressed a kiss to my hair. "You're the amazing one. I don't deserve you."

"You do deserve me, and I hope I deserve you," I whispered.

"How could you even ask that? You deserve everything." We drew apart, and he sighed loudly, although the grin he couldn't bite back ruined the effect he was aiming for. "I guess since Knox isn't here, I'll carry all your make-up shit, Elena."

She laughed, moving behind me to unclip the running belt I'd forgotten I was wearing, smoothing her hand down the back of my dress. "That's sweet of you to offer, but I'll use Quinn's belt. You're both going to be the centre of attention in about five minutes."

I glanced down at my Converse high-tops with a shrug. "I'm not sure these go with the dress, but I'll make it work."

"You make anything work," Roman said.

"You're biased." We smiled at each other.

"Nah, I just have amazing taste." He stepped back, offering his arm first to me and then to Elena. "Alright, let's do this."

34

ROMAN

When we reached the entrance to the hall, Elena left us, and then it was just me and Quinn. I looked down at her to find her already looking at me, her gorgeous eyes wide and apprehensive.

"It's gonna be okay," I said softly, and she nodded, taking a deep breath. Straightening my shoulders, I stepped into the room, holding her close to me.

"Hatherley Hall, here's Roman Cavendish and the woman that should have been his goddess all along, Quinn Farrow!" Tristan's voice boomed from the speakers.

For fuck's sake.

His words were accompanied by a roar from the assembled students, the crowd parting for us, creating a path that led to the centre of the hall. As we walked, the sweeping lights dimmed, and a spotlight lit the two of us, following our path to the dance floor area. No doubt that was also Tristan's doing.

"Students of Hatherley Hall, Roman and Quinn will

now take their first dance!" Tristan proclaimed. That dramatic fucking bastard. When the echo of his words died away, music began playing, and déjà vu hit me when students formed a circle around us. But this was nothing like earlier. This was me, finally getting to dance with the girl I was in love with, right there for everyone to see. Her golden laurel wreath glittered under the spotlight as I wrapped my arms around her waist, and she'd never looked more beautiful.

Her hands slid up my shoulders, and then she clasped them around my neck. A gorgeous smile curved over her lips as we began to move to the music, and I couldn't stand it any longer.

Keeping one arm around her, I tilted up her chin, stroking over her soft skin with my thumb. Lowering my head, our lips almost touching, I spoke her name. "Quinn?"

"Yeah?"

I swallowed hard. I'd never said these words aloud. Not to anyone. But with Quinn Farrow, it was easy. "I love you."

Her beautiful eyes widened, glimmering with unshed tears as she stared up at me. "Really?"

"Really. I love you so much. So. Much."

"I love you, too," she breathed.

My heart fucking stopped. "You do?" She actually loved me back?

"Of course I do. How could I not?" she said, like it was that simple, and then we were kissing, neither of us caring about the people watching us, lost in each other.

"I love you. I love you. I love you." I couldn't stop saying it. Couldn't stop kissing her. I never wanted this moment to end. Never wanted to let her go. After everything we'd been through, somehow, she loved me, and I loved her with every fucking piece of me. Quinn Farrow was mine, and I was never going to let her go.

Except I did have to let her go because a heavy hand landed on my bicep. The headmaster stood there, a hard, uncompromising set to his jaw. "Mr. Cavendish. Miss Farrow. Please come with me."

***

We ended up having a reprieve because it was late in the evening—way too fucking late for a confrontation. The headmaster had gathered us together—everyone he knew was involved, at least, which meant Quinn, Knox, Elena, Tristan, and I were there. I presumed Aria had escaped his notice and that he was dealing with Penelope separately—I hoped. He informed us that Quinn and I would have an official meeting the following afternoon, and in the meantime, *none* of us were allowed to leave the premises. He ended with a veiled threat that referred to the crypts, which I knew for a fact the staff always turned a blind eye to, and then told us the only places we were allowed to go to in the meantime were our own dorms and bathroom, our common rooms, and the dining hall. The rest of the school was off limits until the meeting was over, and under no circumstances were we allowed outside. He muttered something about inspections and random checks to make sure we weren't in the wrong places and then dismissed us.

"No after-party," Tristan cried as we headed upstairs to the Epi common room. "Fuck Professor Lexington."

"I'm sorry. I didn't mean for any of you to get involved." Quinn looked like she was on the verge of tears again, and I opened my mouth, ready to defend my girl, but Tristan instantly realised what he'd said, shaking his head and giving her a reassuring smile.

"Ah, don't even worry about it. You're one of ours, and we look out for each other. We'll have a delayed party when all this shit is over, and in the meantime, I'll kick your boyfriend's ass on *Mario Kart*. What do you say, Ro? A hundred a game? Winner of the tournament takes all?"

"Boyfriend." A wide grin stretched across my face.

"Oh, fucking hell." Tristan rolled his eyes. Grimacing, he threw out his hands. "Why am I surrounded by couples?"

"Get over it," Knox told him as we entered the common room and flopped down on the sofas. I tugged Quinn into my lap, and she happily curled into my arms, placing a kiss on my jaw. Tristan threw me a controller, and I let Quinn pick my character and vehicle options.

"If I lose, it's my girlfriend's fault," I told her, taking the opportunity to run my hand up her thigh before the race began.

Her breath hitched, her gaze flying to mine, and then her lips curved upwards. "I guess I'll accept the responsibility." She rested her head on my shoulder, half her focus on the screen, the other talking in low tones to Elena, who was apparently having a sleepover in her dorm since she wasn't allowed to go to the crypts or to Knox's parents' house, where she normally lived. That also meant Knox would be sleeping in with me and Tristan, with the crypts being off limits. I smiled to myself as I knocked Tristan's vehicle off the track, kissing my girl's cheek. I felt…something. Something I couldn't put my finger on.

It took me until the final race of the tournament to work out what I was feeling.

Contentment.

I was completely content, for what might've been the first time in my life.

Yeah, we still had to deal with the aftermath of tonight —and I needed to give my cousins and probably my uncle a heads-up, but for now, I could relax and enjoy being with my best friends and the girl I loved.

35

Quinn

Between last night and today, the plans had changed. First of all, the headmaster wanted to talk to me with my parents present while he ascertained what had happened. I'd put my foot down and said I wouldn't speak without Roman there because he was as big a part of this as I was…and more importantly, he refused to allow me to be "thrown to the wolves alone," as he put it.

So here we were. The headmaster was seated at the head of the large table, with the head of Epicurus house and my history professor on either side of him. My parents sat opposite Roman's uncle, Arlo, who'd insisted on being there in lieu of Roman's parents, who were somewhere overseas. Finally, I was seated at the other end of the table next to Roman.

He squeezed my hand briefly, before anyone noticed, and then rested his arms on the table. I noticed how perfectly pressed his uniform was and how he'd styled his hair so neatly, and warmth spread through my body. He was trying to make a good impression. I loved him for it.

Honestly, I would have loved him no matter how much effort he had or hadn't made. The most important point was that he was there for me, and I was there for him, and I appreciated him being here more than I could ever put into words.

Professor Lexington cleared his throat. "Miss Farrow. I'd like to begin with addressing the allegations against you…"

My nerves got the better of me, and I tuned him out, concentrating on taking deep, even breaths as he continued to speak. The words washed over me like a wave, with the occasional sentence penetrating. "…forensic IT specialists…" and "…first thing this morning…" and "…the evidence corroborates…"

"Quinn."

I blinked, realising everyone's attention was on me, and my cheeks heated. "I'm sorry. I—"

"I should be the one apologising." My history professor studied me over his steepled hands. "You tried to explain everything to me, and I didn't allow you to. I refused a meeting with Mr. Cavendish when he requested one, too, and perhaps if I had, we would have been able to get to the bottom of this sooner. I—"

"You requested a meeting with my professor?" My entire focus was on Roman.

He gave me a small smile, his gaze soft. "Yeah, of course I did, as soon as I knew what was happening. We both knew you didn't plagiarise and that I'd never have sent the email in the first place. If last night hadn't worked out the way it did, I had a whole plan to show there was no way I'd ever send an email like that, and more importantly, you'd never do anything like that in the first place." His eyes hardened. "Anyone who thought you'd do that is a—"

Arlo coughed discreetly, and Roman gritted his teeth but fell silent.

Professor Fitzgerald cleared his throat. "Your record has always been impeccable, Quinn, and it's clear that you've become an incredibly intelligent woman. I should have taken that into consideration." He sighed. "I suppose…it would never have occurred to me that a student would attempt to sabotage another's work in this manner, let alone have the means to do so."

"I expect a formal apology. Our daughter has gone through a traumatic experience. We entrusted her care to you, and you have failed her. She has been let down by your incompetence."

My brows flew up at my dad's hard tone. Next to him, my mum was nodding.

"My husband is right. I'm frankly shocked by your lax security. Allowing students access to staff systems, allowing them to tamper with voting results…" She exhaled harshly. "Don't you realise Quinn was the youngest goddess in Hatherley Hall's history before she left? There was no question she'd be a goddess again on her return. I'm surprised none of you thought to question it when her name didn't appear."

Of course that was the part my mum would focus on. Not that it mattered. The important thing was they were on my side.

"They're right." Roman cleared his throat, shooting a sideways glance at his uncle. "It should have rung alarm bells when Quinn's name didn't appear."

The headmaster nodded. "I concur. Unfortunately, we are unable to show the video, but we can address the additional allegations. I believe you've all been made aware of the content of the video?"

My parents and Roman's uncle all nodded. I'd known

the word would spread like wildfire—it was the biggest scandal involving Hatherley Hall that I could remember.

"Alright. Putting that aside for now, let's move on to the main purpose of this meeting. Miss Farrow has been falsely accused of plagiarism, and that is the most serious allegation we must address here today. We will, of course, ensure that the false accusations are stricken from her record, and she will be allowed to resubmit her original paper for consideration. The other involved party has been disqualified and will be suitably punished."

"Good." My dad gave me a reassuring smile before his expression darkened. "I'm appalled that this incident could even happen in the first place, and I trust that you will ensure it won't happen again."

Arlo glanced at Roman and nodded, and then shot me a tiny wink. I straightened up in my seat, eager to hear what he had to say.

"I believe my nephew was instrumental in discovering the culprit and getting to the bottom of what happened regarding the plagiarism and rigged voting system."

The headmaster and my head of house exchanged glances, and then the headmaster nodded slowly. "That is correct, in our understanding." His gaze turned to Roman, his eyes narrowing. "We are very grateful to you for bringing this matter to our attention, Mr. Cavendish." The words were forced out through gritted teeth, but they were there, and most importantly, my parents were there to hear them.

Roman remained silent until Arlo gave another discreet cough. His words were directed at the headmaster, but his gaze was focused on my parents. "I wanted to do the right thing, and I wanted to protect Quinn."

"And you did the right thing. I'm proud of you." Arlo gave Roman a genuine smile, and Roman seemed to relax.

"Well, I suppose we should thank you, too," my mum said hesitantly. My dad pinched his brow, shaking his head, but eventually, he sighed.

"Yes… Our sincere thanks, Mr. Cavendish. It appears that maybe we have been a little too hasty to judge you. Perhaps…we've been too hasty to judge situations where we may not have been apprised of all the information."

I could see how much it cost my dad to force out those words, but the fact was, he had said them. Swallowing around the lump in my throat, I steeled myself, ready to face the questions I knew were coming. It didn't take long at all until my dad's full focus was on me.

"Quinn. Your mother and I would like to speak with you in private afterwards, but please know that you won't be punished. None of this is your fault."

My lip trembled, and I bit down on it. They were words I'd wanted and needed to hear for so long. And now…now, I was hearing them, but I knew my parents wouldn't appreciate me showing any perceived weakness in front of the school staff. Not only that, but I didn't particularly want to cry in front of them, anyway. Only with Roman, who let me fall apart and put myself together again, supporting me without judgement.

When we'd been shown into an empty classroom, I buried my face in my hands, trying to breathe. It was just me and my parents, and I had nowhere to hide.

"Quinn." My dad's voice cracked, and my gaze flew to his. Were there tears in his eyes? Surely not.

"We made a mistake," he continued, and yes, there were definite tears.

My eyes filled against my wishes.

"Oh, Quinn," my mum murmured, and then suddenly, they were both hugging me, and I didn't know what to do.

"We should have known. We should never have made you leave in the first place," my dad ground out.

"This is our fault. We're so, so sorry," my mum added, sniffing between her own tears.

My face was wet from my own tears. All I could do was let them hug me. It was healing, in a way. I was under no illusion that our relationship would be easily repaired, but maybe we'd made a start.

36

ROMAN

When Quinn, her parents, and her history professor had all left, my uncle sat back in his seat, his gaze fixed on the headmaster.

"I'd like to discuss the matter of having Roman's record expunged."

The headmaster exchanged glances with Professor Donnelly. "I'm afraid we cannot possibly—"

"I've recently come into possession of a Bugatti Veyron." Arlo paused meaningfully. "A Sang Noir. As I'm sure you're aware, only twelve were ever made. I could be persuaded to part with it for an extremely reasonable price."

The headmaster's eyes gleamed. "A Sang Noir, you say?"

I'd heard that Arlo was the best at negotiating deals—part of the reason his company, Alstone Holdings, had grown so rapidly and successfully. Seeing him in action, cutting straight to the point and having clearly researched the one thing the headmaster couldn't refuse, I couldn't help but admire him. His status as one of the elite wasn't only based on his name. He had power, money, and status because he worked fucking hard for it, and he was the best at what he did.

"Indeed. I purchased it at auction at Sotheby's. It's a beautiful piece of machinery. W-16 engine and, of course, the stunning red interior." Arlo produced a tablet from his briefcase, turning it on. He slid it across the table to the headmaster, who flipped through a series of images of the car.

I caught Professor Donnelly's gaze, and he rolled his eyes at me. Yeah, we were both fully aware of what was about to happen.

"I think we can work out a satisfactory deal..." the headmaster began, and my uncle smiled.

Later, after the negotiations were over, I walked to the visitors' car park with my uncle. "Not a bad day's work. It'll be a shame to be parted from the Bugatti, but it's all for a good cause."

"Thanks. Really. Not just for today, but for, y'know. Everything. I don't know how I can repay you. Even before now. The arson, that time you stopped me from getting expelled with the flood, the times I *was* expelled, and you got me into a different school, the—fuck, every time I managed to get into trouble." My voice dropped to a whisper. "I don't know why you'd do that."

"Don't even mention it. You're family, and that's what we do. I'm here for you, as are your cousins." He clapped me on the shoulder. "Just stay out of trouble, okay? You don't have much time left here."

We came to a stop next to his car. "I will, and I know. I'm ready to get out of here."

"You know, if you're thinking about university, Alstone College isn't a bad place. You'd be accepted there straightaway, as long as you get the grades."

"Alstone, huh? Is that your way of saying you want to keep a closer eye on me?"

Fishing his car key from his pocket, he shot me a grin. "It couldn't hurt, could it?"

"I'll think about it." It was a weird feeling, being wanted by family. Weird, but really fucking good. "My girlfriend's applied for Alstone College, you know."

"I know. History, isn't it? The history department may be small, but it's prestigious."

"Yeah. She's applied for a few different unis, and I just want her to go wherever she'll be happiest."

My uncle stared at me, and then he smiled. "I know your parents would…well, I can't speak for them. But I can speak for myself, as your uncle, and say that I'm proud of you, Roman. You're a good man."

I swallowed around the stupid fucking lump in my throat. "Thanks."

"How did it go with your parents?" I settled back on my elbows on the wooden dock, swirling my feet in the water.

Quinn pushed her sunglasses up on top of her head and then turned to face me. Her lips curved into a gorgeous smile that I had to kiss, because how could I resist my girl when she was so fucking happy and all mine? When I finally managed to drag myself away from her mouth, she smiled even wider. "It went well. They apologised to me. I think…no, I know we've got a lot of work to do, but it felt like a step in the right direction. And I think…maybe, they'll come around about you, too."

"Yeah?"

She nodded before shifting closer to me and resting

against my side with her head on my shoulder. "I love you."

I kissed her head. "I love you, too."

We sat in silence for a while, just lazing in the sun, our feet dipping into our lake, no one else around except for the birds and the insects.

It was peaceful, but my mind wouldn't stop working. I straightened up, curling my arm around Quinn's waist. "I'm sorry for saying you should take the journals from the library. I added to everything you had to deal with it."

"That wasn't your fault, Roman. No one forced me to take them. Whatever you'd said to me, I wouldn't have taken them if I hadn't wanted to. It was wrong, and I shouldn't have done it, and that's all on me. Not you. I don't blame you for it."

This girl was way too fucking good for me.

I had to do something to help make things right. "Now all this shit is over with, let's make a plan for me to win your parents over."

Quinn huffed out a laugh. "How are we going to do that?"

"I'll wow them with my natural charm. Wait. I don't have natural charm. Fuck. Maybe I should take some lessons from Tristan."

"Please don't." Tapping her nails against the wood, she thought for a minute. "You could probably charm my mum with compliments. My dad...I don't know. He used to play lacrosse at school, so maybe talk to him about that? Um...maybe future plans?" She grimaced. "Honestly, I just want them to like you for you. Because you're amazing, and I love you."

"Baby. You're so fucking sweet, did you know that?" I kissed her cheek. "Okay. I have an idea. We'll invite them to my next lacrosse game. We're playing Cheltenham, so it should be an easy win. I'll impress them during the match, and after that, we'll take them for lunch at Nottswood Golf & Country Club. Knox and Tristan are members—I'll get them to make us a reservation."

"You're not a member?"

"Fuck no. I don't like golf, and I don't like snobby rich people. I swim when Knox and Tristan go there."

She laughed. "Fair enough. My parents are members of a different country club—my dad's not much of a golfer, either, but I'm sure they'll enjoy the surroundings. I remember going there with P-Penelope's family once. It's a good choice."

"Speaking of Penelope…did you hear what her punishment was?"

"No, what was it?" Straightening up, she turned to me. "I haven't heard anything."

"Tristan found out. Head boy privileges and his ability to sweet-talk the staff. He said he was gonna resign from his head boy position, by the way."

"He is? Why?"

I shrugged. "Dunno. I think he's over all that shit, and I think he feels a bit responsible that he was the head boy and Penelope was the head girl, and he never had any idea that she was behind it all. Will and Katy are gonna be the new head boy and girl for the rest of the term, not that there's much left of it."

"He shouldn't feel responsible. None of us knew. I was her friend. Or I thought I was." She gave me a sad smile.

"Baby, come here." I pulled her into my arms, and she let her body relax into mine with a sigh. "Nothing's ever going to make up for what she did, but I guarantee she'll regret it for the rest of her life. She's been expelled. I could've pressed for criminal charges separately for the spiking incident, but as it is, the plagiarism, tampering with staff equipment, impersonating two other students—all of that shit is enough to make sure she not only gets expelled, but she has no chance at getting into any of the unis she applied for. Even if they don't do a criminal check or whatever, someone might've uploaded the footage from the ball and emailed a link to all the admissions officers at those unis."

"Someone?" I could hear the humour in her voice.

"What are you implying, Quinn?"

"Nothing at all."

I smiled into her hair. "I'd do anything for you. One of the reasons I didn't want to press charges was because I didn't want to drag this shit out. We need to finish this term and then go somewhere far away. Somewhere you can fucking shine without another person trying to bring you down."

"Somewhere with you."

"Yeah. You and me."

I couldn't imagine anything better.

37

Quinn

"As it stands, I'm obligated to punish you for removing the journals from the library." Professor Fitzgerald shifted in his desk chair, clearly uncomfortable. "I'd like to also offer you a formal apology once again."

I shook my head. "It's… Obviously, I was upset, but I understand why you would think I did it. The evidence was right there in front of you. What other conclusion were you supposed to come to?"

"Even so. As for your punishment, detention in the library, replacing the books on the shelves. Four evenings should be enough. Report to the library on Monday at 6:00 p.m."

"Make it two evenings, and I'll serve it with her. Double the labour."

My history teacher sighed as I spun around to see Tristan casually leaning against one of the classroom desks.

"Any reason, Mr. Smith-Chamberlain?"

He placed his finger to his lips and shot me a wink, to

which I rolled my eyes, trying not to smile, and Professor Fitzgerald pinched his brow.

"I shouldn't need to remind you that journals are not to be removed from the library. Fine. You may serve Quinn's punishment with her if it will help to ease your guilty conscience."

"My conscience is clean," Tristan told him, widening his eyes innocently.

"Out. Both of you. As far as I'm concerned, the matter is closed, and I don't want to hear any more about what you may or may not have done."

I nodded, thanking him before following Tristan out of the history classroom. As we reached the door, Professor Fitzgerald called after me.

"Quinn?" When I turned around, he smiled. "Very good work on your extra-credit assignment. We won't count our chickens just yet, but I have a feeling the panel from *The Historical Review* will be impressed with everything you've achieved."

"Really?"

"Yes, really."

"Guess you'd better come with me to our lacrosse practice so you can give your boyfriend the good news," Tristan said as we left the classroom behind. "We need to get him hyped for tomorrow's game."

"I will. Thanks, by the way. You didn't have to offer to serve my detention with me."

He shrugged. "I've been taking journals out of the library for the past four years. It's the least I can do. Ease my guilty conscience."

"Do you have a guilty conscience?"

"Nope. Not about taking them. But I do about you having to be punished for something I do all the time.

Roman would do the same for me, and anyway, you're one of us now. That means we look out for each other."

A warm feeling spread through me as I took in his words. Coming back to Hatherley Hall, I hadn't known what to expect, but somehow, I'd ended up with an amazing man who loved me, but also a group of people who really, truly had my back.

"Thank you, Tristan. The same goes for me, too."

The conditions were perfect for the lacrosse game. Fluffy white clouds, bright sunshine, and a fresh breeze. The mood in the stands was jubilant as the teams jogged onto the pitch. Roman had said it would be an easy win, and the Hatherley Hall team looked confident and focused. It was too hot to wear Roman's hoodie, but he'd given me a team jersey with a number 18 on the back. *His* number. When I'd shown up with Elena, both of us wearing our boyfriends' jerseys, Aria had sighed and shaken her head at us, muttering that she'd never be caught dead wearing one. We were now seated in the front row along with our friends and families. My parents were to my left, and my mum was currently in a conversation with Knox's mum while my dad stared across the field with a faraway look on his face.

When the teams took their positions, Roman shooting me a huge grin, my dad finally turned to me. "This brings back memories. Being out there on the field, stick in hand…" He trailed off as the game began, his full attention turning to the players. My focus was on my boyfriend, of course, fast, determined, and so gorgeous with that look of concentration on his face.

The first half passed in a blur, and by the end of it,

Hatherley Hall were winning, 7–5. Knox and Tristan had been integral in scoring our goals, and Roman had been instrumental in setting the majority of them up, running and passing the ball with deadly accuracy while avoiding the Cheltenham players. My voice was hoarse from cheering, and I gratefully accepted the water bottle Aria handed to me.

When I lowered the bottle, my dad was giving me a thoughtful look. "Your…friend. Mr. Cavendish. He's rather talented."

I bit back a smile. Roman had already been upgraded from "the Cavendish boy" to "Mr. Cavendish," *and* my dad was acknowledging him as a friend of mine? This was going better than I thought it would.

"He's very talented," I said softly, my gaze going back to the field. "Not only at lacrosse. He…he's an amazing man."

My dad didn't respond other than a brief nod, but it was enough. More than enough. Hope rose inside me, and I let myself smile for real.

In the second half, Cheltenham managed to score again, but we drew ahead, thanks to an amazing play from Lincoln, assisted by Knox. Cheltenham did their best to recover, but it was clear to everyone watching that Hatherley Hall were dominating the game.

With only a few minutes left on the clock, Roman got the ball in his scoop and *ran*, a blur down the field, the crowd roaring their support. He sliced his stick through the air, sending the ball straight into the goal and sealing our win. The game finished 14–9, and when Roman jogged over to me and pulled off his helmet, his eyes sparkling and a huge grin stretching over his face, I didn't even hesitate. I leaned over the barrier at the same time as he reached for me, our mouths meeting in a euphoric kiss that was everything.

Until my dad cleared his throat, and Roman and I sprung apart. My heart sank at his serious, unsmiling face, but then he held out his hand to Roman.

"Good game," he said, and my heart skipped a beat. Roman's eyes widened as he took my dad's hand and shook it.

"Thank you." There was a small pause before he added, "Sir."

My dad's lips tilted upwards in the barest hint of a smile.

38

Quinn

"I knew you'd manage to charm them." I straddled Roman on one of the sofas in the crypts, my arms wrapped around his neck. He rubbed his thumbs over my hips as he kissed me.

"Yeah. The meal went well, I think. Compliments are definitely the way to your mum's heart, but I won your dad over the minute I took my first shot in the lacrosse game."

"I think you won them both over before that, to be honest. When they found out your role in everything and how you'd been dragged into it all against your will. I'm pretty sure your uncle impressed them during the meeting, too."

"He's good at that." Roman grinned. Reaching around me, he grabbed his cider from the coffee table and took a swig before offering the bottle to me. "Do you think they'll be okay with the fact we're together?"

"I…I think if I can show I can keep my focus on my studies, they'll be okay. I get the sense they feel partly responsible for the things that happened—for isolating me, I guess. We don't need to hide. We just need to toe the line for the rest of the term." Sipping the cider, I allowed myself to properly think about the future. A future that included both Roman and the approval of my parents, something I never thought would be possible. Maybe Penelope had done me a favour in her own twisted way.

"Arlo's given me the toeing-the-line talk, too. I guess I can't be the bad boy forever." He pouted, and I laughed, kissing him again.

"Ahh, look at this. All the lovebirds together. How sweet." Tristan threw himself down onto the sofa next to us, slinging his arm across Roman's shoulders. He nodded towards the opposite sofa, where Knox and Elena were reclining. As I shifted sideways on Roman's lap, placing the bottle down, I saw Knox give Tristan a lazy smile, saluting him with his beer.

"Two of the three gods are taken now, Tris. Are you gonna join us?"

"You wish." Rolling his eyes at Knox, he kicked his feet up on the coffee table and then patted Roman's shoulder. "But I am gonna do you a favour, Ro. You can have the room tonight. Literally all I ask is that you don't fuck on my bed or my desk—just stay away from anything that's mine. But if you want the room for you and Quinn, you can have it."

I was swept into a standing position before I even had time to register it, laughing as Roman more or less dragged me away from our friends, through the crowd, and up the stairs.

"Eager to celebrate, are you?"

"What do you think? We have a whole night to ourselves and a bed. All we need to do is sneak you past the prefects—oh, wait, they're not gonna stop us." His eyes sparkled, and the happiness on his face made my stomach flip.

The happiness turned into a slow simmer of heat as he wrapped his arm around me, leading me through the castle, dipping his head to my ear and telling me all the things he wanted to do to me, how I was his, and how he couldn't wait to get me in his bed. All the while, he was sliding his hands over my body, teasing me, torturing me with too-quick touches, driving me wild with need.

By the time we reached his dorm room, the simmer was an inferno, and the second the door closed behind us, Roman was on me, pinning me up against the wall as he yanked down my shorts and underwear with one hand, his mouth at my throat, sucking a mark into my skin. I kicked them off, along with my flip-flops, which went sailing across the room somewhere. I didn't care where—all I cared about was the man that was fucking devouring me.

"Fucking mine," he growled, tugging my top and bra off before getting his mouth on my breasts, leaving them aching, sending tingles all through my body when he sucked and lightly bit my nipples. I arched forwards, so wet and so desperate for friction, his jeans rough against my oversensitive skin.

"Ro. Please."

"I've got you, baby." Lifting me into his arms, he turned us, lowering me onto his desk. "Legs up," he commanded as he yanked down his jeans and boxer briefs. Lying my back flat across the desk, I hooked my legs over his shoulders, and he scooped his hands under my ass and thrust inside me without pausing for breath, both of us too desperate to wait any longer.

I cried out, impossibly full, the delicious, aching stretch of his thick cock inside me making me temporarily lose my breath.

"Fuck. You feel so good." He drew back almost all the way and then thrust back in. Only his hands kept me in place, the force of his movements making the desk slam against the wall as he fucked into me, the angle making him hit so deep inside me.

Something crashed to the floor as his thrusts became harder, but neither of us even paused. One of his hands slid onto my clit, and that was enough to send me over the edge, shaking and gasping as he continued to fuck into me restlessly, pounding in and out until he came inside me with a long, drawn-out groan.

I lowered my trembling legs, and he scooped me into his arms, wrapping them around me as he pressed breathless kisses to my hair.

"That was so good," I murmured, sliding my lips down his throat, his pulse beating wildly beneath me.

"Fuck, yeah. So good." He drew back, a slow smile curving over his lips. "Round two in the bed? I'll take my time with you, make you feel amazing. You can ride me, then I want you underneath me so I can watch your face when you come. I want to see what I do to you."

"Mmm." Winding my arms and legs around him, I let him carry me over to his bed. He stripped out of his clothes and then crawled over my body.

He placed his mouth to my ear, his hot breath sending a shiver through my body. "Don't tell Tristan we fucked on his desk."

"What? I thought that was your desk."

"Nope. His was closest. You were too irresistible; I couldn't wait any longer." His hand stroked down my side. "I think we broke his pen holder. I'll get him a new one."

"Hopefully before he notices and puts two and two together."

Roman laughed. "Or not. I want to see his face when he realises how it happened." His laughter died away, and then he nipped at the shell of my ear. "Enough talk about other people. Enough talking. All I want to hear is you saying my name and those sexy fucking noises you make when I fuck you."

That was a plan I could definitely get on board with.

The next morning, both of us woke early, and after grabbing our swimming stuff, we managed to escape Hatherley Hall without running into anyone. We made our way to our lake, stripping down to our swim clothes, and ran off the end of the jetty, cannonballing into the water.

Summer had definitely arrived. The warm rays sparkled on the surface of the lake, rainbow droplets scattering around me as Roman shot out from beneath the surface, tugging me into his arms and spinning us around in the cool water. I tipped my head back, the ends of my hair dipping into the water as I wrapped my legs around Roman's waist. He grinned and pressed a kiss to my throat before falling backwards, sending us both into the lake with a huge splash, dunking us beneath the surface.

When we resurfaced, both of us laughing and gasping for breath, he gently pushed my hair back from my face. When he was satisfied, he violently shook his head in an attempt at getting the worst of the water out of his hair, sending more droplets flying everywhere. I shrieked as cold water peppered my skin, and a gorgeous smile curved over his lips.

His eyes met mine. "Remember when we first used to come down here? I never thought we'd end up like this."

"Me neither." I reached up, sliding my hand over the wet skin of his jaw. He was so gorgeous, his gaze so intent on me, letting me see everything he was feeling. "I'm so glad it worked out the way it did."

"Me too. I love you, Quinn."

"I love you, too. This…being here with you—this is everything."

Pulling me into him, he tilted my head up for a kiss. "It is. And the best is still to come, you know."

He was right.

The best was still to come.

ROMAN

ONE YEAR LATER

The click of the front door unlocking sounded, and then Quinn bounded into our apartment, waving her phone at me. "Am I reading this right? Another summer internship?"

I took the phone, scanning the email. "Yeah, you read it right. There was no way you wouldn't get another internship. Not after you impressed them last summer with your paper and the internship they extended because they were so pleased with you. And getting published in your history journal. *Twice*. You're fucking amazing, baby."

She gave me a bright, happy smile. "I can't believe it, but I'm so glad." Wrapping her arms around my neck, she stared up at me. "Speaking of amazing, West happened to let it slip that you have the top grades in the entire year of your business degree. The entire *year*, Roman."

I grinned. Us both getting into Alstone College to study for our degrees, moving into a fucking gorgeous apartment in a converted Regency-style mansion, being around my uncle and cousins and knowing what it was like to have family around me and caring about me for the first time in my life…I guess you could say it had settled me. The need I'd always had to act out had somehow disappeared. That itch beneath my skin, that sense I'd always had of never really being wanted…all of it had gone. Dissolved, like it was never there. Although I knew the scars would remain, it was surprisingly easy to put it all behind me.

I owed most of it to Quinn, though. Falling in love with her had changed me for the better. They say you shouldn't rely on someone else for your happiness, and it wasn't like that. It was like together, we were better. We brought out the best in each other. Supported and encouraged and lifted each other up. Yeah, we had our bad days—no one was perfect, least of all me—but we were fucking solid. Quinn Farrow was mine, and I was hers, and we'd made a home together here in Alstone. Whatever we ended up doing in the future after our degrees, we had a strong, unshakeable foundation, and nothing would tear us apart.

Quinn took her phone back, mumbling about letting her parents know the news while her fingers flew across the screen, and my smile widened. When she'd finished and slipped her phone into *my* pocket, I kissed the tip of her nose.

"We need to celebrate. What do you want to do?"

Tapping her fingers on the back of my neck, she thought about it for a minute. "Honestly? I think I'd like to go down to the pier, walk along the beach, and get fish and chips. I know it sounds boring, but—"

Placing my finger over her lips, I shook my head. "It's not boring. Wanna go to the cove after? We can swim. Naked."

She laughed, as I knew she would. "Alright. As long as you warm me up afterwards."

"That goes without saying." I kissed her. And then kissed her again. And then a third time, just for luck. I'd never get enough of my girl.

When we were in my car, heading towards Alstone pier, I placed my hand on Quinn's bare thigh. Out of the corner of my eye, I could see her smile as her hand came down to cover mine.

I stared straight ahead, towards the sea, burnished with an orange glow from the setting sun. I smiled, too, my heart full.

Once upon a time, there was a boy who never knew love.

That boy grew up to be a man who loved and was loved beyond compare.

THE END

THANK YOU

Thank you so much for reading Roman and Quinn's story!
Want more from the Gods of Hatherley Hall? Book 3,
Sinful Storms, is coming. Pre-order now:
https://mybook.to/sinfulstorms

Are you interested in reading more about the Cavendishes?
You can find out more about Roman's cousins Caiden and
Weston and dive into the mystery and suspense
surrounding them in The Four series, beginning with
Caiden's story in The Lies We Tell:
https://mybook.to/tlwt

Check out all my other links at
https://linktr.ee/authorbeccasteele
Feel free to send me your thoughts, and reviews are always
very appreciated ♥

Becca xoxo

ALSO BY BECCA STEELE

Gods of Hatherley Hall Series

(M/F academy romance)

Cruel Crypts

Wicked Waters

Sinful Storms

LSU Series

(M/M college romance)

Collided

Blindsided

Sidelined

*Unwrapped (festive spin-off novella)**

Ignited

Tempted (novella)

The Four Series

(M/F college suspense romance)

The Lies We Tell

The Secrets We Hide

The Havoc We Wreak

*A Cavendish Christmas (festive short story)**

The Fight In Us

The Bonds We Break

The Darkness In You

Alstone High Standalones

(new adult high school romance)

Trick Me Twice (M/F)

Cross the Line (M/M)

In a Week (M/F short story) *

Savage Rivals (M/M)

Other Standalones

Cirque des Masques (M/M dark circus romance)

Reckless (M/M soccer romance)

Mayhem (M/F Four series dark spinoff) *

Heatwave (M/F summer short story) *

After Dark (M/M/M Cirque des Masques short spinoff) *

Boneyard Kings Series (with C. Lymari)

(RH/why-choose college suspense romance)

Merciless Kings

Vicious Queen

Ruthless Kingdom

London Players Series

(M/F rugby romance)

The Offer

London Suits Series

(M/F office romance)

The Deal

The Truce

The Wish (a festive short story) *

Box Sets

Caiden & Winter trilogy (M/F)

(The Four series books 1-3)

**starred books (plus bonus scenes) are available as free downloads from https://authorbeccasteele.com*

***Key - M/F = Male/Female romance*

M/M = Male/Male romance

RH = Reverse Harem/why-choose (one woman & 3+ men) romance

ABOUT THE AUTHOR

Becca Steele is a USA Today and Wall Street Journal bestselling author of new adult romance. Her books have been translated into multiple languages.

Becca resides in the south of England with her family. When she's not writing, you can find her reading or gaming. Failing that, she'll be watching Netflix or making her 500th Spotify playlist.

Join Becca's Facebook reader group Becca's Book Bar, sign up to her mailing list, check out her Patreon, or find her via the following links:

facebook.com/authorbeccasteele

instagram.com/authorbeccasteele

bookbub.com/profile/becca-steele

goodreads.com/authorbeccasteele

patreon.com/authorbeccasteele

amazon.com/stores/Becca-Steele/author/B07WT6GWB2